THE CORPSE AT THE

CRYSTAL PALACE

ALSO BY CAROLA DUNN

THE CORPSE AT THE CRYSTAL PALACE

A Daisy Dalrymple

Mystery

CAROLA DUNN

CONSTABLE • LONDON

CONSTABLE

First published in the US in 2018 by Minotaur Books,
an imprint of St. Martin's Press, New York.

This edition published in 2018 by Constable

A CIP catalogue record for this book
is available from the British Library.

ISBN: 978-1-47212-544-6

Printed and bound by CPI Group (UK) Ltd, Croydon, CR0 4YY

Papers used by Constable are from well-managed forests
and other responsible sources.

MIX
Paper from
responsible sources
FSC® C104740

Constable
An imprint of
Little, Brown Book Group
Carmelite House
50 Victoria Embankment
London EC4Y 0DZ

An Hachette UK Company
www.hachette.co.uk

www.littlebrown.co.uk

To all the fellow authors
whose work has inspired me since I learned to read.

ACKNOWLEDGMENTS

My thanks to Carole Rainbird and her sister Janet Heppell for taking me to the Crystal Palace and Hampstead Heath; to Linda Cummens for help with sculpture studio and goldsmith's workshop settings; to Father John Matusiak for explaining the Russian Orthodox wedding ceremony; to Dmitri Shcherbakov for Russian usage; to Nancy Mayer, as always, my go-to guru for UK legal information; and to librarians Stephanie and Sarah for help in finding a 1920s fashion magazine that I somehow lost in the intricacies of the web.

THE CORPSE AT THE

CRYSTAL PALACE

ONE

"*Mrs. Fletcher*, my lady."

"Daisy, darling," Lucy said languidly, not rising from the Empire chaise longue where she reclined. Her slender figure was draped in a peach silk negligée adorned with a froth of lace, oddly incongruous with her dark, sleek bob.

"Hello, darling." Daisy pulled off her gloves. "It's filthy out." She trod carefully across the Aubusson. Her shoes were damp though she had only crossed the pavement from the taxi and had wiped her feet vigorously on entering the house. Even in St. James's, the streets could not be kept clear of snow and slush.

"Too divine of you to come struggling through the knee-high drifts."

"Not quite that bad, though I think there's more to come. Three inches is a lot for London in March, and of course we have more up in Hampstead. It's beautiful, but messy. Your note sounded urgent, darling. What's up? Are you ill? You're never ill."

"I'll tell you in a minute."

The door to the boudoir opened again, to admit the butler with a tray of coffee and biscuits. As he arranged it on a low table beside the chaise longue, Daisy looked round the room. Lucy had had the downstairs rooms of the Georgian town house done over in the latest Art Deco style, but here, in her private room, mellow antiquity reigned. It contrasted also with her strictly utilitarian studio and darkroom in the basement.

Over the satinwood bureau hung a photographic portrait of Gerald, Lucy's husband. It was surrounded by the original photos she had taken for the book of follies she and Daisy had produced together. Daisy was sure the display was symbolic, but whether of the folly of men or the folly of women entrusting their lives to men, she had never asked.

The warmth of the central heating was supplemented by glowing coals in the grate. Daisy took her gloves and scarf, stuffed them in her pockets, and unbuttoned her coat.

"*Aargh*," moaned Lucy. Clapping her hand to her mouth, she jumped up, sped to the door, and disappeared.

Daisy looked after her friend in astonishment and concern.

"I'm so sorry, madam," said the butler.

"What's wrong, Galloway? Lady Gerald looked awfully pale!" In spite of her usual exquisite maquillage.

"I'm afraid the aroma of coffee . . . discommodes her ladyship, madam. At present."

"Nauseates her? Then why on earth did she order it?"

For a moment he gazed at the ceiling, as if seeking inspiration, before deciding to enlighten her. "Her ladyship is endeavouring to overcome her . . . discomfort by force of will, I believe, madam. I have heard her ladyship remark that it's 'all in the mind.'"

"Oh dear!" Daisy had to suppress a giggle. "How very Lucy. Take it away, please, Galloway, and bring tea. I suppose tea is all right?"

"Oh yes, madam. Very weak China, without lemon. On no account Earl Grey."

"No, I remember when I was . . ." All too clearly. "Thank you, Galloway."

"Madam will await her ladyship's return?"

"Good heavens, yes."

"Very good, madam." He gathered up the coffee set and carried it off.

Daisy also remembered that when she herself was in the same condition, Lucy had told her it was all bosh, she was as healthy as a horse. As a result, she didn't feel as much sympathy as she might have otherwise. She nibbled pensively on one of the ginger nuts the butler had left. Ginger was good for nausea.

Lucy's return coincided with the arrival of the tea.

"Sorry, Daisy," she said, sitting down as the butler unloaded his tray. "That will be all, thank you, Galloway."

The butler bowed and once again departed.

"Darling, you're preggers at last! Congrats."

Lucy grimaced. "I apologise for any sarky remarks I made when you went through this misery."

"It's horrid, isn't it? Let's hope it's as short-lived as mine was. Are you all right later in the day?"

"Yes, as long as I'm careful what I eat for lunch."

"I bet Gerald's thrilled."

"In his quiet way."

"Have you told your people?"

"Not yet. I'll be seeing the parents soon. We're having a big family gathering at Haverhill for my grandfather's birthday. He's very shaky, and it may be his last. Practically everyone will be there, though I do hope that loathesome little toad Teddy won't have the cheek to turn up."

"Your cousin Edward?"

"*Second* cousin, if you please."

"Why, what's he done to earn your ire?"

"What hasn't he done! Obviously you don't read the gossip columns. He was always a bit of a tick, but since he inherited most of Aunt Eva's money, he's been behaving like an unmitigated bounder."

"Oh dear!"

"His latest exploit is getting himself cited in a breach of promise case. Not easy-come, easy-go Chelsea studio people, either, though I gather he frequents their company as well as the smart set. You remember the free-and-easy lot we used to know when we lived there."

"How could I forget?"

"In fact, a thoroughly respectable girl hitherto, or so it's claimed, in spite of being a foreigner. One can only be glad Teddy isn't a Fotheringay."

"Devenish, isn't he? Yes, Angela's his sister."

"Have you kept in touch with Angela? Frankly, I don't know what you see in her. I suppose she'll be at Haverhill, with a dog or two in tow. Thank goodness I'll have a good excuse for withdrawing from the maelstrom when I can't stand it any longer."

"You're going to tell everyone the news?"

"Not likely! Not at this stage. Mother, of course, and she can tell Father if she wants to. And Tim, I expect. They're the only people who'll notice if I disappear from the festivities now and then. Or at least, the only ones whose opinions I care for. Speaking of opinions, what do you think of this?" Lucy looked down at her lacy negligée with a frown.

"Is it the latest thing?"

"Darling, I never wear the latest thing, I wear the *next* thing."

"You don't give a straw for my opinion on fashion, so you won't take any notice, but I wouldn't have said it's really your style. The peach colour suits you, though."

"The lace suits the way I feel, fragile and in need of cosseting."

"Gerald will cosset you whatever you wear, darling. If you look too fragile, he may go all male and bossy and try to make you give up photography."

"I can't work in the darkroom, anyway. The smell of the chemicals is as bad as coffee. Worse!"

"With any luck, it won't last long. Are you going to keep up the photography after the baby's born?"

"Of course. Daisy, how did you find the twins' nanny? I suppose I must start thinking about that sort of thing."

"You haven't got a faithful family retainer on either side who will be devastated if she isn't asked to be Nurse?"

Lucy pulled a face. "Not one I would want in charge of my child."

"Mrs. Gilpin was personally recommended to me by a friend whose children were too old for a nanny. She's very good with the twins."

"But . . . ?"

"I didn't say 'but.'"

"I heard it coming."

Daisy sighed. "But she tries mercilessly to boss Alec and me, not that we knuckle under. She disapproves of parents visiting the nursery whenever they please or taking the babies for walks. Children should appear in the drawing room briefly at teatime."

"The way we were brought up."

"Yes, and truth to tell, my mother being the way she is, I'm glad. But Alec and I enjoy playing with them."

"And you don't mind battling Nanny," Lucy said dryly. "You've kept her on in spite of her attitude."

"She's *very* good with the children. And good or bad, like other servants, nannies aren't so easy to come by in 1928 as they were in 1908."

"I don't suppose you could pass yours on to me. I expect her style would suit me."

"The twins are only just three. Though we are thinking of sending them to the local Montessori kindergarten school . . . If I were you, I'd start asking friends and family for recommendations."

"What a frightful bore. No doubt as soon as I break the news, everyone will start giving me advice."

"I escaped a lot of that because I already had Belinda when I got pregnant. People sort of assumed I must know about child-raising."

"Oh yes, your little stepdaughter. How is she?"

"Honestly, darling, you are hopeless. She's not a little girl now, she's fourteen and long since away at boarding school."

"Don't tell me that. It makes me feel old. Thirty! Are we really thirty this year?"

"It does sort of creep up on one."

They fell silent for a moment, contemplating with dismay the approach of middle age.

"Does having a fourteen-year-old daughter make you feel older?" Lucy enquired, not without a hint of malice.

"Only when people comment on it. Which reminds me, I'm going to be in charge of a sixteen-going-on-seventeen-year-old for a week during the Easter hols. I'm sure that will make me feel old, but no one is likely to presume she's my own."

"What? Who?"

"Geraldine and Edgar's brood, all of them."

"Those West Indians they adopted? The black family? Are they adopting them legally or just informally."

"Legally. The case is wending its way through the courts."

"How on earth did you get yourself landed with them at Easter?"

"I offered. Cousin Geraldine wants them to see the sights of London. As she's never lived in town and rarely visited, she asked my advice about what to see."

"I hope she's not expecting you to give the girls advice on fashion!"

"No fear! They're a bit young to be worrying about that anyway. Anita's sixteen and Dolores just fifteen, I think. We'll be taking them to the zoo and the museums and the Changing of the Guard, that sort of thing. Kew Gardens, perhaps. Which reminds me, have you ever been to the Crystal Palace?"

"No, never. Its heyday is long past. Queen Vicky may have frequented the place in the early days, and our sort of people went on going to concerts there, but it was going downhill even before the war. The Army using it for training didn't help, of course. There was a bit of a revival when the Imperial War

Museum moved in, but they moved out again a couple of years ago. It's strictly hoi polloi now, from what I've heard."

"But neither a haunt of vice nor a desolate ruin?"

Lucy laughed. "Not to my knowledge. I daresay the children would enjoy a visit and you've never worried about consorting with hoi polloi."

"The thing is, my American editor wants an article about it, and Belinda is very keen to go. She's often seen it from Hampstead Heath, as one can on a clear day. One of her friends told her it was fun. It sounds to me like the sort of outing that would be more fun with companions."

"As long as you don't expect me to accompany you," Lucy said with a shudder.

"Not likely! I meant the young people, though I wouldn't mind another adult to keep me company. Hmm, Sakari might like to bring Deva along."

"Your Indian friend? No doubt another brown face or two will make your cousins feel more at home."

"I should hope they'll jolly well feel at home in my house with or without Sakari!"

"In your house? Won't they be using the Dalrymple town house?"

"Legally, Mother has the use of it, you know. As soon as Geraldine broached the possibility of borrowing it, Mother decided she had long-laid plans to spend April in town. Typical of Mother. She claims there isn't room for all of them."

"Bosh!"

"Absolutely, darling."

"More room than in your house."

"No, actually. We have plenty, even if Geraldine changes her mind about leaving them entirely to my care."

"She's not coming to lend a hand?"

"She's very good with the children, especially the boys, but she's also a magistrate and active on all sorts of local committees, as well as the parish council."

7

"Good heavens, how exhausting!"

"She's thriving on it. She's really found her feet and her niche. And of course Mother says such behaviour is beneath the Viscountess Dalrymple."

"What does the Dowager Viscountess say about the African horde moving into Fairacres?"

"They're Trinidadian, not African. In any case, you know I stopped listening to Mother's tirades years ago. Though I gather it's reawakened her grievance about Edgar's inheriting Fairacres, just when I hoped she was coming to terms with that. But that's Mother for you. She still carries on about Alec being a policeman, though we've been married for nearly five years. She's not going to change."

"I expect not. I remember you telling me years and years ago that Gervaise was the son and heir, Violet was the good daughter, and you were the naughty daughter. I wouldn't be surprised if all your unconventional notions come from knowing that whatever you do, she will disapprove."

"Darling, you sound just like Sakari!"

"Sakari?" Lucy raised delicately painted eyebrows. "What *do* you mean?"

"She's a glutton for self-improvement. She's always going to lectures and psychology is one of her favourite subjects."

"Has she told you the same, that you're still rebelling against your mother?" Lucy asked, sardonic but interested.

"Hardly. She's never met Mother and I'm still sufficiently filial not to talk about her with anyone but you and Alec."

"How wise."

"As for unconventional, you're a fine one to talk! Who signed up as a Land Girl when she could have found a nice, comfortable job in a ministry?"

Lucy groaned. "And regretted it. I must have been mad."

"And then set up as a photographer in a Chelsea studio instead of immersing herself in the fashionable world. *And* refused to stop working when she married."

"All right, all right! I concede, at least to some extent. It's a frightful bore not being able to work in the darkroom at the moment. The fumes are altogether too much for my poor tum."

"I'm not surprised. I have a vivid memory of the smell of your shed in the garden in Chelsea."

"One gets used to it. I daresay I shall even grow used to being a mother."

"You're welcome to come and practise on mine, and on Geraldine's brood while they're here."

"Thanks, but no thanks! Be honest, darling, weren't you the least little bit put out at suddenly finding yourself with a horde of negro cousins?"

"It wasn't really so sudden. I'd known for ages that a great-great uncle—or whatever he was—had gone to the West Indies, so it was always a possibility. Besides, when we met them at Christmas, I liked them. Which is more than you can say for your cousin Edward."

"True," Lucy admitted with a moue of distaste. "Very true."

TWO

Daisy's stepdaughter, Belinda, came home for the Easter holidays. The gales that had swept across the country the previous day died down during the night. In the morning it was still blustery, but the sun shone.

Sakari, as had become customary, had offered her car and chauffeur to pick up Belinda along with her own daughter, Deva, and their friend Elizabeth, at Liverpool Street station. After breakfast, Daisy rang up her friend on the telephone to make sure the arrangement stood. Though Sakari usually had the use of the Sunbeam tourer, occasionally her husband, a high official at the India Office, had unexpected need of it.

"Do not worry, Daisy, Kesin will meet the train on time and deliver Belinda to you."

"Oh, good. I've been meaning to ask you whether you and Deva would like to come to the Crystal Palace with us one of these days. 'Us' being the new cousins from Fairacres. I told you they're coming to stay with us in a few days' time."

"The children from the West Indies? I shall be interested to meet them."

Daisy had sudden qualms. "I'm told the Crystal Palace has

gone downhill since the days when Queen Victoria used to pop in now and then. Belinda very much wants to go and I promised to take her, but perhaps you—"

Sakari chuckled. "My dear Daisy, I have already visited it, more than once. The exibits are most instructive, though the display of Indian culture is by no means extensive considering the size and variety of my country. They do however give one a starting point for further studies."

"It sounds interesting for the older girls. I'm afraid it may not amuse the younger boys."

"For children it is excellent. When they grow restive, they can safely go out to run and play in the gardens. Deva and I will certainly go with you, if we are able to arrange a mutually convenient date."

"I've got a feeling I may be grateful for the presence of another adult. Thanks. I must run now, darling. It's such a beautiful day I want to take the twins out on the Heath in case it rains later."

"Let us hope that March will go out like a lamb," said Sakari, with her usual pleasure at the opportunity to use an English idiom.

Daisy went down to the kitchen for her daily consultation with Mrs. Dobson, the cook-housekeeper, then up to the nursery to see the twins. As always, her arrival brought a frown to Nanny Gilpin's face.

However, Daisy had long since won that struggle. Her own mother had visited the nursery so seldom as to make each occasion a terrifying ordeal, to Daisy, at least, if not to her brother and sister. Still worse had been the brief and strictly regimented visits to the drawing room after tea. Daisy's children were not going to regard their mother as a stranger.

The three-year-olds were sitting at the table, drawing with coloured crayons. Nana, sprawled under the table at their feet, raised her head and thumped her tail in greeting.

"Good morning, Miranda. Good morning, Oliver."

They pushed back their chairs and jumped to their feet. "Good morning, Mummy." Both glanced at Nanny, waiting for her grudging nod before rushing to fling themselves into Daisy's arms.

This was Nanny's kingdom and Mrs. Gilpin granted few concessions to modern notions of parenthood. Nor to modern notions of nannyhood, come to that. The hems of her striped dresses had crept up to mid-calf but her waistline had defied the vagaries of fashion by remaining at her waist, and she still wore her hair in a bun, with a stiff white cap skewered to it by a jet-knobbed hat pin. She insisted on the nursery maid, Bertha, wearing a cap, too.

She pursed her lips as Daisy and the twins exhanged hugs and kisses.

"Mummy, come and see my picture," said Miranda.

"Manners, Miss Miranda!"

"Please will you *please* come and see my picture, Mummy?"

"Mine too," Oliver chimed in. "Please, mine too."

"Show me, chickabiddies."

Daisy admired Miranda's Snow White, without a body but with wings in place of ears.

"Because snow flies through the air, doesn't it, Mummy? 'Member when it snowed outside? She's flying away from the wicked queen."

Oliver's train consisted of clouds of steam. "You can't see the engine, Mummy, 'cause there's too much smoke."

"Speaking of trains, guess who's coming home today."

"Daddy!" cried Oliver.

"Daddy may." Alec had been sent to Leeds to assist the local force. "If we're lucky. Someone else—"

"Bel!" Miranda jumped up and down with excitement. "Sister Bel's coming home!"

"That's right, Belinda."

Oliver frowned in thought. "Why because?"

"Because it's the end of term. The beginning of the Easter holidays."

"Bel coming on a train?"

"Yes, darling."

"I go to the station to see the engines."

"Not today."

"Why because?"

"Because Mr. Kesin is fetching her."

"Why because, Mummy?"

"Because Deva and Lizzie are coming home too. Bel will be home by lunchtime. We'll go to see the trains another time, I promise. Now, we're all going to walk to the Heath, to feed the ducks."

At the magic word, the dog sprang up, scampered to the door, and whined.

"We'll take Nana to the Heath," said Miranda.

"I want to see trains," Oliver insisted, pouting.

"Now now, Master Oliver, you'll do as your mother says, and with a smile, if you please! Come and change your shoes and get your coat and cap on." As she buttoned Oliver's coat and the nursery maid helped Miranda with hers, Nanny added in a tone of faint disapproval, "You will be taking the dog, madam, I suppose?"

"Of course."

"Then you'll be needing an extra pair of hands."

"Certainly, but there's no need for you to stir, Mrs. Gilpin. Bertha shall come with us."

Daisy's walks with the twins and Nana always turned into a romp, very unlike the sort of sedate promenade the nurse considered proper.

"I going to ask Mrs. Dobson for bread to feed the ducks," Oliver announced.

"That's a good idea, darling. We'll stop at the kitchen on our way."

When they reached the Heath, each twin clutching a brown paper bag of bread crusts, Daisy stopped to look out over the city. For once a propitious breeze had cleared away the usual haze to an approximation of Wordsworth's vision of London "all bright and glittering in the smokeless air."

"What are you looking at, Mummy?" Miranda asked.

"The view. Everything."

Both children stared solemnly into the distance.

"The view is a long way away, isn't it?"

"Yes. I do believe that glint on the horizon must be the Crystal Palace."

"Why because?" Oliver demanded.

"Because it's on a hill and it's all made of glass, so the sun reflects from it. Can you see that shining spot in the distance? It's one of the places Bel wants to take the cousins when they come to stay."

"I go too."

"I don't think so, sweetheart. It's not really a place for small children. Have you ever been, Bertha?"

"No, madam, but I always wanted to."

"Well, we'll see." Daisy saw Oliver's lower lip begin to quiver and remembered that to a small child *We'll see* generally signifies *No*. "Let's go and feed the ducks," she said quickly. "I bet they're hungry. I'll race you down to the pond."

When they returned to the house, Bertha took the twins up to the nursery to have their lunch, followed by a nap. Daisy retreated to her small office at the back of the house to get her notes in order for an article about Audley End House for her American editor. She wanted to get it finished and posted before the holiday hordes arrived.

Belinda burst in a few minutes later. "Mummy, I'm home!" She kissed Daisy. Her bobbed hair still took Daisy by surprise though Bel had had her ginger pigtails cropped off months ago, at Christmas.

"Hello, darling. Lovely to have you home again."

Bel perched on the corner of the desk. "What are you writing about?"

"An upstairs coal cellar."

"No, really."

"Really and truly. It's at Audley End House. You remember I went to see the house after last time I visited you at school."

"I hope you took a photo. I'd like to see it. But now I have to go and see the twins before their nap. Nanny will be livid if I disturb them once she's put them down. See you at lunch." She

14

raced out, then, a moment later, she popped her head round the door. "Mrs. Dobson said Daddy's away. Do you know when he's coming home?"

"I don't, darling, but he's been gone several days, so soon, I expect."

"Goody. And the cousins are coming on Monday?"

"Yes. Truscott's driving them up to town from Fairacres."

"I can't wait to show them London! I'm going to make a list of places to go. Do you know, they've never been to a zoo?" She disappeared again.

Daisy hoped for sunshine. The zoo in the rain was dismal. If bad weather curtailed outside activities, she was going to have to cope with a houseful of bored children.

The second post brought a letter from Geraldine. She had decided to come up to town after all. Daisy's thoughts flew to bedrooms. Where on earth was she to put her? One could hardly offer Lady Dalrymple a child's room. Bel would have to sleep in Alec's dressing room, then the older girls could have her room, and . . .

Daisy's blank gaze caught her mother's name farther down the page.

Geraldine had had it out with the dowager viscountess, who had been forced to concede that there was plenty of room in the town house for her successor and two of the children. Anita and Dolores naturally had very different ideas from Ben and Charlie about what they wanted to see in London. The girls' choice would be museums, St. Paul's and Westminster Abbey, a concert perhaps, and hat shops. The boys would like to visit the zoological gardens, the Tower of London, and Madame Tussaud's, and to witness the Changing of the Guard. Which—Geraldine wondered—would Daisy prefer?

Daisy turned the question over to Belinda, who, after serious consideration, voted in favour of Ben and Charlie.

"You see, Mummy, next year I'll be older and I'll probably want to do the same things as Anita and Dolores. I mean, I'll start caring about hats and things. But I had such fun with Ben last summer, before the others came, I don't want him to think

I don't like him anymore. By next year, he'll probably be like Derek and not want anything to do with girls." Her cousin Derek's defection when he started at Harrow was a sore point.

Daisy wondered whether her stepdaughter regarded the mayhem of last summer at Fairacres as just part of the fun, but she only said, "I'll write and tell Geraldine right away."

"I'll take it to the letter box. Maybe Nanny Gilpin will let Bertha and the twins come too, and we'll take Nana. You know, Mummy," she added, "I bet Grandmother Dalrymple will be relieved to have the girls instead of the boys."

"I shouldn't be surprised," Daisy agreed, laughing. "But I shouldn't be surprised if she decides not to come while they're here after all."

Unexpectedly, Alec came home that day in time for dinner. He listened to Belinda's plans to entertain the cousins.

"It sounds as if you're going to keep them busy, pet. Daisy, if you're going to the Crystal Palace, you'd better avoid the days, usually Saturdays, when they have football or motor racing. Those events often bring out the rowdies."

"I'll check their schedule, darling."

"I wish you could come too, Daddy." Belinda was a bit of a worrier; Daisy blamed the years her martinet mother-in-law had had the upbringing of the child.

"I'll see what I have on at work, but I doubt it."

"Let's invite Uncle Tom and Mrs. Tring, Bel," Daisy suggested. DS Tring, Oliver's godfather, had been Alec's right-hand man for years. Since retiring, he had regained his youthful step and his joie de vivre. "I expect they'd enjoy it."

"Oh yes, do let's. No one would dare to be rowdy with Uncle Tom there. I'll write to them after dinner."

The Trings accepted. The days that suited them also suited Sakari. Daisy and Belinda started to make plans.

"Though there won't be nearly enough time to do everything," Bel said with a sigh.

THREE

Belinda sat in the windowseat in the living room. She had a book in her lap but her attention was on the cobbled sweep enclosing the communal garden. A blustery wind tossed the trees and cloud shadows raced across the grass. At last her patience was rewarded. Lord Dalrymple's new green Wolseley Landaulette turned into Constable Circle and proceeded up the slope at a stately pace.

Dropping her book, Belinda sprang up and hurried to Daisy's study. "Mummy, they're here!"

"Oh, good, just in time for tea. I'll be there in a minute."

Belinda sped back down the hall. She opened the front door just as the car pulled up at the foot of the steps. When she was halfway down, Ben jumped out of the front, where he had been sitting next to the chauffeur, Truscott.

Charlie, a year younger and therefore relegated to the back seat, hopped down a moment later. He was quite a bit smaller, as well as younger, not having yet had what grown-ups called a "growth spurt." The European side of his ancestry showed more than Ben's, lighter skin and wavy rather than tight-curled black hair.

They both called hello and waved to Belinda as she ran down the last few steps, but they turned to thank Mr. Truscott before coming to meet her. It was lucky they had good manners, Bel thought, or Aunt Geraldine wouldn't have adopted them. Ben would have returned to Trinidad after last summer and Bel would never have seen him again.

She crossed the pavement to join them as the chauffeur climbed out, a bit stiffly. "Hello, Mr. Truscott. Thank you for bringing Ben and Charlie."

"My pleasure, Miss Belinda."

"I hope you and your family are well." She had often heard Daisy enquire after their well-being. Truscott had been in the family since Daisy's father first bought a motorcar. "My mother said Mrs. Dobson is expecting you for tea in the kitchen. She's made a cake specially."

"Thank you, Miss Belinda, I shan't turn that down." He headed for the boot. "I'll just bring in the suitcases."

"We can carry them," said Charlie. "You drove a long, long way. You must be tired."

"You're a good lad, Master Charlie. It's all in the day's work. Suppose you carry the small bags and I'll bring the big ones?"

"Hello, Ben." Daisy came down the steps. "Hello, Charlie. How nice to see you both again. Bel, will you take them up to their room and show them where to wash? Good afternoon, Mr. Truscott."

"Afternoon, Miss Daisy." The chauffeur handed the boys a couple of satchels and touched his cap. "You're looking very well, if I may say so."

Daisy stayed chatting to Mr. Truscott, while Belinda took her cousins into the house and upstairs.

"Mummy thought you'd like to share a room, but if not, one of you can move. There's plenty of space."

"Let's share." Charlie sounded anxious.

"That's all right with me," Ben said good-naturedly.

Bel showed them their bedroom and pointed out the bathroom and the lav. "I'll come back in ten minutes and we'll go down to tea."

"I hope Mrs. Dobson baked a cake for us, too," said Ben.

"A big one. And lots of little ones."

"Good. Hurry up and wash, Charlie. Hands *and* face, and don't forget to brush your hair."

"You think you can order me about, just 'cause you're a year older," grumbled Charlie, but he went off to the bathroom.

The day of the Crystal Palace outing was sunny and warm. Belinda was glad, because her cousins were less interested in the contents of the building than the maze and the statues of prehistoric monsters, which were in the park.

Besides the Trings and Deva and Aunt Sakari, the twins were to go with them, along with Nanny and Bertha. When Daisy had told Mrs. Gilpin she was considering taking the twins, with Bertha to help look after them, Nurse Gilpin had said grudgingly that she herself had never seen the Crystal Palace and would quite like to. Bel thought privately that Nanny would be a frightful wet blanket, but after all, she'd be stuck with Mirrie and Oliver and so unable to interfere with other people's fun.

"How will we all get there?" Charlie asked. "By tube?" They had taken the Underground to the zoo the day before, and the boys had been just as impressed by it as by the animals.

"No, it's too complicated with so many people, 'specially with Nanny saying the twins have to leave at midday to come home for lunch and their nap. Aunt Sakari's going to bring her big car—"

"What kind of car?" Ben wanted to know.

"It's red. A Sunbeam tourer, I think. Mummy was going to drive her car—it's a Gwynne Eight—but Aunt Geraldine said she'd send Mr. Truscott with the Wolseley. Uncle Tom and Mrs. Tring live quite near the Palace, so they'll get themselves there."

"Uncle Tom's a detective, like Uncle Alec?"

"That's right, only he's retired now."

"And he's not our uncle, silly," Ben pointed out. He had met the sergeant the previous summer. "He's Mr. Tring to us and don't you forget it. And Aunt Sakari is Mrs. . . . . Mrs. what, Bel?"

"Mrs. Prasad." She noticed that Charlie looked worried. "But neither of them would mind if you made a mistake. They're nice."

The two cars arrived on time. Mrs. Gilpin and Bertha, wearing identical black capes and black felt hats, packed the twins into the Dalrymple Wolseley. Belinda and Daisy joined Sakari, who was alone in the back of the Sunbeam.

"I bring a disappointment, Belinda. Deva has come down with a feverish cold. She is not fit to go out."

"Poor Deva! I hope she gets better quickly. My father couldn't come either. He's gone away again, to Bristol."

Though sorry for Deva, Bel didn't really mind her absence. She was a good friend for quiet times, but keeping up with Ben and Charlie called for plenty of energy.

The boys, having been introduced to Aunt Sakari, vied to sit beside Kesin in the front.

"Two may come," the chauffeur said good-naturedly. "You sit still, yes?"

They passed through the centre of London in a stately procession. The Wolseley led the way, as Kesin knew the route. Sitting on a fold-down seat, facing backwards, Belinda couldn't see where they were going, only where they had been. She could hear the boys commenting on the passing scene but she had to twist round to see what they were talking about. It was very frustrating.

After crossing the river, they drove on for what seemed like ages and ages. The close-packed city streets gave way to bigger houses with proper gardens. They turned right, then left, then right again, until Belinda was sure they were going in circles. Did Kesin really know the way? Truscott, with the twins aboard, followed trustfully.

Another turn, then Charlie said, "Golly!" in an awed voice, and Ben said, "Gosh! Look, Bel!"

On the left side of the car was a wall of glass, stretching as far ahead and up as she could see. Through it, dim shapes were visible but she couldn't make out what they were.

A moment later the cars pulled up. Ben and Charlie immediately tumbled out, jumping over the running board straight to the pavement. Charlie stood staring up in awe at the towering entrance arch. Ben, after a glance upward, came to open the rear door, while Kesin descended in a more dignified manner and went to open the other door.

"You get down first, Belinda," said Sakari.

Bel did, wondering whether she—or she and Ben—ought to try to help Sakari out. She was rather a large lady, almost as large as Mrs. Tring, whom Belinda saw approaching along the pavement with Uncle Tom. Luckily Truscott hurried from the other car to offer Sakari a strong arm.

Uncle Tom was biggest of all, and his blue and green checked suit did nothing to disguise his size. As he raised his bowler to the ladies, revealing the hairless expanse of his head, Charlie whispered an awed, "Gosh!" He hadn't met ex–Detective Sergeant Tring before.

Ben grinned. "You'd better behave yourself, young 'un, or Sergeant Tring'll be after you."

"Don't tease," said Bel. "It's all right, Charlie, Uncle Tom is really nice, and he's not a policeman anymore, anyway."

The twins arrived, holding hands, the other two little hands firmly grasped by Mrs. Gilpin and Bertha.

Miranda broke away, ran to Belinda, and hugged her round the waist. "I want to go with Bel," she announced.

"We're all going together," said Daisy. "You may hold Belinda's hand until we're inside. I'll go first to buy the tickets."

"I sent Kesin yesterday to get them." Sakari delved into her capacious handbag and triumphantly produced a sheaf of papers and a roll of tickets. "Here's a pamphlet for each of you, with plans of the building and the park."

"Mrs. Prasad, you're a wonder," said Uncle Tom.

"I have the guidebook if you desire further information, Mr. Tring."

"We need not all stay together," said Daisy. "We ought to have a rendezvous."

"I suggest the north end of the nave," said Sakari, "at the Monti Fountain, which you will find on the plan. The fish in the fountain will keep the little ones amused if they tire of running about."

"It sounds ideal. We'll meet there at a quarter past noon. Truscott is coming back to fetch the twins and Mrs. Gilpin at half past. Let's go in."

It was early, not much past ten, and few people were queuing for tickets. Sakari handed her roll to the attendant at the gate, who counted everyone off as they went through.

The hall they entered was huge, almost as high as St. Paul's dome but all glass. The sun shone through the roof, though not as brightly as Belinda would have expected. She decided the glass hadn't been cleaned for while. It must be an awfully difficult job, and scary with nothing underneath but glass.

Enough sunlight came in for all sorts of plants, big and small, to grow along the sides of the hall, among a multitude of statues.

Ben was studying his map. "Here's the Monti Fountain. Let's start there and go right round all the stuff and end up back there."

"I want to see the monsters," said Charlie.

"They're in the park," his elder brother informed him, studying the plan. "We'll go outside this afternoon."

"Why not now?"

"Because I bet later there will be more people, so it won't be so much fun inside. We'll see the monsters after lunch."

"Come on," Belinda urged. "Let's not waste time arguing."

"There's a Navy gallery upstairs, Charlie. Our dad was in the Royal Navy, Bel."

"Look, there's a round and round staircase over there."

"Spiral," said Bel and Ben simultaneously.

"Does it go to the Navy?"

"Yes, look at the map."

They had all reached the place where the nave that ran end to end of the palace crossed the central transept. Bel told Daisy their plans. "Is that all right, Mummy?"

"Of course. You've got your watch on? Keep your eye on the time."

Ben and Charlie at once ran off to the left along the nave. Hurrying after them, Bel glanced about. On her right was the Opera House, not in use at ten on a Wednesday morning, and then the Italian Court, which was closed off, with a notice saying it was open to Crystal Palace Club members only. On her left was the Egyptian Court, the entrance guarded by gigantic statues wearing funny-looking false beards like the ones she had seen at the British Museum.

In fact there were statues all over the place. Bel passed the Renaissance and Mediaeval Courts on one side, Greek (closed for renovations) and Roman on the other. Through each entrance she saw vistas of rooms within rooms, full of statues and pillars. Between the Alhambra and Byzantine Courts, according to the pamphlet, she caught up with the boys.

They were gaping at a fountain, or rather at its pedestal. Or was it a plinth? Bel wasn't sure. Whatever it was called, the lower part seemed to be all bosoms.

"They're naked!" Charlie blurted out.

"Hush!" hissed Ben.

"Nude," Belinda said firmly. "When it's art, they're called nude. Lots of old statues are nude. Stop staring."

Ben looked down at his guidebook. Charlie, unabashed, asked, "Have they got heads?" and crouched to peer up under the shroud of greenery hanging from the upper basin of the fountain. "Yes," he said, satisfied. "I wonder—"

"There's a gallery with telescopes." Ben's sweeping gesture took in the upper reaches of the palace. "Up on the top level. Let's go there first. It sounds more interesting than all these courts."

"All right, how do we get there? Where are the stairs?"

"Look. See this circle thing on the plan? In the corner there, behind the . . . um . . . Al-ham-bra Court. Would that be stairs?"

"Another spiral staircase. But let's go through the Alhambra Court."

"What's Alhambra?" Charlie asked.

"I don't know. What does it say, Ben?"

"It's a palace in Spain that was built by the Moors."

"Who are the Moors?"

"People from Morocco," said Belinda. "That's in Africa."

"Our mother's people came from Africa, didn't they, Ben."

"Yes, and France. Come on."

Belinda loved the Alhambra Court. It was very colourful, with bright patterned tiles and mosaics, sweet-scented flowering plants, and fountains. The central fountain was surrounded by four giant statues of lions, greatly preferable to embarrassingly nude women, though Bel didn't think they were as good as the ones in Trafalgar Square.

The boys admired them, but they didn't let Bel linger. They all sped across the first hall and turned right in the second, scarcely even glancing at the elaborate pillars and arches. An opening led into a passage, at the end of which an iron staircase circled upward.

When they reached it, Bel saw another passage at right angles, running behind the Alhambra. Ladies and gents conveniences opened off it, she noted. It was always useful to know where those were.

She hurried to catch up with the boys, round and round and up and up two dizzying flights.

The top gallery, high up under the glass roof, ran through big iron hoops. When Belinda looked along its length, it was like looking through a telescope backwards, narrowing into the distance. In the spaces between the hoops, real telescopes were set up to give a view through the glass wall over the whole of London, all the way to Hampstead Heath. No one else was up there yet, so each of them bagged one. Belinda explained how to find St. Paul's dome, and once they'd spotted it, she directed them to other landmarks she recognised.

"Golly," Ben exclaimed, "London is enormous!"

"I bet it's as big as the whole of Trinidad," said Charlie.

"Maybe." Ben didn't like the idea, Belinda could tell.

"I shouldn't think so, but we can look it up in Mummy's encyclopaedia when we get home. Let's look over the rail and see if we can see the others. Hold on tight, Charlie."

From their height, even the biggest statues looked like toys and the people Lilliputian. Mrs. Gilpin and Bertha in their uniforms with the twins, coming out of one of the courts opposite, were unmistakable, but Bel didn't see any of the others.

"I feel sick," Charlie announced.

"You're just giddy," Bel assured him. "Sit down for a minute, and when you get up don't glance down. Keep looking right across to the other side. Then we'll go down the steps and you'll be all right."

The lower gallery had the naval museum. Ben and Charlie were thrilled.

"As well as our dad being a sailor, Uncle Frank works in the dockyard," Ben explained. "We used to spend quite a lot of time there."

"He's our stepfather."

"I remember him. I met him at Fairacres last summer."

There were models of all kinds of ships in all stages of construction and paintings of great sea battles and storms at sea. The boys were fascinated. Belinda found it quite interesting, but gradually she drifted away from them into the next section of the gallery.

It was full of statues and pictures from India. She had learnt a bit about Hindu gods and goddesses from Deva, so it was fun identifying them—blue-faced Krishna with his milkmaid lover Radha, elephant-headed Ganesh, Hanuman the monkey-god. She happened upon a statue of the Buddha with the most beautiful smile she'd ever seen, and then became absorbed in a display of miniature paintings in brilliant colours.

"Bel, where are you?" Two pairs of feet thudded towards her.

"Here." She emerged into the main aisle.

"Are you ready to go down?"

"Are we late?"

"No, a bit early." Ben glanced round the Indian stuff. "Do you want to stay longer?"

"Come *on*!" Charlie was already starting down the stairs at the end.

"We've hardly seen anything on the ground floor," said Bel. "Let's go."

They were halfway down when Charlie said, "Is that your nanny, Bel?"

The woman in a nursery nurse's uniform was hurrying—almost trotting—towards the stairs, along the wide passage behind the courts. She wore a black cape and black hat but her head was bowed, so Belinda couldn't see her face. When she passed below, her hat looked different from Mrs. Gilpin's. Not that Bel had looked at Nanny Gilpin's hat very closely. She was pretty sure, though, that it was the winter one, made of felt, with a black silk rose on the band and a rose carved in ebony on the end of the hat pin. The one passing below was shiny straw and the brim was broader.

"I don't think so. No, here comes Mrs. Gilpin now. Without Oliver and Miranda. How odd! I wonder where she's going."

"Let's follow her," whispered Ben, close behind her on the next step up. "Like we did last summer."

Privately, Belinda thought she was too old to play Red Indians. She reminded herself that her cousins were her guests and she didn't want to be a wet blanket, as Derek was to her nowadays. "All right. But I bet she just goes back to the twins."

The stairs were in a corner. The first nanny had turned left, towards the nave, and so did Mrs. Gilpin. Belinda had the impression she was following the unknown woman. There was no other way to go, though, so she was probably imagining it.

This passage wasn't crowded with statues and plants. In fact it was mostly bare except for pictures on the walls. Luckily the children were all wearing rubber-soled plimsolls; they wouldn't make any noise if they were careful. They waited till the two nannies were about halfway to the nave and then crept after them.

When the stranger reached the nave, she glanced back over her shoulder. Mrs. Gilpin half-raised her hand, as if to stop her, but instantly she vanished round the corner to her right. Nurse Gilpin paused for a moment, hands on hips, a picture of stiff outrage, then quick-marched in her wake.

"The rendezvous is the other way," said Ben, as Belinda and the boys ran to the corner and peered round. "Do you think she's lost?"

"No," said Bel positively, "but where on earth is she going?"

Both uniformed figures were crossing the central aisle towards the main doors to the park. The huge hall was quite busy now, some people gawping up in wonder at the glass dome high overhead, some studying their guidebooks, some heading confidently in one direction or another.

"I'm sure Mrs. Gilpin is following that other nanny on purpose," said Belinda. "I can't imagine why."

"If we don't hurry we'll lose them and never find out," Ben said impatiently. "Come on."

They dodged through the crowd. Belinda caught glimpses of the nannies until they disappeared into a jungle of marble and greenery.

"More statues and more plants!" Charlie exclaimed in disgust as they reached the outskirts. "We'll never find them."

"Split up," Ben advised. "We'll meet at the end, by the doors to the park."

"*Then* can we go and see the monsters?"

"It'll be time to go to the rendezvous, I should think," said Bel. "Monsters after lunch."

She went round to the right, Ben to the left, and Charlie down the centre so that they could keep an eye on him through the gaps. Bel soon saw Mrs. Gilpin's hat bobbing along above a massive plinth, visible between the legs of a monstrous horse.

Dodging about to keep her in sight, she approached the glass doors to the terrace just in time to see her push through them. Ben and Charlie had arrived ahead of her and were lurking behind a giant sea serpent with a man and two boys struggling in its coils. Charlie popped out, grimacing and gesturing at her to hurry.

Not waiting for her, Ben dashed off. Belinda and Charlie caught up with him on the terrace outside, crouching behind the balustrade and practically fizzing with impatience. He paid no heed to the few people promenading there who gave him curious glances.

"Do hurry! Look, she's going down the steps. The other one *ran* down."

"Nannies don't run," said Belinda.

"That nanny does. If we don't want yours to see us, we can't follow till she gets farther away, then we'll have to be pretty nippy."

"Blast! I mean bother. You're not to say that, Charlie, and don't tell that I did. Which way did the other nurse go at the bottom, Ben?"

"Right. Down the steps on the right, and then round that path that curves off to the right."

"Oh yes, I see her. She's going to get behind those trees any minute. We'd better go now or we'll lose her."

"Which one are we following?" Charlie demanded.

"Both of them," said Belinda. "There, Mrs. Gilpin's going down the right side steps, too. If we stay close to the balustrade, I don't think she'll see us if she looks back."

"Keep your heads down," Ben advised.

Bent double, they scuttled down the wide stone steps. At the bottom, the steps divided into narrower flights to left and right. They paused to reconnoitre.

Nurse Gilpin had reached the foot of the second flight. She was marching stiffly but remarkably rapidly along a broad paved path that curved away to the right. It had lawn on either side, edged with alternating bushes and statues, perfect for trailing without being spotted.

Ben and Belinda exchanged a glance and ran down the steps. On their heels, Charlie said, "But where's the other one? I can't see the other one."

"I bet Mrs. Gilpin can," Ben reassured him. "Let's not lose sight of her."

Dodging from bush to bush, they were close behind when Mrs. Gilpin crossed another terrace, went down a few more steps, circled a fountain, and disappeared into a wooded area.

The children ran. They came to a rose garden with paths going all over the place in an intricate pattern. Most of the roses were just well-pruned stumps, with red shoots sprouting here and there, but round the edge were climbing roses tied to trellises. Nanny Gilpin, down in the sunken centre, hesitated before setting off along one of the curved spokes of the circle. Reaching the path round the rim, she doubled back, then turned to the right. Belinda and the boys had stopped behind the trellises and they were able to take a shortcut without going into the garden.

From this they emerged into a wide, straight avenue of plane trees. Mrs. Gilpin, slowing now, was a short way down the gravelled walk. As the children ducked back into the trees, Belinda glimpsed the other nanny's hat vanishing downward, presumably down another flight of steps.

The trees grew in a double row, so they slipped along between the rows. The cover ended at the steps. They watched Mrs. Gilpin trudge heavily down the double flight. Whatever she was up to, Bel had to admire her persistence.

Their mutual quarry was already halfway down the next long stretch of the avenue.

When Mrs. Gilpin reached the foot of the steps, she trod heavily onto the gravel with a crunch. The other nanny glanced back, then broke into a run. Nanny Gilpin plodded on, fading but game.

"She's got a bee in her bonnet," Belinda whispered.

"A bee?" said Charlie. "Won't it sting her?"

"Never mind. Come on."

They stole down the steps and took to the trees again.

The nanny in front came to the end of the avenue, turned off to the right, and was lost to sight. Mrs. Gilpin's pace picked up remarkably.

"Shouldn't we get closer?" Ben hissed. "We'll lose them."

"Better not. She'll be furious if she finds out we've tailed her." Belinda looked at her watch. "We shouldn't really. We ought to go back—"

"Not yet!" The boys were unanimous.

"We ought to find out what she's doing, so we can tell Aunt Daisy," Ben said persuasively.

" 'Sides, we ought to tell her about the bee in her hat," said Charlie, "so she can get rid of it before it stings."

Belinda regarded him with disfavour. "There's no bee. That's just a saying. All right, we'll go a bit farther."

At the end of the avenue, Nanny Gilpin turned the same way as the other one. When the trio came to the spot, there was no sign of the two nannies. A narrow winding path led between trees, bushes, and beds of daffodils and crocuses. Many of the bushes were evergreen, so even though the rest were just beginning to put out leaves, Belinda couldn't see much except for occasional glimpses of water as they trod cautiously along.

On the sandy path, their footsteps were almost silent. Mrs. Gilpin wouldn't hear them coming. On the other hand, they couldn't hear where she was. Peering ahead, they crept round the first bend.

"Gosh! A monster!"

"Hush!" Ben clapped his hand over his brother's mouth.

"It's just a deer," said Belinda. "Three deer. I suppose they might be prehistoric deer. Reindeer maybe, with those antlers. Come on, we can't stop for every statue."

This resolve was put to the test when Charlie spotted another sculpture, definitely a monster, rearing its misshapen head above the shrubbery. To stop him diving into the bushes to get a closer view, Belinda and Ben each had to grasp one of his arms and hustle him past. At least he protested in a whisper. He was rewarded round the next bend by a much better view of the enormous creature's hairy back.

"I bet there's even better ones farther on," said Ben.

And there were; monstrous beasts lurking among the trees, with massive heads, gaping tooth-filled mouths, and taloned feet. Now Charlie had to be held back from racing on to the next wonder. They came to a pond infested by crocodilians with long narrow snouts, and nightmarish flippered horrors with long snaky necks ending in tiny heads, and, on an island, giant toads and tortoises.

After a glance, Belinda's attention returned to their quest, but Charlie's alarmed voice made her turn back.

"Look." He pointed. "What's the black thing over there next to the frog?"

"That's Mrs. Gilpin's hat floating by the croc," said Ben.

"So the black thing must be Mrs. Gilpin," Belinda deduced, shocked. "What on earth happened to her?"

"She went for a swim?" Charlie said doubtfully.

"Don't be silly. She's not moving. We've got to get her out. Ben, we'll have to do it." Bel sat on the ground and untied her shoes. "She'll be heavy, 'specially with wet clothes. We're stronger than Charlie. Charlie, you have to go for help."

"But—"

"Go on. Find Mr. Tring. Or Mummy, or anyone. Go on, hurry, run as fast as you can. Come on, Ben. I don't think it's very deep but I'll go first and you come right behind in case I lose my feet."

"We'd better hold hands."

"All right." Shivering, Belinda stepped cautiously into the water.

FOUR

Daisy and Sakari stepped out of the Byzantine Court into the nave.

"My favourite so far," said Daisy. "Though the Alhambra Court is wonderful too. I love all that intricate decoration, and so colourful. All so different from anything one sees in this country, or in museums. I'm looking forward to the Indian displays."

"They are very skimpy, Daisy. What there is, we will see after lunch. At present we should go to the rendezvous. I see your nursery maid and the twins by the fountain."

Miranda and Oliver leaned on the rim, dabbling their hands in the water, apparently unaware of the abundant bosoms looming over their curly heads, one dark, one as red as Belinda's.

"Don't splash, Miss Miranda," said Bertha. "It's cold outside. You won't like having wet clothes." She cast an anxious look backwards and saw Daisy. "Oh, madam, I'm that glad you've come. I didn't know what to do."

"You seem to me to be doing very well. Where's Nurse?"

"That's just it, madam. I don't know where she's got to, I'm sure."

"She didn't tell you where she was going?"

"Oh yes, madam. Master Oliver, there's no need for you to copy your sister. You can't reach the farthings you threw in, not anyhow. Come away from the water now."

The children obeyed, at last noticing and succumbing to the rival charms of their mother. "Hello, chickies!" They embraced her legs as she asked, "Well, Bertha, where? Where did Mrs. Gilpin go?"

Turning pink, Bertha glanced round and whispered, "To the ladies' convenience, madam. Ever such a long time ago."

"I daresay she's not feeling well."

"She didn't say, madam. I thought she was just going to spend a penny."

Daisy frowned. "I'd better go and see. Sakari—"

"But of course, Daisy, I will stay with the little ones."

"It's over there, madam, behind the heathen place, Mrs. Gilpin said."

"The heathen . . . ? Oh, the Alhambra Court. Thank you, Bertha. You stay here with Mrs. Prasad and the twins. I'll send for you if I need your help. Miss Belinda and the boys should be along any minute, and Mr. and Mrs. Tring."

Daisy hurried off, taking a quick detour through the splendours of the Mohammedan palace. In contrast, the ladies' room—or rather rooms—were frightfully Victorian. The anteroom, doubtless known in its heyday as the retiring chamber, had flocked wallpaper in a pink that was obviously faded from crimson. Plush, overstuffed horsehair chairs and sofas with sagging seats no longer offered weary sightseers a comfortable repose. Daisy wasn't surprised to see no one had taken advantage of their invitation. A faint but pervasive odour of Jeyes Fluid was an additional deterrent.

But if not resting with her feet up, where was Nurse Gilpin? It wasn't at all like her to entrust the twins to Bertha's sole supervision for so long. She was nothing if not reliable.

Between the outer room and the inner was a sort of cubbyhole or closet. There lurked an attendant, ready to pop out with an offer of a clean towel for sixpence for anyone who looked askance at the common roller towel. Such at least was the usual practice. Daisy found an aged crone in a shapeless black dress and cardigan, nodding on her stool, who started awake when addressed.

"Towel, madam?" She peered through bleary eyes.

"No, thank you. Did you notice a nanny in here this morning? A nursery nurse?"

"Nannies? There was a bunch of 'em come in. Odd, I thought. We don't get many 'ere, not in uniforms, anyways. Not many of anyone. They mostly go the other end, near the restrongs."

"A bunch? How many?"

"I dunno, madam. Three or four mebbe."

"And did they all leave again?"

"I'm sure I couldn't say. It's not my job to count people in and out. Though why anyone'd want to stop in there longer'n they need—"

"No, I suppose not." Daisy didn't bother to explain. "I'll just check."

The "ladies' conveniences" were a reminder that high society as well as hoi polloi had once frequented the Crystal Palace. The walls were hygienic white tile but the hand basins were marble and the screen concealing the lavatories was mahogany. The doors to the cubicles, wide enough to accommodate crinolines and bustles, were also mahogany, with frosted glass panels. They swung inwards, a luxurious waste of space the average modern public convenience couldn't afford. Daisy walked along the row at a distance that allowed her to read the VACANT/ENGAGED signs without, she hoped, looking nosy if anyone came in.

All read VACANT except the farthest from the entrance. She moved closer and said in a low but urgent voice, "Mrs. Gilpin? Are you there?"

No answer. No sound but the gurgling of plumbing.

The doors were pretty solid, made to muffle indelicate sounds emitted by Victorian ladies. Daisy took another step forward. She was about to speak when she noticed that the door wasn't properly closed. Though the latch was turned to "occupied," the bolt was resting against the jamb, not in its socket, leaving the door just a crack ajar.

"Mrs. Gilpin?" Pause. "Is anyone there?" Still no response.

Daisy's suppressed irritation gave way to alarm. Slowly she pushed the door a few inches, till she saw a corner of striped skirt.

"Nanny!"

No indignant squawk followed her intrusion so she swung the door all the way open.

The figure sat on the old-fashioned bench seat, slumped against the wall in the corner of the cubicle, her cape crumpled about her. Her face was half-hidden by her hat, and the light was poor, just what the mirrors in the room beyond reflected through the doorway. Daisy could see, however, that the hat was not Mrs. Gilpin's. It appeared to have been knocked forwards when she fell backwards, disarranging her hair. Or rather, the poor woman appeared to be wearing a wig. The hat was attached by a pearl-headed hat pin, so when the hat slipped it took the wig with it, exposing her ear and the side of her neck above the collar of her dress.

And that was the best place to check her pulse, as she was wearing tight gloves that looked difficult to take off. Daisy stripped off her own right glove and pressed two fingers to a likely spot on the nurse's pale neck.

The skin was warm, but she couldn't find a pulse. Either the woman was dead, or Daisy was touching the wrong place. She was not very good at finding pulses, even her own. She shifted her fingertips. Still nothing.

Whether the nurse was dead or just ill, she would have to be moved. She was too hefty for Daisy to shift her singlehanded, not to mention that the floor of the ladies' room hardly seemed a suitable place to lay her. The dim attendant wouldn't be much help. Tom Tring was the person she needed.

Especially if the nurse was dead. She hadn't stirred since Daisy's arrival on the scene.

In the meantime, where was Nanny Gilpin? If she hadn't gone astray, Daisy wouldn't have found herself unwillingly involved with this stranger.

In which case the unfortunate woman might have remained undiscovered for hours.

Stepping out of the cubicle, Daisy sighed. On the whole, she couldn't regret having turned up, since her arrival might save a life. However, she could imagine all too easily what Alec would say if she once again inadvertently got herself mixed up in a suspicious death. And as for Superintendent Crane . . .

But he was on the brink of retirement, and Alec was quite likely to step into his shoes.

In any case it didn't make any difference to what she had to do.

"Towel, madam?" offered the attendant as she approached.

"No, thanks."

"Oh, it's you, deary. Find the nanny, did you?"

"Not the one I was looking for, but a different one. I'm afraid she's very ill."

"Deary me!"

"I have to go and get help, and you must keep everyone out. Have you got a key to this door?"

"That I don't. Never been no need to lock it," the old woman said, puzzled.

"Don't you want to keep people out when you mop the floor?"

"I just puts out me sign, WET FLOOR KEEP OUT."

"Oh, well, that will do. Put it out now, please."

"Is the floor wet, then?"

"No."

"Then why—"

"The police will be coming."

"The perlice? What for?"

Obtuse, not argumentative, Daisy decided. In her most authoritative voice she said, "Put the sign up now, Mrs. . . . I don't know your name?"

"Mrs. 'Atch, and 'as bin these fifty year."

36

"All right, Mrs. Hatch. I'll be back in just a minute *with the police*." Looking back from the door to the passage, she saw the attendant struggling with a folding wooden notice board.

She hurried on to the fountain. The Trings had joined Sakari, Bertha, and the twins, but there was no sign of the older children. Belinda was usually very punctual. She had the boys to shepherd, of course, but this was a bad moment to go missing. Someone would have to wait here for them.

No sign of Mrs. Gilpin, either. It was too bad of her! Truscott would arrive any minute to chauffeur the twins back to Hampstead. Miranda and Oliver were tired and growing fractious, splashing water at each other despite Bertha's admonitions. They ought to go home, not to wait about for their nurse. Though the nursery maid could manage them in the car, a responsible adult ought to see that they reached the car and got into it.

Tom Tring came to meet her. "Trouble, Mrs. Fletcher?"

"I'm afraid so, Tom."

"In the ladies' room? Could be ticklish. I'm not on the force anymore, remember."

"Once a policeman, always a policeman. Give me a minute to organise everything and I'll explain. Sakari, Mrs. Tring, I need your help, one of you to wait here for the children, and one to see off Bertha and the twins in the car. And oh dear, ask Truscott to come straight back if Lady Dalrymple will allow him. We'll never all fit in your car, Sakari, with Mrs. Gilpin along. May I leave it to you to decide who does what? Thank you! Bye-bye, babies." She kissed them. "I'll see you at home. Bertha, I trust you to look after them."

"Of course, madam. Mrs. Gilpin, is she—"

"I didn't find her. I'm sure she's all right. Off with you, now. Truscott will be wondering where you've got to."

As Daisy turned back to Tom Tring, Mrs. Tring went off with Bertha, each carrying a twin.

"All right, Mrs. Fletcher, what's happened?"

She tucked her hand into his arm and led him along the corridor, feeling like a tug with a great liner. "I don't know, exactly. Probably nothing out of the way. But someone with some degree of authority will have to be told and I want your opinion before I report it."

"Report what, Mrs. Fletcher?" Tom asked patiently.

"There's a woman, a nursery nurse, and I think she's dead. But I'm not sure."

"Ah. Sounds to me like you need a doctor first, not a copper."

"I don't know where to find a doctor."

"That's a point. But is there any hurry?"

"I doubt the ladies' room attendant will hold off anyone insistent on going through to the . . . the inner room."

He grinned at her. "Come now, Mrs. Fletcher, it's not like you to be mealymouthed. The lavatories?"

"Yes. She's actually sitting on one."

Tom groaned. "In a state of undress?"

"No, thank goodness. At least, only her hat. And wig."

"Her wig? She's wearing a wig?"

"I think so." Daisy tried to picture the woman's head. "Either that, or she has an awful lot of hair."

"Hmm. Well, here we are." He braced his wide shoulders theatrically. "Best brave the lion's den, I suppose."

"She's no lion. More like a mouse. I'll go ahead and warn her that you're coming."

"I doubt she'll need much warning." Tom patted his midriff with a comfortable chuckle.

"You'd be surprised. She seems to be half blind."

As they approached the closet, the attendant popped out. "Sorry, madam, you can't go in. We got the perlice."

"I've brought the police, Mrs. Hatch."

"Oh, it's you, madam." She peered past Daisy at Tom. "That's the perlice? Where's 'is 'elmet?"

"He's a detective in plainclothes. He'll know what best to do for the unfortunate woman."

"I'm sure I 'opes so, madam."

"Did you take a peek at her, Mrs. Hatch?" Tom asked.

"Catch me!"

"And no one else has been in there?"

"Not a soul. There was just three come in. I sent 'em to the south end ladies'."

"Did you mention the police?"

"No. Never 'ave got rid of 'em, would I."

"Very true."

"Thank you, Mrs. Hatch." Daisy was relieved that the attendant had proved trustworthy. She and Tom went through to the inner room. "It's the far end. The last door. I left the door exactly as I found it."

"You didn't touch her?"

"Only to try to find a pulse in her neck. I didn't . . . disarrange her at all."

Tom nodded approval. He went on and Daisy followed a few feet behind, noting sadly how he had lost the lightfootedness that had always characterised his walk, despite his bulk. Stopping halfway, she watched him enter the last cubicle.

Not more than a minute and a half later, he came out and beckoned to her.

"She's dead. No obvious sign of injury. I hate to ask this, Mrs. Fletcher, but seeing I'm not strictly a copper, I'd like a corroborative witness. Would it upset you to take a quick look? Just so you could say it's the identical body you found and I've left it as you found it."

"No visible injuries? I don't mind, then."

"Just one thing. I've moved the hat and wig—you were right about that—to show the face. I'll put them back when you've looked at the face. Seeing your nurse has gone missing—"

"I'm sure it's not her."

"I'm sure you're right. But maybe it's a friend of hers you've seen before."

"She wouldn't have a friend come to the house, or stop and talk to one if I were with her."

"Still, you never know. Not that it's my business these days, but humour an old man's curiosity, will you?"

"You'll never be old, Tom, but all right."

"Here." He handed her a small electric torch. "Never go anywhere without one."

Daisy took it and went past him into the cubicle. Though willing, she wasn't exactly keen on examining the dead woman. Keeping the torch beam on the floor, she gave her a cursory glance below the neck. Everything looked the same as before. Then she flashed the beam quickly on her face. She frowned, puzzled.

"She does look sort of familiar," she admitted, leaving the cubicle, "but I can't place her. And she seems a bit odd, too, though I'm not sure why."

Tom was wearing his inscrutable expression. "Ah. No doubt you'll mention that to the officer who comes to investigate."

"It's just a feeling. Alec would say—"

"*Aunt Daisy!*" The anguished cry came from the entrance.

Daisy and Tom swung round. Mrs. Hatch had Charlie by the ear. At least the children had turned up, Daisy thought thankfully as she hurried over.

"Charlie, you shouldn't come in here!"

"Mrs. Aunt Sakari said to. Make the old witch let me go!" He aimed a kick at the attendant's skinny ankle.

Mrs. Hatch dodged with surprising agility, keeping a hold on his ear and screeching an unprintable comment about heathen brats.

"Let go of him," said Daisy in the grande dame voice she'd learned from her mother. "Charlie, apologise for being rude."

"Sorry," he muttered. "But, Aunt Daisy, it's *urgent*. We found Mrs. Gilpin in the water with the monsters and she's not moving and Ben and Bel went in to try and pull her out and Bel told me to fetch Mr. Uncle Tom Tring. So will you come, please, sir, *quick!*"

FIVE

Ex-Detective Sergeant Tring took charge. After a piercing look at Charlie—and Tom could do piercing looks with the best of them despite his usual geniality—he said, "Calm down, young shaver. I'm coming. Just hold your horses a minute. Mrs. Hatch, you've done a good job and I'm going to have to ask you to hold the fort again. Can I rely on you?"

"Don't 'ave much choice, do I."

"Mrs. Fletcher, you're going to have to find a doctor and . . . Ah. Here comes Mrs. Prasad."

"Sakari!" Daisy hurried to meet her friend. "Good timing."

"I thought you might need assistance, Daisy. What can I do?"

"Mrs. Prasad, Mrs. Fletcher must find a doctor. Have you any idea—?"

"There is an office at the far end of the Palace. If they have no doctor employed here, they must at least have a telephone."

"Thank you. And a copper, Mrs. Fletcher."

"I'm on my way." She noticed that Charlie looked anxious. "Charlie, you've done well. Mr. Tring will take care of you, just do what he tells you."

At the door, glancing back, she heard Tom say, "Mrs. Prasad,

I'd take it kindly if you'd stay here and help Mrs. Hatch keep everyone out."

"Willingly, Mr. Tring. I am more than ready put up my feet."

Glancing back, Daisy saw Tom and Charlie following her as Sakari sank into one of the sagging sofas.

Tom said, "All right, lad, tell me the whole story. Monsters, eh?"

Then the door swung closed behind Daisy. Not knowing which way they would go, she didn't wait for them.

Monsters indeed, she thought. The prehistoric creatures were somewhere in the park, she was sure. What on earth had taken Nanny Gilpin into the park? And what had taken the children after her?

No doubt she'd find out sooner or later. In the meantime, she ought to plan what she was going to say to the police. She was torn between ringing Scotland Yard and asking for Detective Sergeant Piper—who had probably gone to Bristol with Alec, come to think of it—or talking directly to the local division like any ordinary citizen.

If the division were in charge, perhaps Superintendent Crane would never find out she was responsible for the discovery of the corpse in the Crystal Palace, though she could hardly keep it from Alec. The Super would be even less pleased than Alec. Honestly, anyone would think she did it on purpose!

The nave was quite crowded now. Coming to the central aisle, Daisy spotted Mrs. Tring between people, statues, and greenery and managed to catch her attention. They both altered course to meet.

"Did the twins get off all right, Mrs. Tring?"

"Yes indeed. Mr. Truscott was waiting. They hopped right into the car, such good poppets. I gave them each a lollipop."

"That was very kind of you." How lucky Mrs. Gilpin wasn't there to object! Whatever had happened to Mrs. Gilpin?

"I hope my Tom sorted out your trouble, Mrs. Fletcher?"

"He's been very helpful but it's still a work in progress. I'm on my way to ring for the police."

"I hope your nanny is all right?"

"I'm not exactly sure. But I'd better not stop to explain. If you go to the ladies' room, Mrs. Prasad will tell you what's going on."

Daisy hurried on along the nave. It seemed endless, being even longer than the one she had come from, since the end of that had burned down long ago and never been rebuilt. When she came to the Crystal Fountain, she spared it hardly a glance in passing. Somewhere beyond it was the office—Ah, there was a sign.

The restaurant was nearby and appetising smells wafted to her nostrils. If not for Mrs. Gilpin's strange behaviour, they would all by now be sitting at a table ordering lunch. What had possessed the woman to go traipsing out to the park and fall into a lake?

Pushing open the door of the office, Daisy came upon a young girl almost in tears. In her hands was a spool of type-writer ribbon, one end of which disappeared into the bowels of her machine. Her fingers were liberally splotched with ink, some of which had transferred to her face.

"Having trouble?" Daisy said sympathetically.

"It's a different make from the one I learned on!" she wailed, then cast a hunted look at a door into an inner office. "I've only just started, and now I'm bound to get the sack."

"I expect I can sort it out for you, but first, I need to use your telephone."

"Oh, but I'm not allowed to let anyone use it. There are public telephones—"

"I've got to call the police. It's urgent. I haven't time to go hunting for a public phone."

"Why, what's happened?"

"Listen and you'll know as much as I do." Daisy sat down on a chair beside the desk, pulled the phone towards her, and lifted the receiver. The girl cast another glance at the connecting door but didn't object again. "Hello, operator. Give me the police, please." She covered the receiver with her hand. "Have you got a doctor here?"

"It's my first week. I don't know."

"Go and ask him." She gestured at the door.

"I daren't!"

"Go. I'll deal with him. Hello?"

"Sydenham Police Station, Sergeant Wimbish."

"Hello, Sergeant. My name is Fletcher, Mrs. Fletcher. I'm reporting a dead body in the ladies retiring room at the Crystal Palace."

The girl squawked and fled to the inner office.

"A body?" said the sergeant in the gruff voice of sceptical officialdom. "Dead?"

"Yes, that's right."

"You're having me on. Wasting police time is an offence—"

"This is not a hoax. Ex–Detective Sergeant Tring of the Yard told me to telephone."

"Sergeant Tring? He's there? Let me speak to him."

"He's here at the Palace, but not here with me in the Palace office."

"Oh?" Scepticism became suspicion.

"He's seen the body. But he couldn't come with me." Should she mention Nanny's plight? Better not, until and unless it turned out to be relevant. "Someone had to stay there to keep people away," she added, truthfully if misleadingly.

Nothing but heavy breathing came to Daisy's ear for a moment, then the sergeant said, "Please hold the line a moment, madam."

Daisy agreed to hold. She looked up to see a small, fat man, crimson in the face, breathing stertorously at her, his eyes popping. The girl hovered behind him.

"Madam, this is a private telephone!"

She raised her eyebrows. "So I was informed. I assumed you wouldn't care to obstruct police business."

His small mouth pursed. "Are you claiming there really is a body?"

"Do I look like a practical joker? I assure you—"

"Mrs. Fletcher?" That was the phone.

44

"Excuse me. Hello?"

"Mrs. Alec Fletcher?"

"Ye-es," Daisy admitted.

"This is Detective Inspector Mackinnon."

"Mr. Mackinnon? What a relief! I mean—"

"Never mind, Mrs. Fletcher." The redheaded Scot's amusement was all too obvious over the wire. "I know what you mean. Now tell me what you've got yourself into this time."

"I . . ." She remembered just in time that she had listeners. The man had edged closer, his head cocked. "I'm in the Palace office—Sergeant Wimbish told you I'm at the Crystal Palace?—and I'm not alone. Can't you just take my word for it that you need to come? Or send someone?"

"Willingly, but my superiors like their *i*'s dotted and their *t*'s crossed."

"Oh, of course, I don't want to land you in hot water. Just a minute. Please, Mr. . . . ?"

"Ledbetter. I must protest—"

"Will you please go into the other room, and close the door behind you?" She knew she was being high-handed but she had taken an instant dislike to the man, a rarity for her. "This is a private matter."

"This is a private office," he stormed.

"Yes, I'm sorry to trouble you, but—"

"Let me speak to him." He grabbed the receiver from her hand. "Who is this? I wish to protest in the strongest terms the invasion of my private office."

"I am Detective Inspectorr Mackinnon of the Metropolitan Police, P Division." His voice was loud enough for Daisy to hear, and very Scottish now. "To whom am I speaking, sirr?"

"My name is Ledbetter. I'm the manager of the Crystal Palace. This young woman—" He quailed at Daisy's glare. "This young lady barged into my office with a cock-and-bull story about—"

"Mr. Ledbetterr, let me get this strraight. Arre you saying you do not wish the prrroper authorrities to investigate the rreport of a possibly crrriminal incident in the establishment you manage?"

"Of course not!"

"I beg your pardon. Then you would have preferred that Mrs. Fletcher telephone from a public box, where anyone could have overheard her and spread the story through the crowd—"

Ledbetter ran his finger round inside his collar. "Well, no."

"Of course not. In my opeenion, Mrs. Fletcher has acted verra prroperly. Now I require further details, such as are not to be bandied before the public, being in this case your good self. Therefore I officially request, sir, that you provide for Mrs. Fletcher a telephone and a place of privacy to use it."

"Oh, if it's *official*, that's another matter. Come along, Miss Carr. Don't dawdle." As he handed the receiver back to Daisy, with a scowl, he noticed the devastated typewriter ribbon and transferred the scowl to his secretary. "You've already wrecked the machine!"

As the door to the inner office closed behind them, Daisy heard the girl attempting to excuse her contretemps with the ribbon.

"Mrs. Fletcher? Do I gather that Mr. Tring is with you?"

"With me at the Crystal Palace, but not with me at this moment. He checked that the woman is really dead."

"He's making sure no one goes near, I assume."

Daisy was happy to let him assume. She told him the whole story, omitting only that Mrs. Gilpin had not rejoined the twins and the nursery maid, and that Tom had gone looking for her. That had nothing to do with the dead nanny. She hoped.

"You'll send someone?" she asked when the tale was told.

"I'll come myself, and bring the divisional surgeon, or another doctor if he's unavailable. It'll take a while—they patched me in from Peckham—but I'll send a couple of local officers, with instructions to put themselves under Mr. Tring's command. Should they ask for the Palace office?"

"No fear! Tell them to go straight to the north end ladies' room. I'm persona non grata here."

46

Mackinnon laughed. "Right you are. I'll see you as soon as I can make it. Let me have a word with the irate gentleman."

"Don't mention my husband!"

"I won't," he promised, laughing again.

" 'A source of innocent merriment,' " Daisy quoted silently as she fetched Ledbetter to the telephone. If only Superintendent Crane viewed her propensity for finding bodies in the same light.

She hurried back along the endless nave, the size of the building now more an irritant than a source of wonder. Just after crossing the central aisle, she heard Belinda's voice behind her.

"Mummy, wait!"

"Darling! What's going on? Is Mrs. Gilpin all right?"

"No. Oh, Mummy, it's awful. Ben and I pulled her out of the water, but she's awfully cold. She's all muzzy in her head, too, and she can't remember what happened. Uncle Tom says she probably hit her head on the snake-neck monster. Her face is sort of greeny white. I expect she was sick after I left."

"Poor Mrs. Gilpin! Did she say why she went out into the park instead of going home with the twins?"

"No. We saw her following the other nanny, but we don't know why. Mummy, Uncle Tom said to get hold of a doctor and someone to help carry her."

"All right." Daisy contemplated returning to the Palace office and decided discretion was the better part of valour. "Have you noticed a public telephone?"

"Yes, by the entrance where we came in."

"Good. There's an attendant there, too. We can ask for help. Come along. You'll have to explain where to find them. By the way, darling, I'm proud of you for going to the rescue."

"And Ben."

"And Ben, of course. And Charlie for coming on his own to tell us."

The attendant at the gate, an Australian by his accent, was a different kettle of fish from his superior at the office. He not only gave Daisy the name—Merriam—of a local doctor who was occasionally called in when a visitor needed attention, he lent her change for the telephone, taking it from his till.

"And don't you worry, madam. While you ring up, I'll organise a couple of chaps with a stretcher."

"Thank you. My daughter here can describe exactly where to find the vict—the patient."

"Good on you, young lady."

"Oh, I nearly forgot, Uncle Tom said blankets and hot drinks, too."

The man nodded to her. "I'll get ahold of a thermos of something. Alf! Alf, come over here a minute! There's blankets go with the stretcher, right?"

Daisy left them to it. The telephone operator knew Dr. Merriam's number and put her through right away. The doctor's wife answered the phone and said crossly that her husband had just sat down to his lunch. Daisy persuaded her to at least pass on a message. Counting her pennies, she found she had enough for another six minutes, but he came on the line before the first three were up. She explained the situation.

"Well, that's a change," he said cheerfully. "It's usually children who go climbing those prehistoric beasts and fall in the lake. They're bringing her up to the Palace, you said. To one of the ladies' retiring rooms?"

"I imagine so. The north end, I expect, as it's already closed off. The man at the entrance should be able to direct you." Besides, the police would want to talk to Mrs. Gilpin, as she must have been there about the time of the other nanny's death.

"Oh? What—"

"Sorry, I mustn't talk about it. And I really must run."

When Daisy found Belinda, she was with the gatekeeper, Alf, and a third attendant, poring over a map of the park. The gatekeeper had identified her "snake-neck monster" as a plesiosaur. As Daisy reached them, Bel triumphantly put her fingertip on the map. "Here it is. Next to this island. We waded across."

Daisy hadn't noticed Belinda's dampness before but the hem of her skirt was still dripping.

48

The gatekeeper marked the spot with a cross and gave the map to Alf.

"Right you are, miss. We'll find it easy without troubling you to lead the way. We're off." He picked up a folded stretcher and the pair departed.

Daisy thanked the gatekeeper. "We'll go back to the ladies' room," she said to Belinda. "Sakari and Mrs. Tring will be dying to know what's going on."

"I wanted to go with them."

"I want you to stay with me, darling. One less to worry about. What a morning!"

SIX

Daisy and Belinda found Sakari and Mrs. Tring chatting comfortably on a sofa. Mrs. Tring was knitting. She never went anywhere—even the pub, Tom had once revealed—without her knitting.

"Did anyone go in there?" Daisy asked.

"Only the two of us," said Sakari. "It was necessary."

"We didn't poke about."

"Mrs. Tring would not let me."

"Good."

"I might have noticed something of interest."

"And you might have mucked up evidence. Not that there's any reason to suppose it wasn't a natural death." Daisy frowned. "Except . . . I only had a brief glimpse, but she seemed awfully young to drop dead unexpectedly."

"Daisy, the child!" Sakari protested.

"I don't mind," said Belinda earnestly. "When your father is a detective, you hear all sorts of things. Besides, Aunt Sakari, remember when Deva and I, and Lizzie, found—"

"All too well. I hope the local police here are less obnoxious than the ones we faced at that time."

"He was frightful, wasn't he?" said Daisy. "DI Mackinnon is on the way. I know him, and he's altogether a different kettle of fish. He's coming from Peckham, though. A couple of men from the Sydenham Station should get here first. If one is the sergeant I spoke to, he'll be sticky, unless Mackinnon gave him what-for."

"Well," Sakari observed comfortably, "you and I did not quail before Detective Inspector Gant—was that not his name?—and I expect we can hold our own with this sergeant fellow. However, I am sorely in need of fortification. If Belinda will go with me to help, I shall obtain sandwiches for everyone and bring them back here."

"That sounds like an excellent idea!"

Belinda looked as if she'd rather stay, but she was a well-mannered child. "Of course I'll help, Aunt Sakari."

They went off together. Though Daisy was hungry, she was sorry to lose her friend's support in the face of Sergeant Wimbish's hostility. Sakari on her high horse was an awe-inspiring phenomenon.

"Don't you worry your head about that sergeant, deary," said Mrs. Tring, patting her hand. "I never met a copper yet I couldn't put in his place."

Daisy laughed. "I expect you've had plenty of practice with Tom."

"So've you, with the Chief, don't forget. I can't believe a uniform sergeant's going to bother you."

"Not for long, anyway, with Inspector Mackinnon on his way."

She didn't have to test her mettle against Wimbish. Perhaps cravenly, he sent two constables, as Daisy discovered when she went to answer a knock on the door. The elder of the pair was a grizzled veteran. The other was very young and very red-faced.

"Come in, officers," she invited. "I'm Mrs. Fletcher."

"Are there any ladies," the senior asked warily, "in a state of undress?"

"No." Daisy suppressed an urge to add, "Not even the deceased."

He took off his helmet. Stepping in, he glanced round the room as if half-fearful, half-hoping that a scantily clad houri would appear out of the woodwork. Mrs. Tring, large, placid, and busy with her knitting, both disappointed and relieved him. "Just two of you, are there?"

"As you see. This is Mrs. Tring."

"Where's Sergeant Tring? I was told he's here."

"He was needed elsewhere," said Mrs. Tring tranquilly. "He'll be back before the inspector gets here." She laid a slight stress on the word "inspector."

The reminder of the imminent arrival of his superior punctured the constable's officiousness. "Thank you, madam." Suddenly he swung round, pointed, and snapped, "Who's that?"

Startled, Daisy looked. No one was visible, but he must have caught sight of Mrs. Hatch, she realised. Hearing the male voice, she must have popped her head out to see what was going on. Not that she could see much, poor woman.

"The attendant, Mrs. Hatch," she said to the constable. "I forgot about her. Inspector Mackinnon is sure to want to talk to her."

"Why? Did she see what happened?"

"Doubtless that will be one of the questions he asks her."

Disconcerted, he snapped at the young constable, who had followed him in and stayed uncertainly by the door. "On guard outside. Don't let anyone in."

"What about Inspector Mackinnon?"

"Well, of course."

"And Sergeant Tring?"

"I suppose so."

"As if that pipsqueak could stop my Tom!" Mrs. Tring murmured just loud enough for Daisy to hear.

They smiled at each other and Daisy sat down beside her to wait. The constable paced back and forth. To Daisy, he seemed to be approaching closer and closer to the unfortunate Mrs. Hatch, huddled invisibly in her cubby. Daisy wondered if she'd need to go to the rescue.

Before she had to decide, the door opened. Tom entered. "Constable, come and lend a hand."

Responding to his authoritative voice, the man didn't argue. They both went out, leaving the door open. Through the doorway came the confused sound of a crowd.

"I can't abide people with nothing better to do than gawk at other people's business," said Mrs. Tring.

Outside, the voices of the two constables rose: "Move along, there. Move along, please."

Tom returned. After him came two tired attendants wheeling a folding stretcher, then Sakari and Belinda carrying baskets, and last Ben and Charlie, both soaked to the skin. Daisy was afraid their lips would have been blue if not for their dark skin.

"I rescued Mrs. Nanny's hat," Charlie explained proudly.

Mrs. Gilpin's lips *were* blue although she was swathed in blankets. She lay inert on the stretcher and didn't stir as the men transferred her to a sofa. As Mrs. Tring bustled about rearranging cushions to make her comfortable, Daisy tipped the stretcher men generously.

"You fellows," said Mrs. Tring, "and Tom, please go away. We must get her wet things off."

"Bring dry blankets," Sakari commanded.

"Boys, don't go," said Daisy. "Into the other room with you and don't touch anything. Don't you dare open any of the doors. Mrs. Tring, I'll get you some towels. Belinda, come and help."

As Daisy hoped, Mrs. Hatch had a good supply of replacement roller towels. Though the same thin linen cloth as the hand napkins, their size made them much more useful. After another generous tip to the attendant, she was permitted to carry off two-thirds of them. She kept four and had Belinda take the rest to Mrs. Tring.

The four she took through to the lavatories. The boys stood sodden and shivering in the middle of the floor.

"We're frightfully cold, Aunt Daisy."

"Here." She handed each two towels. "Strip off. Use one to

dry yourself. I'm sure you have sufficient ingenuity to turn the others into some sort of toga to make yourselves decent."

Leaving, she heard Charlie ask in a loud whisper, "What's 'sufficient ingenuity'?"

"Clever enough."

"What's a toga?"

"It's a thing the Romans wear. I learned about them in Latin. I'll show you a picture when we get home. Come on, get undressed."

"I can't undo my tie. It's got in a knot."

"Here, I'll do it."

Daisy turned at the door. "By the way, I'm proud of you both. I'll be telling Aunt Geraldine and Uncle Edgar what a good job you did. You may have saved Mrs. Gilpin's life."

Mrs. Gilpin had been stripped and dried by Sakari and Mrs. Tring, as attested by a heap of crumpled towels and a neat stack of wet, folded clothes. They were wrapping her in a blanket that presumably wasn't damp.

"How is she doing?" Daisy asked, approaching.

"Nasty bump on the back of her head," said Mrs. Tring.

"I would put ice on it," said Sakari, "if she were not so cold."

"Is she bleeding?"

"It's just a graze. Mrs. Tring cleaned it."

"Mrs. Fletcher?" The nurse's voice wavered. Her eyes blinked open. "What happened?"

"Mrs. Gilpin! How do you feel?"

"My head aches terribly, madam. What happened? Did I fall?"

"We're hoping you can tell us."

She closed her eyes. "I can't remember." Suddenly her eyes opened again, wild with alarm, and she struggled against the enveloping blanket. "The twins! Where are the twins?"

Daisy put a hand on her shoulder and pressed her back, saying, "They're perfectly all right. Bertha looked after them and took them home in Lady Dalrymple's car."

"Oh, thank heaven." Tears sprang to her eyes. "I should never have left them!"

Though Daisy agreed, this was not the time to say so. "What *do* you remember?"

"I went to the . . . the ladies' convenience. Is that where we are?"

"Yes. In the retiring room."

"So the pool and the monsters were just a bad dream."

Daisy saw Belinda begin to speak and gave her a slight frown.

Nurse Gilpin went on, "I don't see how I came to fall. The floor wasn't slippery. And how did I get so wet?" Her wandering gaze fell on Bel and filled with suspicion. "Unless Miss Belinda threw a bucket of—"

"I did not! I wouldn't play such a scurvy trick. I and the boys *rescued* you—"

"That will do, Bel. I heard a knock on the door. Go and see who it is. Mrs. Gilpin, you were found in the pond at the far end of the park. Concentrate on that and perhaps you'll remember why you went there."

"Do not press her now, Daisy." Sakari came with a steaming cup from the table where she and Belinda had set down the baskets. "Whatever occurred, she has had a most distressing experience. Here is some soup."

"And here are dry blankets," said Belinda. "The stretcher man brought them. Mummy, Detective Inspector Mackinnon presents his compliments and wants to know if he may come in."

"Five minutes," Mrs. Tring said firmly.

"I'd better go and talk to him," said Daisy with a sigh. "I didn't tell him about Nurse Gilpin."

"Uncle Tom's telling him."

"I'll bring him up to date on her condition. He mustn't press her too hard."

"Will he want to ask me questions too? Me and the boys?"

"I expect so. Yes, I'm sure he will. So will I! Don't worry, he's a nice man. He's worked with your father more than once."

"And with you?"

"Well, if you want to put it that way, yes."

"Oh, all right. Are we going to have lunch soon? I'm awfully hungry. Aunt Sakari got two picnic baskets, each for four people. People buy them to picnic in the park. There's different kinds of sandwiches and cold chicken and hard-boiled eggs. Cakes and biscuits, too, and bottled lemonade and ginger beer."

"As far as I'm concerned, everyone had better eat when they have a moment, but ask Sakari, darling, I'll leave it to her."

Daisy went out to the passage. The local police had left, she was glad to see. An unknown bobby was moving on the curious onlookers. Two plainclothesmen, one with a camera and the other with a satchel, stood looking bored. Tom, Mackinnon, and a third man, who carried a doctor's black bag, were talking together in quiet voices. She went over to them.

"Mrs. Fletcher." Mackinnon greeted her with a smile and a handshake. "We meet again. This is Dr. Merriam, a local practitioner."

"How do you do, Doctor. We spoke on the telephone. Thank you for coming so quickly."

He nodded acknowledgement. "I should like to see my patient as soon as possible, Mrs. Fletcher."

"Of course. Please go right in, Doctor—at least, that's all right, isn't it, Inspector?"

"Certainly. My police surgeon is on his way. When are we to be allowed in?"

"Mrs. Tring said five minutes. But as Dr. Merriam will be examining Mrs. Gilpin, I'd better check before you all troop in there."

"Nae dout, nae dout. I can't call to mind ever having to invade a ladies' sanctuary before. Ye've talked to yon nanny?"

"A little. She seems not to be able to remember anything after leaving the twins to go to the ladies'."

Mackinnon pounced on the doubtful word, just as Alec would have. "'Seems'?"

"I didn't really mean anything by it." Daisy considered. "She

56

says she can't remember. I have no reason to doubt her. But it's hard to believe she could forget walking all the way to the other end of the park and falling in a pond."

"Not surprising," rumbled Tom. "It's often the case with head injuries."

"Then, will she remember later? I'm not just being nosy. If I'm going to continue to trust her with my children, I want to know whether she had a good reason to go off when she was supposed to be looking after them. A really good reason."

"Understood," said Mackinnon. "I'll keep it in mind. Would you go, please, and find out if it's all clear?"

Daisy returned to the retiring room. Dr. Merriam was bending over Mrs. Gilpin. Sakari, Mrs. Tring, and Belinda had all seized the momentary calm to possess themselves of sandwiches. Still no sign of the boys: Daisy wondered briefly if they were having trouble with their togas. Then the doctor came over to her.

"Mrs. Fletcher, you're my patient's employer?"

"Yes. How is she?"

"I don't foresee any major problems, except possibly the memory loss. But she will need to keep very quiet for a few days, with someone keeping an eye on her. Will that present any difficulty?"

"Not at all."

"I'll tell the detective to postpone talking to her, if possible, and if not to treat her with the utmost consideration."

"He's not here because of what happened to her. He may not want to question her at all."

"That would be ideal. You may, of course, call me in if need be, though I have no objection to your consulting your own doctor."

"We live in Hampstead. It would be frightfully inconvenient for you. I won't bother you unless my doctor wants to consult you. Here's my card. Send the bill to me, please."

He bowed and took his leave. Daisy followed him to the door.

"You can come in now, Inspector." She stepped back and he

came through into the retiring room, with his plainclothesmen at his heels and Tom bringing up the rear.

At the other end of the room, the boys appeared, precariously draped in roller towels. Ben's was slipping off his shoulder. Charlie's dangled round his feet, in imminent danger of tripping him.

"Aunt Daisy, we need pins!"

"So I see." She also saw that Mackinnon was valiantly striving to keep a straight face.

"Don't worry, Daisy." Sakari hefted her handbag. "I have pins. Boys, come into this corner out of the way."

Charlie had spotted the food. "I'm *ravenous!*"

"You shall eat as soon as you're safe from indecent exposure."

"What's—"

"Come on, Charlie," his brother urged. "Don't keep Mrs. Prasad waiting."

"My cousins," Daisy explained to Mackinnon. "They got soaked to the skin."

He grinned. "Boys that age have a knack for it. Just as you have a knack for—"

"Please don't say it!"

"All right. I shall want some details from you, though, so don't fold your tent and steal away."

"I shan't."

"Mr. Tring?"

Tom led the three detectives into the inner room. Mrs. Hatch was too cowed to protest as the four large men passed into the inner sanctum.

Daisy seized the momentary lull to snabble something to eat. The boys came to join her, looking, after Sakari's efforts, as if they'd just stepped off the stage of *Julius Caesar*. "All secure?" she asked.

"As secure as a sari, Aunt Sakari said," Ben assured her.

"And I have never lost one yet, Daisy, I promise . . ."

"It feels funny," said Charlie, squirming.

"But I do not wriggle," Sakari said severely.

Charlie froze, gripping the front of his toga as if he'd been stabbed by Brutus. "I'll be careful. What is there to eat?"

Belinda came over just then with a request from Mrs. Tring for more soup for the invalid. After dealing with this and making sure Mrs. Tring was well fed, Daisy turned back to the boys to find Charlie with a thick slice of Battenberg cake in one hand and cherry cake in the other.

"He is on holiday, Daisy," Sakari pointed out.

"So you let him stuff himself with—" She laughed. "Oh, all right. But you must eat some proper food after."

"I was going to anyway," said Charlie, injured.

"Mrs. Fletcher?" One of the detectives called her from the attendant's cubby. "Mr. Mackinnon would like to speak to you, please."

"In there?"

"Yes, madam."

"Shall I go with you?"

"No, thanks, Sakari. I'd rather you kept an eye on the children."

Ben looked as if he wanted to object that they didn't need to be kept an eye on, but his mouth was too full.

Daisy went through, bestowing a consoling pat on Mrs. Hatch's shoulder as she passed. The first thing she saw was a small pile of wet clothes in the middle of the room.

"Oh those boys!"

"Never mind those. At least: You confirm that they belong to your young cousins and were not here when you originally came into the room?"

"Yes. You saw them in their togas."

"Very ingenious, too," murmured one of the sergeants.

Mackinnon gave him a quelling glare. "I'm sorry to ask this, Mrs. Fletcher, but would you mind taking another look at the deceased?"

Daisy wanted to say that she'd mind very much. However, the inspector knew that if not exactly accustomed to dead bodies, she was by no means inexperienced. "I'd rather not, but if you think it could help . . ."

"Let me ask this first: Mr. Tring mentioned that you had a vague feeling the face was familiar. Have you had any further thoughts, any brain wave, about who it might be?"

"I would certainly have told you if I had!" she said indignantly.

"I'm not suggesting otherwise. It's possible that seeing it again might jog your memory."

"I suppose so. I don't claim to have looked awfully closely."

"I can't blame you. However, our first job is to identify the—"

"*One* of your first jobs." The speaker, who had approached unobserved, was a tall, painfully thin man with a stoop and a sharp nose that gave him the air of a cockerel hunting for insects. He carried a black bag. "Ascertaining time of death ought not to be delayed."

"Hello, Doctor, glad you made it. Our divisional surgeon, Mrs. Fletcher. You can give us two minutes, Dr. Watchett."

"And not a second longer."

"Aweel, noo." Mackinnon looked at Daisy.

"Very well." She steeled herself as they crossed to the end cubicle. "Her face isn't . . . disfigured, is it? I don't recall . . ."

"Not a bit of it. Not a mark on it. Did you touch the handle?"

"N-no. No, I didn't. I noticed the door was ajar and I only had to push." She put out her hand, stopping short of the polished wood. "About here."

"Excellent."

"But dozens of people must have touched the knob. Dabs aren't going to help much, are they?"

"Very likely not, but you never know." The inspector reached past her to wrap the knob with a handkerchief and delicately turn it with two fingers. The door swung open. "Do exactly what you did before, as closely as possible."

Daisy stepped in. Her hesitant glance showed everything just as it had been before. "With her hat and wig all askew, it didn't seem possible she was just sleeping. I couldn't tell whether the poor thing was ill, unconscious or . . . or dead, so I tried to find a pulse. In her neck as she's wearing gloves." Reluctantly she touched the woman's neck. It had cooled noticeably. Repressing a shudder, she drew back and turned to the inspector. "Like that. I can't be sure of the precise spot."

"You couldn't find a pulse?"

"No, but I often can't find my own. Her neck felt quite warm, warmer than it is now. I decided it was better to go for help than to keep trying."

Mackinnon nodded. "Your touch didn't alter the position in any way?"

"Not at all."

"Two minutes is up," came the impatient voice of the doctor.

"Another thirty seconds. Does the face still seem familiar?"

"I don't know. I honestly can't say."

He sighed. "No, a fleeting impression is hard to rediscover. Look more closely, please."

Daisy complied. She stared at the short blond hair under the wig, at the petulant mouth and obstinate chin. Or was she reading too much into the features of a dead woman? "I still think there's something odd, but I can't pin it down."

"Excuse me." He joined her in the now-cramped space. Lifting one of the limp hands, he eased off the glove. "And now?"

The hand revealed was square and strong, not really surprising. Nannies needed capable hands. The fingers were blunt-tipped, with short, manicured nails. Daisy couldn't see any distinguishing mark—ring, scar, or missing finger—by which she might be expected to recognise it.

"No," she said, puzzled. "But . . . Good heavens, she's not—" In spite of a vague suspicion, a glance at the body's torso startled her. No bosom! How had she failed to notice? "It's a man? I don't believe it!"

SEVEN

"*And then* the doctor put his foot down," Daisy told Sakari, "and insisted on making his examination. Mr. Mackinnon didn't get round to confirming or denying my guess."

"Perhaps the inspector is not certain, Daisy, until the doctor has examined her . . . or him. Or perhaps it is a *hijra*, one of those unfortunate creatures such as we have in India that are neither one nor the other."

"A hermaphrodite? I suppose it's possible," Daisy said doubtfully. "It wouldn't explain the disguise, nor what he's doing dead in the lavs. Nor why he seems familiar."

Charlie came over so they dropped the subject.

"Thank you for the lunch, Aunt Sakari," he said with a punctiliousness probably coached by Belinda, to which he added his own enthusastic coda: "It was a smashing spread! Aunt Daisy, may we go and explore some more? We may never have another chance," he said mournfully.

"In your togas? Good gracious no!"

"I didn't get a chance to look at the monsters properly. No one would notice us in the park. We could sneak behind the bushes like we did before."

"Not even in the park. Besides, Detective Inspector Mackinnon may want to talk to you."

Charlie heaved a sigh. "Then when are we going home?"

"Patience! Not until Nanny Gilpin is fit to be moved. And Truscott gets back here."

"By the way, Daisy, when Belinda and I fetched the lunch baskets, I rang home to tell Kesin not to wait until five o'clock but to bring the car back here right away."

"Oh, good. I'll go and see how Mrs. Gilpin is doing."

"Mrs. Tring seems a very competent nurse," said Sakari.

"She was a VAD during the war."

Daisy went over to the sofa where Mrs. Gilpin lay, with Mrs. Tring sitting close by knitting. Eyes closed, the nurse was very pale, her lips bloodless. "How is she?" Daisy asked in a low voice.

"None so bad, considering. She's best not fussed, and so I shall tell the inspector. I hope Tom's just watching and listening, not interfering?"

"He's being very discreet. I forgot he was there."

Mrs. Tring sighed. "He does miss the job, and that's the truth."

"I'm so very glad he's here. I don't know what we'd have done without him."

"Managed very well, I don't doubt, Mrs. Fletcher," she said tartly, but she looked pleased.

"And that goes for you, too."

"Nonsense!"

"Truly. Nursing is not my forte. I'll hire a nurse to take care of Mrs. Gilpin at home."

"I was wondering if you might let me take care of her. I take an interest in the poor creature already, and besides, you wouldn't have to worry about her rambling in her mind and maybe saying things none but the police ought to hear."

"What a good idea! I'd much rather have someone I know and trust. I'd pay you the same as any agency nurse, of course."

"That's not necessary, Mrs. Fletcher, though I don't deny I wouldn't mind earning a bit of pocket money."

"So you shall."

"You'll let me break it to Tom, if you don't mind. There's no knowing how he'll take it."

"Tell him you'll be doing me a favour. How soon shall we able to take her home?"

"She could be moved now, if we can get the stretcher back. Better wait for the inspector, don't you think?"

"Truscott and Kesin won't be here for a while yet, anyway."

Belinda came over. "Mummy," she whispered, "mayn't we *please* sneak into the back of the Roman gallery, just to show Charlie what a toga ought to look like? The entrance is only just across the passage from the ladies' room. If anyone's there, we won't go in, and if anyone comes, we'll leave right away."

"All right, go! Back here in ten minutes flat. And if you start any rumours about the ghosts of ancient Romans—"

"Oh, Mummy, no one will see us, honestly." Bel fled before Daisy could change her mind.

"Weak of me, I know, but they've been pretty patient."

"They're the heroes of the hour, remember."

"Their hour is past. I wish Mr. Mackinnon would get on with it."

"More haste, less speed."

"I daresay. But I, for one, am heartily sick of sitting about in a ladies' room, and I do believe the smell of Jeyes gets stronger by the minute."

"Have you had anything to eat?"

"No," said Daisy, surprised. "I recall picking up a sandwich. I must have put it down somewhere. I haven't had a moment to think about it."

"You have a moment now, and I expect you'll feel much better for it."

Sakari, foreseeing her need, had poured a mug of soup and prepared a plate of food. Daisy was finishing off a second sandwich when the children returned, giggling. Though quite certain she'd be happier to remain in ignorance of the cause of their glee, she was equally certain she ought to investigate.

Mackinnon's reappearance allowed her to evade the decision. He came towards her. She noticed that he had left Tom Tring at the cubby between the two rooms, talking to Mrs. Hatch. If anyone could extract information from that poor bewildered woman, Tom was the man. Alec had always relied on his way with servants, especially female. Mackinnon was sensible to utilise his abilities even though he was retired.

Daisy wished she could hear what was being said.

"Mrs. Fletcher, I'd like to talk to the children now."

"Before Mrs. Gilpin?"

"Yes, I'm hoping they'll give me a better idea of what I need to ask her. Besides, you must be wanting to get them home, dry, and properly clothed." He had a straight face and a twinkle in his eye.

"We've got to wait for our cars. I can't imagine how I'm going to get the boys out to them without causing a scandal."

"That, I'm happy to say, is entirely up to you."

"If you have any bright ideas, let me know. The same goes for Mrs. Gilpin as for them. She ought to be in bed."

"I'll wait until she is before I see her."

"You don't believe she just slipped and fell and knocked her head?"

"I'll not rule out the possibility, Mrs. Fletcher, but there are altogether too many nannies in this story to just ignore them. When she's more comfortable, likely she'll be better able to give her mind to remembering. You may take her home as soon as convenient."

"Thank you! Sakari," she called to her friend, who had moved to a discreet distance, "we can take Mrs. Gilpin home as soon as Truscott or Kesin gets here, if we arrange for a stretcher to carry her to the street. Would you mind awfully—"

"Leave it to me, Daisy."

"Mrs. Prasad, please make use of the uniformed constables outside as errand boys."

Belinda and Ben exchanged a swift glance.

"We don't mind running errands," said Ben.

"We'd *like* to run errands," said Charlie. "It's pretty dull here."

"Dressed like that?" said Sakari dryly. "I think not."

Mackinnon intervened. "I want to talk to the three of you."

The glories of being interrogated by the police narrowly outshone those of running errands in togas. Mackinnon sat them down in a row on a sofa opposite a pair of chairs for Daisy and himself. Bel and Ben were solemn. Charlie wriggled.

"I've heard what happened from Sergeant Tring," said Mackinnon. "Now I want to hear from you, all the details, and why you acted as you did."

"Are we in trouble?" asked Charlie, not visibly troubled by the prospect.

Mackinnon grinned. "Not from me, laddie. You probably saved Mrs. Gilpin's life. The police like people who save lives, when they don't put themselves in danger."

"Good."

"We didn't put ourselves in danger," Ben affirmed. "We hid behind statues and trees and bushes all the way."

"Nearly all the way," Belinda corrected conscientiously. "There weren't any in the passage, at the beginning."

"Tell me about the beginning, what got you started."

They all started talking at once. The story proceeded with many interruptions and digressions, Mackinnon patiently sorting out the relevant from the irrelevant. As for Daisy, she continued to veer between dismay at their having embarked on the quest in the first place, gladness that they had been on hand to rescue Nanny Gilpin, and admiration at their persistence.

To those mixed emotions was added intense curiosity about the third nanny. If she had nothing to do with the male masquerader's death, why had she fled?

Daisy could think of only one reason, and Mackinnon seemed to be thinking along the same lines.

"How tall was the nanny Mrs. Gilpin was following?" he asked.

"Ever so tall," Charlie said promptly. "Tall as a tree."

"He's such a shrimp, he thinks everyone is tall."

"Most grown-ups look tall to us," Belinda pointed out.

"You didn't happen to notice how the nurse's height compared with the people you passed?"

"Too many statues," said Ben succinctly.

Bel agreed. "You feel as if you're surrounded by gigantic people all the time. All the real people are like midgets."

"Och, I know well what you mean. Didn't I feel like a dwarf myself walking among them!"

"But other people are still bigger than us."

"And lots of the statues are rude," Charlie added sotto voce.

Mackinnon bit his lip and hastily asked, "Did you notice, by the way, how the nanny walked?"

"Fast," said Charlie. "We had to run."

"Show me. All of you: Walk across the room pretending you're imitating . . . her."

The exercise didn't seem useful to Daisy. Belinda walked fast with small ladylike steps; Ben strode along; and Charlie pranced.

Mackinnon shook his head. "Thank you. Did you happen to see her face well enough to recognise it if you saw it again?"

Three more heads shook in unison.

"She only ever glanced back."

"And she was too far away, anyway."

"When we first saw her," said Bel, "she was close and coming towards us, right past us, but she kept her head down. All you could see was her hat."

"Not her hair? The colour of her hair?"

They all shook their heads again.

"Too much to hope for. Thin or fat?"

"She was wearing a cape," Belinda told him. "You couldn't tell."

"All right, that'll be all for now. I'd like you to keep thinking about it, though. You might remember something more. Thank you for your help."

"We haven't been much help," said Ben, "not really."

"You'd be surprised. So far, I'm just getting a feel for what's happened. You have filled in parts of the picture. Like a jigsaw puzzle. Every piece you add gives you a better idea of what the rest is like."

"I like jigsaw puzzles," Charlie said thoughtfully. "Perhaps I'll be a policeman when I grow up."

"Sounds like a good plan, laddie. Off you go, now."

"Ask Aunt Sakari and Mrs. Tring if there's anything you can do for them."

"What do you think, Mrs. Fletcher," said Mackinnon, "can I rely on their evidence?"

"They didn't contradict each other, not seriously. I'm not sure I'd trust Charlie once he's had time for his imagination to get to work. The other two are reliable."

Tom joined them.

"Any luck, Sarge?"

"Not much, sir." He glanced at Daisy, who tried to look as if her attention was elsewhere. The inspector gestured to Tom to go on. "Mrs. Hatch is the name, Mavis Hatch. Nice old bird, still working to support a couple of great-grandchildren. Eighty-three years old, she informs me, and a one for the boys in her youth. The truth of the matter is, she remembers those days better than she does today's doings."

"She can't remember anything at all?" Mackinnon asked in dismay.

"Very little. Her eyesight and hearing aren't anything to write home about, either, and she dozes a lot. She has a vague impression of noticing several nannies all at once, but she can't say how many. She remembers being surprised at not noticing any children with them. The Palace isn't a place people bring babies, which they might leave outside the ladies. Little kiddies have to tag along and they usually make enough disturbance to draw her attention."

"Hm, I'm not sure where that gets us. She couldn't even say whether more than two nannies had gone through to the lavs at the same time?"

Tom shook his head, the electric light gleaming on the hairless dome. "If she had, I wouldn't take her word for it."

"Anything else?"

"Nothing worth hearing. I'll write you up my notes same as if I was still on the force."

"Thanks, Sarge. If there's anything good about this case, it's that you were on the spot."

"And Mrs. Fletcher," Tom said loyally.

"A mixed blessing," Mackinnon muttered almost silently, softly enough for Daisy to ignore it.

Besides, it was hard to disagree. One way or another, it was going to be impossible to keep Alec in ignorance. She shuddered when she considered his probable reaction. Unless Mackinnon had picked up some thread to follow that she had missed, he was likely to ask for help from the Yard. Her involvement made it almost certain Alec would be put in charge, if he came back from Bristol in time.

Assuming the masquerader had not died a natural death: As if in answer to Daisy's thought, the divisional surgeon appeared from the inner room, followed by the photographer and finger-print officer.

The latter pair sketched salutes towards the inspector. At his nod, they departed. The doctor came over. He glanced at Daisy and gave Mackinnon a questioning look.

"Thank you, Mrs. Fletcher. I'll call in Hampstead tomorrow to see whether Mrs. Gilpin is recovering and whether you or the children have remembered anything more. If you need help with getting everyone out to the street, just call on the constables outside the door."

"Thanks." Reluctantly Daisy rose. Tom followed suit, but Mackinnon waved him back to his seat.

"Please stay, Mr. Tring."

Fuming, Daisy rejoined Sakari and Mrs. Tring. They had worked out a plan to get everyone away without having to parade through the length of the Palace.

"Thanks to Ben," said Sakari, "the more because he and Charlie would have liked to show off their togas. He consulted the map in his guidebook and found a gate to the street quite close by, if we go out by the north end. At my request, one of Mr. Mackinnon's men went to instruct the bobby on duty outside the main entrance to keep an eye out for the two cars and redirect them thither."

"Oh good. Where are the boys?" Daisy asked.

"As soon as Tom finished with Mrs. Hatch," Mrs. Tring explained, "we sent them to beg, borrow, or buy a laundry bag from her and collect their wet clothes."

"What a good idea. I'll go and ring Cousin Geraldine to make sure Truscott is on his way. If not, I'll hire a car." As she turned to the exit, Mackinnon was already leaving and Tom was coming towards them. "I just want a quick word with Mr. Tring first."

"How can I help you, Mrs. Fletcher?" asked Tom.

Daisy drew him aside. "Did the doctor find out what he died of?"

"Ah." Tom ruminated, his eyes twinkling. "I've been told not to talk about it, but seeing I can't get the sack, and seeing it's you, Mrs. Fletcher, I'll say this much. Dr. Watchett discovered the immediate cause of death, but not what caused it."

"That's a riddle, not an answer!"

" 'Fraid so."

"What was the immediate cause?"

He shook his head, his moustache twitching as he grinned. "Sorry, it's not for me to say."

Daisy made a moue. "What about the time of death? Did he give you that?"

"At least half an hour, not more than two hours, before he arrived. But he could have been some time dying."

"How horrible! Do you . . . do they know who he is?"

"No idea. He had no papers on him, no laundry marks on his clothes, nothing. DI Mackinnon is counting on you to come through, to identify the elusive familiarity you claimed."

"Oh dear!" said Daisy.

EIGHT

The next morning, as soon as she had bathed and dressed, Daisy went up to the nursery. Bertha had all under control, the twins chattering happily as they dipped toast fingers in their soft-boiled eggs.

"Oh yes, madam, they're behaving ever so well. After breakfast, we'll do our ABCs, won't we, kiddies, and then walk to the Heath when it's warmed up a bit. Lovely day it is."

"Let me know when you're going to walk and I may come too." She went down to the bedroom now occupied by Mrs. Gilpin and tapped on the door.

Mrs. Tring called, "Come in."

Mrs. Gilpin was sitting up in bed, leaning against plumped pillows, with a breakfast tray on her lap. Pale and heavy-eyed, she glanced round as Daisy entered, then winced and put a hand to her head.

"Good morning, Mrs. Gilpin. I hope you slept well."

"Yes, thank you, Mummy—madam," she said listlessly.

"Do you—" Daisy hesitated, glancing at Mrs. Tring, who guessed her question and nodded permission. "Do you remember anything more? Why you chased after the other nanny?"

"I shouldn't've done it, madam! Leaving the babies alone in a place like that!"

"They weren't alone. Bertha's perfectly capable of looking after them." To her dismay, far from being comforted, the poor woman pushed away her tray and burst into tears. "I'm sure you had a good reason for going, even if you can't recall what it was."

Mrs. Tring bustled her out and she was only too glad to leave.

She went downstairs to breakfast, to find that Belinda and the boys had almost finished theirs. After an exchange of greetings, Daisy asked Elsie for scrambled eggs and toast, poured herself a cup of coffee, and enquired what their plans were for the day.

"The zoo," said Bel.

"I'm going to ride an elephant, Aunt Daisy," Charlie proclaimed, "and a camel and in a llama carriage."

"If it's not too expensive," Ben reminded him. "You already spent almost all your pocket money."

"I should think I might find some spare change in my handbag. Bel, when you've finished eating, go and fetch it from my bedroom and I'll see if I can contribute to the exchequer."

"Gosh, thanks, Aunt Daisy."

"May we take sandwiches, Mummy, so we don't have to come back to lunch? The rides aren't till the afternoon."

"Yes, but make them yourselves if Mrs. Dobson is busy. Without getting in her way."

Three or four letters lay by her place at table, and the newspaper, which she was making a conscientious effort to read regularly now that she was allowed to vote. She left them until the children had excused themselves and dashed off.

Nothing from Alec: Elsie would have put it on top. The top letter was the weekly screed from her sister, Violet. She set it aside for later. Under it was a scribbled note from Lucy: Having got over the morning sickness, she was constantly hungry; could Daisy meet her for lunch?

Daisy could, Bel and the boys having obligingly taken themselves off for the day. Unless she ought to stay in and wait for

DI Mackinnon . . . No, if he didn't telephone to make an appointment, he'd just have to risk her being out. Mrs. Gilpin and Mrs. Tring wouldn't miss her for a couple of hours.

The next envelope was addressed in untidy handwriting she didn't recognise at once, though there was something familiar about it. On the back flap was the discreetly embossed insignia of the Ritz Hotel.

Inside, as well as a folded sheet of Ritz notepaper, was a second envelope, with just her name written on it.

"Gloria!" she said aloud in surprise.

Her American friend, meticulous about Christmas and her birthday, rarely wrote at other times. And of course the outer envelope had Phillip's scrawl. Phillip Petrie had been her dead brother's best friend. Having promised Gervaise to take care of his little sister if he were killed in the war, he had done his best to marry Daisy when she failed to find herself a husband. She had refused him at least a dozen times, she thought affectionately. It had been a great relief when he fell in love with the daughter of an American millionaire whose passion, like his, was automobiles.

Setting aside Gloria's thick letter with Vi's, for later, Daisy unfolded the notepaper. As she had already guessed, Phillip was in London on business and looking forward to seeing her. "And Alec," he had inserted as an afterthought. Though horrified at her marrying a policeman, he had come round in the end.

The last letter, atop a pile of bills and circulars, was from Alec's mother. The usual litany of complaints, no doubt, leavened by a list of errands the elder Mrs. Fletcher hoped the younger would spare a few minutes to perform for her in London. "Leavened" was the wrong word. Not only would the errands certainly take several hours, but Daisy would earn no expression of gratitude for their performance.

What's more, she'd be unable to complete at least one task in a satisfactory manner, so it would be the subject of the next letter's complaints, and proof, besides, that her aristocratic upbringing had made her unfit to be a middle-class housewife.

Daisy poured another cup of coffee and spread another slice of toast thickly with butter and marmalade. Thus fortified, she slit open her mother-in-law's letter. Best to get it over with.

It was every bit as sticky as she expected, even without the marmalade fingerprints acquired in the reading.

Dealing with its demands would have to wait until Belinda went back to school. On the way to her office, Daisy dropped off on the hall table Mrs. Fletcher senior's enclosed notes to Bel and Alec. She rang up and left a message for Lucy, then Mrs. Dobson came in for their daily consultation. They were discussing the vagaries of the coal merchant and whether to try a different firm when the telephone rang.

"Good day, Mrs. Fletcher. Mackinnon here. How is the patient this morning?"

"Much better. She doesn't seem to remember anything more, though."

"Aweel, that's a pity. Perhaps I can jog her memory. Would it be convenient if I dropped by in about half an hour?"

"Yes, that's all right. Did you want to talk to the children, too? I'm afraid I let them go to the zoo."

"Never mind. I'll catch up with them later. Will you be at home?"

"Until about noon. I doubt I can help you. I must have imagined his face was familiar."

"I'll bring a photograph looking more like his normal appearance—"

"Except that he's dead."

"It's not obvious, I promise. They do wonders these days. You won't find it too upsetting."

"Less upsetting than finding the body, I daresay!"

"I daresay, although if I've learnt anything in this job it's that you never can be sure how people will react. I'll be with you shortly, Mrs. Fletcher."

Before Mackinnon arrived, Tom Tring turned up, ostensibly to see his wife. Daisy heard Elsie admitting him and went out to the hall to greet him.

74

"How is Mrs. Gilpin?" he asked.

"Not too bad, I gather. Mrs. Tring is better able to tell you. You're in luck," Daisy continued as she walked with him down to the kitchen where, according to the parlourmaid, Mrs. Tring was taking a cup of tea with Mrs. Dobson. "D.I. Mackinnon will be here in a few minutes."

He grinned. "Far be it from me to seek out the inspector. As the missus keeps telling me, I've got to learn to mind my own business."

"I can't count the number of times I've been told that."

"Didn't work, did it?"

"No. I'm so very glad and grateful it didn't work on you yesterday. I don't know what I'd have done without your help, Tom."

"You'd have managed, you and Mrs. Prasad between you." They reached the kitchen. "Good morning, Mrs. Dobson. How's it going, ducks?"

Daisy left them and went back to the office. As she finished the letter she'd been writing, the front doorbell rang again.

Elsie came in. "It's the police, madam. That nice detective, the Scottish one, that came when we had that nasty business in the garden, remember?"

"Show him into the drawing room—no, make that the sitting room, please, Elsie. Ask if he'd like tea or coffee."

"There's two of them, madam. A DC Potter."

"All right. I'll be there in a moment."

After combing her hair, powdering her nose, and putting on a bit of lipstick, Daisy joined the detectives in the small sitting room at the back of the house, a less formal place than the drawing room. Elsie followed her in with a tray of coffee and biscuits.

Mackinnon took out his pocketbook, extracted a photograph, and handed it to Daisy. "Ring any bells?"

As he had promised, it didn't look too terribly like the face of a corpse. Definitely male; young—mid-twenties, at a guess; fair hair, cut short, as she had already noted, so it fit under the wig, and close-shaven, showing no shadow of a beard; his eyes were closed, thank goodness. Perhaps that was why he seemed to have no expression whatsoever, nor any signs of his character in his face.

"Definitely familiar. I haven't the foggiest who he is or where I met him."

"He's barely medium height; slender. Manicured hands and expensive linen. No laundry marks so possibly new, bought specially for this—I suppose it was a bet or a dare, though he looks too old for such shenanigans. They usually grow out of pranks like this in their teens."

The door opened and Tom looked in. "Sorry to disturb you, Mrs. Fletcher, Inspector. The missus asked me to say, Mr. Mackinnon, being as she's nursing the nurse, so to speak, if you want to talk to her patient, she wants to be present. Or at least nearby, in case of need."

"By all means, Mr. Tring. Since you *just happen* to be here, would you care to take a peek at the photograph of the deceased?"

"I don't mind if I do. You never know your luck, and I did think—Well, blow me down! Mrs. Fletcher, I don't want to put anything in your mind, but if you think back a couple of years to an affair you got mixed up in, in the country, a chum—"

"Let me look." Daisy took the photo from his hand. "Teddy Devenish!"

"Miss Lucy's—Lady Gerald's, I should say—cousin, wasn't he? And a royal pain in the neck, if my memory serves me."

"He sneaked into the house the night his grandmother was murdered. Oh blast, I suppose I'll have to break it to Lucy, not that she'll be heartbroken. And Angela!" Daisy groaned.

"Now hold on," exclaimed Mackinnon. "You'll have to break it to me before you talk to anyone else. You both identify the deceased as Teddy Devenish? That's Edward?"

"Yes, and Devenish with two Es. I don't know his middle name. He's heir to a baronet."

"Lucy?"

"Lady Gerald Bincombe."

"Nobs," muttered D.C. Potter. "We got trouble."

76

"She's some sort of cousin of Teddy," Daisy continued. "We were—"

"In a minute, please. Angela?"

"Miss Angela Devenish. His sister, or one of them."

"His parents?"

"Sir Somebody and Lady Devenish."

"Sir James," Tom put in.

"Got that, Potter? He's the one will have to make the formal identification. At least, was the deceased married, Mrs. Fletcher?"

"Not that I know of. Not that Lucy mentioned." Daisy recalled what Lucy had said. "Oh, no, not married."

"Do you happen to know his parents' address?"

"No idea. Somewhere in the country. He's a huntin', shootin', fishin' squire. Lucy might know. Or I could write and ask Angela. We aren't exactly close, but we correspond occasionally and I sometimes see her when she comes up to town. She'd wonder why on earth I was asking. I'd have to tell her."

"Never mind. It'll be in the *Baronetage*. You don't happen to know the victim's address?"

"So he *was* murdered!"

"Yes, Mrs. Fletcher, he was murdered."

"Ah," said Tom. "Like the Empress of Austria." He sketched a wink at Daisy.

Mackinnon gave him a repressive look, to which Tom returned a bland smile.

"Please keep that under your hat, both of you. Thank you for your help. Knowing who he is, we can get on with the job. Mr. Tring, would you let your good lady know I'd like to see Mrs. Gilpin now?"

Tom went out.

"I'm desperately trying to think how the Empress of Austria was killed," Daisy confessed. "Not an 'infernal device'—that was the Archduke and Archduchess, wasn't it?"

"Don't expect me to enlighten you, Mrs. Fletcher. The *ex*-sergeant shouldn't have told you."

"I suppose not. I won't pass it on, I promise." Except to Alec, possibly.

Mackinnon read her mind. "Don't worry. Given the prevalance of nobs, I'll be asking the Yard for help. If Mr. Fletcher isn't assigned to the case, I'll eat my glengarry."

"Do you have one?" she asked with interest.

"I do indeed. It went through the war with me, so it's a wee bit shabby. Now, you'll excuse me, Mrs. Fletcher. I must talk to your nurse."

"I feel I ought to be present."

"But you don't want to," he said shrewdly. "Mrs. Tring will protect her from our persecution."

Daisy smiled, a bit guilty for her reluctance, and nodded as they went out. She heard D.C. Potter enquire, "What's a glengarry, sir?"

"A rrelic of the brraw old days of Scots independence, laddie." He closed the door.

She hadn't got round to telling him she was lunching with Lucy. No doubt he would have views on exactly what she was permitted to tell her friend. She'd have to make clear that she couldn't possibly fail to inform her of her cousin's death. Lucy would never forgive her.

Though tempted just to fail to inform Mackinnon of her luncheon date, Daisy realised he'd be justifiably annoyed. Which was all very well, but if Alec took over the case . . .

She heard the tramp of police feet on the stairs. She'd catch the inspector when he came down.

In the meantime, what was it she ought to know about the assassination of the Empress of Austria? Unlike the Archduke's, it had taken place before she was born, a couple of decades earlier, she was pretty sure, and in Switzerland. Time to consult the encyclopaedia in her office.

But Nelson's failed her. The only Empress of Austria she recalled from history at school was Maria Theresa, who was too long ago and hadn't been assassinated. Skimming the article on Austria's history since 1850, she found no mention of any assassination. Lucy would know. Lucy possessed much more enthusiasm for things royal and aristocratic than Daisy had ever been able to summon up.

She went up to see the twins, nobly resisting the urge to listen at Mrs. Gilpin's door as she passed.

NINE

Whenever Lucy invited Daisy to meet her, she chose the most fashionable restaurants. Entering the Café de Paris, Daisy hoped last year's spring costume was not impossibly dowdy.

It wasn't that she hadn't the money for a new costume. Since inheriting Alec's long-lost great-uncle's estate, the Fletchers had been very comfortably off. But Daisy hadn't the figure required for modern styles. As a result, she found visits to her dressmaker frightfully depressing and therefore simply couldn't find the time.

She asked the maître d'hôtel for Lady Gerald Bincombe and was led at once to a table in a discreet corner. However flamboyantly modish Lucy might be, at least she never insisted on flaunting the latest acquisition in the most public spot in the room.

Daisy sat down, hoping Lucy wouldn't be late.

"Today's menu, madam. May I recommend the coquilles St. Jacques? The sole bonne femme is also particularly good today."

"Thank you."

The wine waiter appeared at her elbow.

"Would madame care to order a cocktail?"

"I'll have a half and half vermouth with soda, please."

"Certainly, madame. Ah, here is Lady Gerald."

Lucy being Lucy, the maître d'hôtel and the wine waiter vied to take her furs and seat her. She was wearing a black and sunshine-yellow costume, the jacket longer and the waist lower than any Daisy had seen before. A little black cap, fitted close to her head and flaunting a topaz aigrette, supplanted the cloche hat that had been ubiquitous for several years.

"Evian with a dash of bitters, Alphonse," she ordered.

"*Tout de suite*, milady," he promised with a look of commiseration as he hurried away.

"He thinks I'm liverish," Lucy said crossly, her high, fluting voice lowered for once. "I promised Gerald to go easy on the cocktails, because of you know what. Honestly, anyone would think I'm a confirmed toper!"

"Darling, no one looking at your complexion could think anything of the sort. I'm glad you're feeling better."

"I'm dying of hunger all the time. And I have a craving for asparagus. If they haven't got fresh asparagus I shall scream."

"Please don't. Cousin Edgar sent us some from Fairacres and it's even reached High Street, Hampstead. Covent Garden must be bursting with the stuff."

They settled on their lunch, including asparagus, and Lucy leaned back. "How is it going with the horde of visiting relatives?"

"We only have two. I've hardly seen anything of Cousin Geraldine and the girls. The boys are delightful—on the whole—and keep Belinda busy. She's taken them to the zoo today."

"The most delightful children are those one seldom sees. Which reminds me, have you decided yet whether you're going to let me have your nanny?"

Alec and Daisy had decided that they wanted the twins to attend the local Montessori school. More accurately, Daisy had decided and convinced Alec. However, when last she talked to Lucy on the subject, she hadn't been certain whether they would still need Mrs. Gilpin's care. After seeing them settle happily with Bertha in charge, she was satisfied.

Yet she hesitated to tell Lucy that Nurse Gilpin would be free to accept an offer in a few months. After her strange behaviour, it was impossible to give her an unqualified recommendation. That business must be sorted out first.

"I don't want to rush you, Daisy, but I'm going to have to look about for someone else if you're keeping her."

"I'll let you know as soon as I can."

The arrival of the soup distracted Lucy from the subject. It was some time before Daisy found an opening to ask about the assassinated empress.

"Elisabeth? Yes, of course I know about the Empress Elisabeth. She was Rudolf's mother."

"The murder-suicide Rudolf?"

"That's never been proven," Lucy said disapprovingly.

"All right, the one who died at Mayerling under mysterious circumstances. Along with his mistress."

"Yes, that one. Elisabeth lost her son, and she didn't get on at all well with Franz Josef. She was travelling alone in Switzerland—"

"Alone with a train of ladies-in-waiting and servants, I assume. And military guards, presumably?"

"I expect so. But when she was attacked, she had only a lady-in-waiting with her. They had just walked from a hotel to board a steamer on Lake Geneva. A man ran up to her. She thought he'd just pushed her, perhaps in an attempt at robbery and she walked aboard before she collapsed."

"Oh, yes, I remember that much. He'd stabbed her with a filed-down dagger, or something of the sort, hadn't he? It was so narrow she didn't feel it enter but she died of internal bleeding."

Lucy was disgusted. "I might have known you'd only be interested in the gory details. For pity's sake let's change the subject."

Daisy was willing. The Empress Elisabeth out of the way, her next interest was in Lucy's relatives. Tactfully, she started with her parents, whom she knew well from visits exchanged since childhood. "How are Aunt Vickie and Uncle Oliver?"

"Same as ever. Mother's always happy as long as she has something to fuss over. There's never any lack. Her last letter was full of some newcomer to the village who simply can't be trusted to make a decent job of the church flowers."

"And how are Nancy and the Rev. Tim? And your niece and nephews?"

"Darling, do you intend to go through everyone on my family tree making polite enquiries? Spit it out: Who is it you're really interested in?"

Pinned down, Daisy said, "Your cousin Teddy. Bad news, I'm afraid."

"Any news about Teddy is bound to be bad news. People always assume I'm dying to hear the latest gossip about my nearest and not so dearest. I can't imagine why. The last I heard about was one of those stupid pranks of his. He never refuses a bet or a dare, they say, and the more disruption it causes the better. He doesn't give a hoot for anyone's opinion."

"Even his nearest and dearest?"

"Especially us. Has he done something outrageous since he was bound over for driving the wrong way round Marble Arch in the rush hour? What is it now? Weren't you asking about him just the other day?"

"No, you were telling me about him. You hoped he wouldn't be at Haverhill for your grandfather's birthday."

"He wasn't. Uncle James was furious. Aunt Josephine was upset but as always she excused him. 'Young people are all so busy these days,' or some such folderol. Busy making mischief, my dear cousin Teddy."

"And Angela?"

"Angela?" Lucy said vaguely. "I saw her, I think, but I didn't talk to her. I've never heard her say a word to anyone except her dratted dogs."

Daisy could not deny that Angela Devenish was far from loquacious, though she could be eloquent in defence of the mistreated animals she rescued. "She gives talks for the RSPCA to Women's Institutes."

"Animals are her only subject of conversation. What her relations are with her brother, I haven't the foggiest. Come on, you were about to tell me about his latest shameful exploit. Does he deliberately set out to embarrass the family, one wonders? Or is it merely a side effect?"

"Now you'll never find out."

"What? You don't mean . . . Daisy, he's dead? In suspicious circumstances, knowing your proclivities. Not, by any chance, stabbed while boarding a Swiss steamer?"

"No, much worse, I'm afraid. At least, once the press get hold of the story—"

"Spare me the details! You're not expecting me to break the news to his grieving parents, I trust."

"Heavens no. That's a job for the police. I only told you because of meeting you today. I could hardly sit here eating with your cousin lying dead and not even mention it."

"True. I'd just as soon hear it from you, in any case. You won't expect me to pretend I'm grief-stricken."

"Hardly. What I want is more information about why you aren't grief-stricken. What exactly has he been up to?"

"*You* want or Alec wants?"

"Alec's away. He has nothing to do with this." Daisy made a moue. "Not yet."

"So you're in a hurry to involve yourself before he comes back to stop you."

"Well, yes, of course. Not that he's ever had much success with that."

"What do you want to know? I do my best not to listen to stories about Teddy."

"I don't suppose you know who his friends are? Were?"

"Not friends of mine! I see—used to see—him in nightclubs now and then. Ciro's, the Kit-Cat, Murray's. Those are the only ones Gerald and I ever go to, but I daresay Teddy frequented some less respectable places, the kind that have gambling rooms upstairs."

"You didn't see whom he was with? Any particular girl?"

"Darling, once having spotted him, I kept my eyes turned away for fear of meeting his. It was only a couple of times, anyway. I've seen him at fashionable parties, too, where it would be more difficult to avoid acknowledging him if it weren't that he seems equally anxious to avoid us."

"So some hostesses still invite him, in spite of his reputation."

"He is well connected, Daisy, and very well off, and a bachelor."

"Hmm. Which suggests he's not associated in people's minds with any particular young lady. Didn't you say something about a breach of promise suit, though?"

"That would be a young *woman*, not a young lady."

"Of course, darling, but you'd think it would put off any hopeful mamas."

"Not the more ambitious of them."

Daisy sighed. "Awful though the war was, at least it spared us the horrors of coming out. I would have hated to be a debutante."

"I might have rather enjoyed it. Still, we had fun in Chelsea, being independent."

"Even living on sardines and mousetrap cheese. It was inspiring living amongst artists and writers and musicians."

"Teddy had his independence handed to him and I don't believe for a moment he was seeking inspiration when he frequented the artsy-craftsy set. Free love, more likely."

"I remember you said he's in with the Chelsea set. In reference to the breach of promise suit?"

"Possibly. Russian émigrés, I've heard. The father claims to be a prince, like most who aren't anarchists."

"Some really are princes. Or were."

"He might have been, for all I know. He's selling off jewels, I believe, and it's conceivable that he came by them honestly."

"Not likely to be advocates of free love, then, like the anarchists! I don't suppose you know their name?"

"No." Lucy shrugged. "One of those unpronounceable Russian names, no doubt. Darling, you're not going to try to investigate them? It could be dangerous. Don't foreigners go in for stabbing more than the English?"

"For pity's sake, don't tell a soul I said he was stabbed! That's the sort of detail the police are most anxious to keep from the press."

"I shan't tell. All the same, Daisy—"

"I'm not going to sweep in and start asking questions. I'd just like to find out who they are before Mackinnon even knows they exist. He never did get round to asking me whether I'd heard anything else about Teddy from you."

"From *me*! You didn't tell him I was Teddy's cousin, did you? *Second* cousin."

"I couldn't help it." That sounded rather feeble and unconvincing, so she rephrased it more forcefully: "It was unavoidable."

"So your inspector's going to come and bombard me with questions? Insufferable!"

"How can he investigate without asking questions of people who know the answers? Your attitude is exactly why he'll need my help. Teddy's respectable friends and acquaintances will all climb up on their high horses and refuse to cooperate, and the artsy lot will go bolshie and refuse to cooperate."

Lucy laughed. "More than likely," she conceded. "All right, I'll be good. Within reason. I suppose the ends of justice must be served, even if Teddy's no great loss to the world."

"He was still young. Who knows? A lot of great statesmen sowed their wild oats in their time."

"Name one."

"Well, I'm sure there were a few. And great authors and artists, too. Did you stay in contact with any of the Chelsea crowd?"

"Ah, I wondered when you'd get to that. Yes, as a matter of fact. One or two. Do you remember Genevieve Blakeney?"

"Vaguely. Sculptor?"

"Painter. She started doing designs for dress material and some of her stuff has become quite fashionable."

"You? Patron of the arts? Or, no, patron of fashion."

"It doesn't have to be one or the other. That's beside the point. Do you want an introduction? A *re*introduction, rather?"

"Hmm." Daisy pondered. "What I really need is to speak to

as many people as possible. Best would be one of those infor-mal parties, where if one turns up with a bottle no one worries about invitations."

"Then you don't need me to wangle an invitation for you," Lucy pointed out.

"No, but you could find out the where and when."

"I expect so."

"And go with me. If you were feeling well enough."

"That's another matter! I suppose I might, if you couldn't find someone else."

"It wouldn't be at all Phillip's cup of tea."

"Phillip? Who's Phillip and what has he to do with taking you to parties?"

"Phillip Petrie. You must remember him."

"Of course. But he went to America."

"He's over on business. I'm going to have him escort me to some nightclubs."

"Daisy! You could always wrap him round your little finger, but won't his wife object? Not to mention Alec."

"Gloria stayed over there. She's in the same 'interesting con-dition' as you. When Alec comes home, I'll tell him I'm think-ing of writing an article about today's *bohémiens*. Which isn't a bad idea, come to think of it."

"From all I hear, our nightclubs aren't a patch on American speakeasies. Besides, Alec would offer to take you himself. That would put paid to your investigation."

"Most unlikely. I think it's a jolly good scheme."

Lucy sighed. "I suppose you can't come to much harm with Phillip. As long as you stick to the respectable places. Promise you won't go to the dives Teddy frequents—frequented."

"Even if I wanted to," Daisy said regretfully, "Phillip would never agree. As far as he's concerned, I'm still Gervaise's little sister."

TEN

When Daisy reached home, she found several messages on the hall table notepad. She glanced through them, half-relieved, half-disappointed that none was from Alec. Much as she missed him, if he had been going to return home tonight, she would have had to postpone her planned outing with Phillip, or even cancel it.

Sakari had telephoned and wanted her to ring back. She went into the office and dialled the number.

"Daisy, good afternoon. How is your unfortunate nurse?"

"She's doing well but she still can't remember anything. It's madly frustrating."

"For her, too, I expect."

"I daresay. And for the police."

"You have seen them today?"

"Oh yes, bright and early. They showed me a photograph of . . . him, not too frightfully grisly, and I was able to identify him. I'd better not tell you on the phone. Not someone you'd know, anyway. Did the inspector visit you as well?"

"He sent a sergeant. I had no useful revelations for him. *Him?* You said 'him'?"

"Yes, darling. A young man disguised as a woman."

"How odd! I cannot see the purpose of such a trick."

"I imagine it was a bet, or a dare."

"Young men do foolish things. But this does not explain his death. It was not an accident, I assume?"

"Apparently not. Or probably not, I should say. Insofar as I'm in the confidence of the police, which is not far."

"He must have been killed by the other nanny," Sakari reasoned. "The one Mrs. Gilpin followed."

"Presumably. There doesn't seem to be any hint of anyone else in the vicinity, barring the attendant."

Sakari laughed. "By all means bar the attendant. Is it known—"

"Caller, your three minutes is up. Do you want another three?"

"Yes, please! Daisy, are you still there?"

"I am. You were asking . . . ?"

"Is it known whether the second nanny is man or woman?"

"Not to me, and I think not to the police."

"He or she was responsible for your nanny's misfortune?"

"So it would appear. Thanks for asking that, Sakari. You've clarified in my mind why I'm so keen to help catch him. Or her. It's not as if I care a hoot about Teddy. He was an obnoxious youth when I met him, and it doesn't sound as if he improved much. Rather the reverse, in fact. But an attack on one of my employees is definitely my business."

"Oh, Daisy, is this not rationalisation?"

Sometimes Daisy wished her friend had not attended so many lectures on psychology. "You mean it's just an excuse for being nosy?"

"I did not put it so." Amusement suffused Sakari's voice. "Let us call it curiosity, a trait we have in common. But your kind of curiosity can be dangerous. Remember that the person about whom you are curious has killed one and seriously injured another. Is not the hunt best left to the police?"

"I can help them. I know people who can find out who his friends were."

"I will not attempt further to dissuade you. If there is anything I can do to assist your investigation, you can count on me."

"Thank you, darling! As a matter of fact, I was thinking of lunching at the Café Royal, the haunt of the artsy crowd. Would you like to go with me?"

"I should love to. I have met interesting people there, as well as a few poseurs."

"Let's go tomorrow. I'll ring you later to make definite plans."

They said good-bye and rang off.

Daisy dealt with the rest of the messages, wrote a couple of letters, and dropped in to see the twins on the way to change for tea. Not that she usually changed for tea, but when a gentleman who had proposed to one several times—however unenthusiastically—came to tea after a long absence, one put one's best face forward. Especially when about to ask a favour.

Phillip arrived promptly, presented her with a bunch of yellow roses, and assured her she didn't look a day older. Nor did he. Tall and blond, he was good-looking in an indeterminate way, with a generally amiable expression. In his mid-thirties, he still had a youthful loose-limbed suppleness of movement, valuable in a profession that involved a good deal of diving into the innards of motorcars. By the time they had exchanged news of their respective families, they were on the old informal footing.

Daisy passed the biscuits and refilled his teacup. "Phillip, will you take me to a nightclub?"

He spluttered and tea dripped on his old school tie. "Dash it, old thing, you ought to give a chap a bit of warning before springing something like that on him!" He dabbed ineffectually at the tie with his handkerchief, then gave up, tucked it away, and smoothed back his already sleek hair. "Why don't you ask Fletcher?"

"He's out of town, I told you."

"Lucky man. Wait till he comes home."

"I really want to go tonight."

"You never used to care for nightclubs. What are you up to, Daisy?"

"What a nasty suspicious mind you've developed in America!"

"That's the way they run business over there. No sealing a deal with a handshake. All the *i*'s have to be dotted and the *t*'s crossed. I'm glad I'm on the technical side. But that has nothing to do with your sudden passion for nightclubs."

"I haven't got a passion for nightclubs! I just thought it would be fun to go to one this evening."

"Come off it, old girl. I wasn't born yesterday, and I've known you since you were a babe in arms. You've got some bee in your bonnet. You haven't got yourself mixed up in one of Alec's cases again, have you?"

Considering Phillip knew of only two or three such cases, Daisy considered his assumption unwarranted. Besides, the case was not Alec's—so far. "No. Will you take me? Or I'll have to find someone who—"

"Not on your life! I'll take you. Any particular place you have in mind?"

"I was thinking of the Kit-Cat?"

Phillip approved. "I was a member before I left the country. A respectable place. In fact, more respectable than it used to be. I heard it was raided by the police and reopened as a restaurant with dancing and entertainment."

"It sounds to me like a nightclub."

"Pretty much, but one is expected to eat, not just drink champagne. By the way, have you learned to dance yet?"

"No. I still have two left feet."

"Oh well, I expect they still have good bands and an amusing cabaret. It's no use going till half after ten, though. That's when they start rolling out the best stuff. I say, would you like to make a night of it, Daisy? Dinner and a show first, I mean?"

"That sounds like fun, but I've got the children to think of."

"Surely the twins will be—Oh, your stepdaughter."

"And the visiting cousins. Belinda and Ben are too old to be fobbed off with nursery tea instead of dinner downstairs." Besides, perhaps she was old-fashioned, but she didn't think dining tête-à-tête, even with an old friend, would be quite comme il faut. "Why don't you join us? We can go on afterwards to a show."

"Er, these cousins, would they be the coloured . . . ?"

"Yes. What difference does it make? I'm surprised at you, Phillip."

"None, none at all," he said hastily. "Things are a bit different in America, that's all."

"It's not all sweetness and light here," Daisy admitted.

"I'll be happy to come to dinner. Is there any show you particularly want to see? Don't say Ibsen, please, or anything on those lines!"

"I've no idea what's on."

"How about *The Yellow Mask*? It's a musical comedy thriller, still going strong after a couple of months at the Carlton."

"Suits me." She checked the teapot and added hot water. "A refill?"

"Yes, please. The one thing I can't get back home: a decent cup of tea."

" 'Back home,' is it?" she teased.

"Home is where Gloria is. We'll never forget what we owe you and Alec."

"Nonsense." Daisy put down this unwonted and unwanted lapse into sentimentality to his five-year sojourn in foreign parts. She passed the gingersnaps. Mrs. Dobson made superb gingersnaps and their crunchiness might avert a further embarrassing display. "Will seven o'clock be all right for you for dinner? I've been dining a bit early while the boys are here. It'll give us plenty of time afterwards to get to the theatre."

"Fine. I have to get the tickets, so I'd better get going."

"Will you be able to get them at such short notice?"

"Oh yes. I know a fellow at my club who—"

"Your club! Why didn't I think of that? I wonder . . . Most men belong to clubs, don't they?"

"Most gentlemen. And there are clubs for working men, I believe."

Daisy dismissed the working men with a wave. "How many gentlemen's clubs are there in London?"

"Good lord, Daisy, I've no idea."

"How on earth can I find out which he belongs to? Lucy might know, though I doubt it, or Angela but she's not on the phone. Gerald? Might be worth trying."

"Daisy, for pity's sake, who are you talking about?"

"Teddy, of course," she said abstractedly.

"Well, if you can supply a surname, you might as well ask me, for a start. I'm a bit out of touch, but I've kept up my club subscriptions. Not that I ever did more than pop in now and then to two of them, stuffy sort of places my father signed me up for. The RAC is the one I mostly frequent. Lots of good chaps there, and naturally I pick up the odd tip useful to my papa-in-law, so—"

"Do stop blathering, Phillip, and let me think." A distant echo came to her in Angela's voice, saying something about a sporty little Lea-Francis. She couldn't attach a name to the car but Angela wasn't likely to have been talking about anyone other than her brother. Teddy was—had been—interested in motorcars at least to some degree. He might well have belonged to the Royal Automobile Club. "Teddy Devenish. Was he by any chance a fellow member?"

"Devenish? The name's familiar. Wait, yes, I don't know him. Ten years my junior, isn't he? But I've heard one or two nasty stories, and there's been some talk about booting him out."

"What sort of stories?"

"The sort I wouldn't sully your ears with."

"I'm an adult, Phillip, however long you've known me."

"No," he said obstinately. He was manifestly relieved when the door opened to admit a horde of children.

"Is there any tea left, Aunt Daisy?" asked Charlie, always single-minded. "I'm starving."

"Charlie," his brother admonished, "mind your manners. There's a visitor."

"Oh!" The hand reaching out for cake was drawn back.

"Sorry, sir, I didn't see you 'cause I'm *starving*. I was riding an elephant, you see."

"Hungry work," Phillip agreed, with more patience than Daisy expected. Of course, he had his own children now.

"This is Mr. Petrie, an old family friend who lives in America now. I expect you've met some of his family in Worcestershire."

"Sort of," said Ben enigmatically. "How do you do, sir."

Belinda and Charlie greeted Phillip, Charlie following up with, "Have you got elephants in America?"

"Only in zoos and circuses, not wild."

"Oh." Losing interest in America, he turned back to the tea table, with an imploring glance at Daisy.

"Mr. Petrie was just leaving. Ring for more tea, Bel, while I see him out."

In the hall, Phillip said, "Honestly, Daisy, if half the stories are true, Devenish isn't at all a desirable acquaintance. Why on earth are you so interested in him?"

"I can't tell you. Read the late editions. I doubt they'll have a name yet but you'll probably be able to guess. Only, for pity's sake, don't tell anyone who they're writing about."

"I shan't have time to read the paper if we're dining at seven," he grumbled. "I assume he's gone to meet his maker in some sordid manner."

"Assume what you like, as long as my name isn't associated with your assumptions! Sorry to be so vague."

"Not vague enough. The police are involved, aren't they? I'll probably be arrested for aiding and abetting, whatever that is."

"Phil, you're not going to abandon me, are you?"

"Of course not, old thing. I promised Gervaise I'd look after you and I will. But I must say, you make it deucedly difficult!"

ELEVEN

Daisy knew as soon as she stepped through the glass door of the Kit-Cat that her best evening frock was hopelessly inadequate for the occasion. The hemline was all right: It could hardly be otherwise when she saw in the vestibule everything from floor-length to above the knee; many were zigzagged or dipping wildly, but hers was not the only straight hem. Her dress didn't expose nearly enough of her, though. Bare backs, bare shoulders, and all but bare bosoms were everywhere. And jewelry flashed on every bosom.

Phillip, immaculate in Savile Row's best evening duds, didn't seem to notice anything amiss in her attire.

Downstairs, the main room was filling up but there was still a choice of tables. The dance floor in the centre was already filled with frenetic-looking two-steppers. Daisy wanted to be at the back of the room, not too close to the musicians on the low stage at the end. Al Starita and his Kit-Cat Band were making quite a din.

Phillip passed on her request to the headwaiter. He pointed out a suitable spot near the entrance to an underling, who escorted them thither and took Phillip's order for a light supper and champagne.

"Perfect," said Daisy. "We'll be able to spot anyone we know, and they'll see us."

"If there is anyone. Neither of us is what you might call 'in the swim.'"

"Don't be such a pessimist, darling. Do you and Gloria ever go to nightclubs over there? Speakeasies, that is. Or are there nightclubs that don't serve drinks?"

"That'd be pretty flat! No, we don't go to speakeasies. Old Arbuckle has nothing against liquor but he's keen on staying on the right side of the law. I say, Daisy, you were right!" he added in a surprised and congratulatory tone. "There's Fenella." He waved to his sister.

Fenella Petrie—or rather, Mrs. Elliot Kerston—waved back. She was making her way into the restaurant with her husband and two other couples. She pointed out Phillip to Kerston. After a brief consultation, the whole group headed their way. Amidst general introductions, a pair of waiters smoothly moved Daisy and Phillip and settled all eight at a large round table.

It was nearer the band and therefore noisier, but Daisy was pleased anyway. Being part of a large group meant no reports of her gadding about with an ex-suitor would filter back to her mother or—less likely but more distressing—to Alec. Also, the Kerstons and their companions appeared to be habitués of the Kit-Cat, so the number and variety of people Daisy was able to speak to was much larger than if she'd had to rely on her and Phillip's aquaintances.

For some time, she chatted with several people and refused several invitations to dance without finding an opening to introduce Teddy's name. Then the dance floor cleared, and the cabaret started.

The third performer was an athletic young woman in extremely short shorts, who produced back flips and splits and such tricks. Daisy had had her fill of acrobatics when she took Belinda and her friends to the circus, so she didn't pay much attention, until Elliot Kerston, sitting next to her, lowered his quite-unnecessary opera glasses and said to the woman on his other side, "Fay Fanshawe—isn't she the girl Teddy Devenish is besotted with?"

"Oh, I wouldn't call him besotted. I don't believe Teddy was ever besotted with anyone but himself. That's the person he was pursuing, yes. One of them."

"Was?"

"Who knows?" Kerston's neighbour shrugged. "Still is, perhaps. Oh, look, there's Jimmy Pontefract." She waved madly at someone seated at a distant table and no more was said of Teddy Devenish.

Miss Fanshawe was joined by a top-hatted dancer and together they did a cleverly timed skit where he failed to catch her after her tricks. She always rolled to her feet, and finally caused him to lose his own balance, ending triumphantly with her foot on his prone body and his top hat on her blond curls. Daisy wondered whether she had a sense of humour to match her timing or was merely performing moves planned by someone else.

Daisy was determined to speak to her as soon as her performance ended, in case she hurried away afterwards.

Miss Fanshawe and her partner took their bows and cart-wheeled off the stage. A new performer came out, a sultry brunette in a slinky sequined crimson frock that clung to a figure considerably lusher than the ideal of fashion. Daisy picked up her handbag and started to push back her chair. Kerston rose to help her.

"I'm just going to powder my nose," she murmured, and paused behind Phillip's chair to repeat her excuse, as he gave her an anxious look.

The brunette started to sing in a sultry voice that riveted every male gaze not already attracted by her appearance. All over the room, ladies rose to their feet. Fenella apparently voiced a common concern when she said, "I'm not staying to watch her vamping every man in the house. Phil, don't let Elliot make a fool of himself."

Daisy had intended to slip away down the passage leading backstage without visiting the ladies' cloakroom. With so many on her heels—she glanced back at the twittering flock and saw beyond them the chanteuse ruffling the hair of a chubby, beaming man sitting near the stage—she couldn't hope to waltz off without being seen. On the other hand, did it really matter if someone noticed her and wondered what she was up to?

What if she simply turned the wrong way when she came out of the ladies'? It would look accidental. If anyone called her back she'd say . . . Well, she would think of something.

A cold shiver ran down Daisy's spine as she pushed open the door to the ladies' room. The bright, swirling patterns of Art Nouveau were so different from the austere Victorian splendours of the Crystal Palace, though, that her uneasiness quickly passed.

A few minutes later, she stepped back into the passage and looked both ways. A few women were still coming from the hall, heads together, loudly deploring the vampish singer. They paid Daisy no heed, so she turned the other way and walked briskly, as if she knew where she was going.

Inevitably she came to a stage door. She was in luck: It was unguarded, perhaps because a performance was in progress.

The corridor narrowed and grew both shabby and grubby. On either side, closed doors bore placards, first the green room, then the names of performers. Daisy found Miss Fanshawe's and tapped tentatively.

"Dammit, who's there?" came a male voice. Before Daisy could retreat, the door was flung open to reveal Miss Fanshawe's male partner. His narrow face twisted, he appeared to be in a towering temper. "What do you want?" he snarled.

" 'Oo is it, Jase?"

"Damned if I know."

"Then either find out or get out." The cockney voice was quite calm. "Preferably get out. And stay off the booze and fags or you'll bugger up your wind."

Casting a venomous glance over his shoulder, he barged past Daisy and hurried away.

Daisy stepped in and shut the door behind her. "Gosh, he's in a bit of a bait," she remarked.

"Silly nit," Miss Fanshawe replied dispassionately, not looking up from filing her nails. Wrapped in a brown flannel dressing gown and a towel turban, she was sitting in an easy chair by a flickering gas fire. "Tries to come the toff, which 'e may 'ave bin but ain't no more. 'E says that last move, where I ends up wiv me foot on 'im, is 'demeaning.'"

"It gets the biggest laugh of the lot. You couldn't do without it."

"Just what I tells 'im. If 'e wants to be a straight dancer and earn 'alf the screw, good riddance to 'im, I says. Though where I'll find summun else wiv 'is timing, I dunno. Comes of playing squash, 'e says." Bright blue eyes in a gamine face at last turned to Daisy. "And 'oo might you be, if you don't mind me asking?"

"My name is Fletcher, though I write as Daisy Dalrymple."

"Cor!" The acrobat sat up and laid down her nail file. "I seen your name in one of them fancy magazines. You gonna write about me?"

"I may, as part of an article on cabaret in London. But don't get your hopes up because I can't promise. It would depend on whether I can find enough material and whether my editor is interested. May I ask a couple of questions?"

"Take a pew, ducks." She waved to the chair on the other side of the grate. "Cuppa? Won't take two ticks."

"If I won't be keeping you . . . ?"

"Nah, nuffing doing till the next show, 'alf past midnight." She busied herself with a kettle over a gas ring attached to the fire. "It's ever such a boring business, reelly. Why so many gets bitchy, I reckon. Me, I takes the rough wiv the smooth."

"Have you ever wanted to go into the theatre? Acting, I mean?"

"Nah, I can't act for toffee, ducks. 'Aven't got the voice, 'ave I, for a start. Never even got the 'ang of talking proper. Took lessons, but it don't seem to stick. Me family's buskers, see, since way back. Out on the streets in all weathers. I was doing back flips for theatre queues when I was knee high to a wharf rat. Cushy berth, this. Milk? Sugar?"

"Just milk, thanks. I enjoyed your act, by the way."

"So you won't write something sarky about it? Only, last time I was promised a mention in the paper, that bloody sod—pardon my French—Teddy Devenish wrote that the act belonged in a third-rate circus. I could have killed 'im."

Daisy was so startled, she said blankly, "What?"

"He came round after a show. Well, that was nice. A girl like me doesn't get a lot of stage-door Johnnies, and they don't stay long, seeing I was brought up proper. But it's nice being taken out to supper and—"

"Teddy took you out to supper?"

"Yes. He treated me like a lady, send in his card instead of barging in and all, and he didn't try to make love. He said he was a writer for the *Evening Dispatch*, a weekly column about people, and he wanted to write about me 'cause I have an interesting job. I don't read the papers much but you better believe I got hold of the *Dispatch*, and there it was. Just a couple of lines, but nasty! Why pick on me? I never done nothing to him."

"*Was* he picking on you? That is, were you the only person mentioned? Or if not, was he complimentary about the others?"

"Not 'im. A bad word for everybody, four or five of 'em, but mostly he used initials for people."

"So he wrote gossip columns for the *Evening Dispatch*!" Daisy wondered whether initials would be any use to the police, if they studied the back numbers of the *Dispatch*. "Not under his own name?"

"No, somefing different. But I know it was him. He was the only writer I ever talked to, before you. That's why I wasn't sure, when you said—"

"I wouldn't say anything you'd object to. That's not the sort of article I write. But I don't want you to count on a cabaret article. I may not write it, in the end. At the moment I'm busy with one about the Crystal Palace."

Miss Fanshawe showed not the least sign of uneasiness at the mention of the site of Teddy Devenish's death. "Int'resting is it, the Palace? Would you believe, I never been there, and me a Londoner born and bred!"

"I expect you'd enjoy it. Well, I'd better be getting back to my friends. I've enjoyed chatting. I'll let you know if I ever do write that article."

"Ta, ducks. It's been a treat, talking to a lady."

Daisy returned along the corridor, earning a suspicious stare from the stage door–keeper. He couldn't very well question her credentials as his negligence had let her pass.

Phillip, alone at their table, was fretting over her lengthy absence. "Where on earth have you been, Daisy? You said you wanted to leave early."

"Sorry, Phil. What's the time?"

"Nearly midnight."

"Gosh, is it really? Yes, I ought to go home. There's not the slightest chance the children will sleep late in the morning. Ought we to wait and say good-bye to the others?"

"No, they'll be dancing till the next act comes on. It's not as if we came with them; they're chance-met. Besides, it's only Fenella." With this cavalier dismissal of his sister, they departed.

The streets were empty and Phillip's powerful car made nothing of Hampstead Hill. They pulled up in front of the house scarcely quarter of an hour later. Daisy was tired and sleepy, but though Phil was a very old friend, she owed him common courtesy as well as much gratitude.

"Will you come in for a nightcap?"

"No thanks, old bean. I'm off to Cowley at crack of dawn. I wish I knew what you're up to."

"I don't know why you always think I'm up to something."

"Because you usually are." He got out to open the door for her and escorted her up the steps.

The electric porch light was on, as well as the hall light inside.

On either side of the door, the Victorian stained-glass panels glowed welcomingly in purples and greens. Daisy had told Elsie not to wait up, so she used her latch-key, then turned to give Phillip her hand. "Thanks, Phil, it was sweet of you to take me out."

"I must have been mad," he grumbled. "Explain to Fletcher that you bullied me into it." He kissed her cheek and loped down the steps with a farewell wave.

She closed the door and pushed down the locking button. As she took off her gloves, she noticed that the light was on in the narrow hall leading back beyond the stairs, not usually left burning at night. Investigating, she saw that the door of the small sitting room was ajar, with a light on inside.

Though not normally of a nervous disposition, she had the mysterious death of Teddy Devenish on her mind, as well as the mysterious actions of Mrs. Gilpin and her present state of mental disorder. Daisy crept forward and peeped round the door.

Alec! He sprawled in his favourite armchair, fast asleep. Looking down at him, she was reminded of the time at Wentwater Court, shortly after their first meeting, when he had drifted off with his boots on in the middle of a strenuous double investigation. Was that the moment when she had fallen in love with him? She wasn't sure, but by the time the two cases ended with him furiously angry at her, she had known she badly wanted to see him again.

His hair was still crisp and dark, but now threaded with silver, and the tired lines in his face were not all temporary. Crow's-feet punctuated the closed eyes that would open to a steely grey capable of freezing malefactors with a single glance.

He wasn't much over forty, she reassured herself, still young. Dark hair often did turn white or silver early. He needed a holiday. Assuming he had wrapped up the Bristol case, perhaps they could go away for a few days.

Probably not, given that she was mixed up in the Devenish investigation. She sighed.

TWELVE

Without moving a muscle, Alec snapped to attention, certain that someone was in the room with him. Where was he?

Ah, at home. He opened his eyes.

"Daisy, where the deuce have you been?"

"Didn't Elsie tell you?"

"Some folderol about the theatre and Petrie."

"I didn't know you were coming home today. Last night."

"I didn't have time to send a telegram. We wrapped up the case unexpectedly and caught the express by the skin of our teeth. But it's nearly one. No theatre stays open this late."

"We joined Phillip's sister and her husband for a bite of supper afterwards," Daisy explained disingenuously. "We went to the Kit-Cat. Not for long. You know I hate dancing. I was thinking I might suggest an article on London nightclubs to Mr. Thorwald, but from Phil's description of American nightclubs, he wouldn't be interested."

Alec was no longer in the least sleepy. "And?"

"What do you mean, 'and'? I didn't want to dance and Phil has to depart at break of day to visit a car factory in Oxford, so we left early. By their standards."

"Daisy, when you use that tone of voice with that ingenuous face, there's always an 'and.' Spit it out."

"We-ell . . ." She perched on the arm of his chair and he put his arm round her waist. "You went to the Yard before coming home?"

"I did. I've read Mackinnon's report."

"And?"

He couldn't help laughing. "And he wants the Yard's help, given the deceased's lack of ties to his division and his social prominence. You identified him, I gather."

"Tom Tring recognised him, too. Did Mr. Crane put you in charge?"

"He asked me if I was willing. And he asked Mackinnon whether he had any objection, given your involvement."

"He *asked*? Don't tell me he's softening in his old age!"

"He's put in for retirement, which sometimes has that effect."

"Oh, Alec, will you—"

"Don't say it. It depends on the powers that be, and I'm not sure I should accept if it were offered to me. It's a very different life."

"You'd be at home much more," Daisy said reproachfully.

"That's the positive side. Let's not discuss it now. I'm tired."

"All right. But are you going to take over from Mackinnon?"

"I'm taking charge, yes."

She sighed. "Then I suppose I'd better tell you what I found out tonight."

"I knew it!"

"Someone happened to mention that Teddy Devenish had been pursuing one of the cabaret performers. I didn't say anything to suggest his name, honestly. But knowing what I know, you could hardly expect me just to let it pass."

"No," he admitted resignedly. "Knowing you, I wouldn't expect that. What did you do?"

He was not surprised to learn that she had gone backstage to talk to the young woman. Nor was he surprised that, despite

Miss Fanshawe's excellent reason for holding a grudge against Devenish, Daisy was quite certain she couldn't possibly have murdered him. She sounded like just the sort of young woman his tenderhearted wife was bound to take under her wing.

"I suppose you'll have to talk to her," she said. "I'd hate her to think I gave her away."

"I'll send Mackinnon. He doesn't need to know you found the connection."

"He'll guess."

"That's the penalty of being notorious in police circles."

"Oh, darling! Though he can't actually tell her I reported her if it's only a guess, can he? Isn't it against the rules or something?"

"Hm, I don't know that there's a specific rule, love, but I shouldn't worry too much that he'll give you away. Only, for pity's sake, don't ever again have a midnight meeting with a possible murderer!"

"She would hardly dare do me in in her own dressing room."

"That's debatable."

"Besides, she's quite small."

"Strong for her size, if she's a good acrobat. And she must surely understand her own body well, even if she has no formal knowledge of anatomy. The murderer must have had some idea of what he or she was doing."

"I suppose so," Daisy said doubtfully.

"She didn't happen to give you the names of any other friends, acquaintances, or victims of Teddy Devenish?"

"I couldn't very well ask her."

"No, I'm glad to know you had so much sense!" Alec yawned hugely and levered himself out of his chair. "Come on, it's long past my bedtime."

"You haven't got a bedtime. Acquiring one would be another advantage of becoming superintendent."

"Don't get your hopes up. They may not offer me the post."

"Tommyrot! You're the best. Of course they will."

Alec kissed her and they went upstairs arm in arm.

Later, when he was drifting into sleep, his pertinacious wife asked, "Darling, did you look in on Nanny Gilpin?"

"No. Mackinnon's going to have to handle her. The twins seem to be all right with Bertha?"

"Perfectly all right. She's learnt a lot from Mrs. G. What I'm wondering—"

"I'll wonder in the morning, love. Sleep tight."

He had forgotten about the children. Though he had told Elsie to call him early, Bel, Ben, and Charlie reached the breakfast table before him, bright-eyed and bursting to tell their story.

For the most part, it varied only in wording from what they had told DI Mackinnon, though much more vivid than any police report was ever allowed to be. The excitement of the chase, the colourful crowds inside and the nearly deserted park, the shock of finding Mrs. Gilpin injured, all became almost real to Alec, as recounted in their eager young voices.

He picked up a couple of details new to him, too, forgotten at the time or omitted as irrelevant from Mackinnon's report. Belinda said she had seen no hat pin in the second nurse's hat, the "nurse" presumed to have murdered Devenish and attacked Mrs. Gilpin. She had noticed the hat because it had made her sure the woman was not Nanny Gilpin.

"I couldn't see her face, you see, Daddy, because we were up above on the stairs. But I know Nurse was wearing her felt with the black rose hat pin. She has a different pin she wears with her caps. The other nurse, the one who was running away, her hat was a sort of shiny straw. She didn't have a pin at all."

"Are you quite certain, pet?"

She gave him a look. "As certain as I can be. Absence of evidence is not evidence of absence."

"Ye gods, where did you learn that?" Many adults—many policemen!—didn't properly grasp that concept.

"I read it somewhere. It makes sense. Isn't it true?"

"Yes, in an absolute sense, but we police are human and often have to work with the preponderance of the evidence."

"What—"

"You'll have to look it up."

"She didn't have a handbag, either," said Charlie.

"She didn't?" Had there been any mention of a handbag in the report? Alec thought not, but he'd been so tired he could have missed it. "Bel? Ben?"

"I didn't *see* one," Ben said cautiously.

"Nor did I, Daddy. I noticed, but I'd forgotten. I thought it was odd at the time, because grown-up ladies always carry a handbag. Almost always."

"Do you recall exactly when you noticed, Bel? Right away?"

"No, I couldn't see her properly from the gallery steps, and as long as we were in the building there were people and statues and plants and things in the way."

"*I* noticed," Charlie said, "when she was running down the steps, the long outside steps, because when ladies run their handbags bump-bump-bump against their sides. It looks funny. And hers didn't because she didn't have one."

"Good point, Charlie. Do you others agree she didn't have one going down the steps?"

Belinda and Ben consulted each other with a glance.

"I can't say for sure," said Ben, and Bel shook her head. "There were lots of steps. We were concentrating on not losing sight of them and not being seen."

Alec sighed. "A pity. Looks as if we'll have to search the whole park as well as the palace itself."

"I can show you exactly where she went, Uncle Alec. At least as far as the pond where we found Mrs. Gilpin. After that, I don't know."

"Ben's really good at maps, Daddy."

"In that case, how would you like a visit to Scotland Yard, Ben? We have a large-scale map of the park. If you can trace her route on it, you may save us a lot of work."

"Yes, *please!*"

"Right now, Daddy? We were going to go to Madame Tussaud's, and then Maskelyne's Mysteries this afternoon."

"You'd better all come. Maybe you'll be reminded of something helpful. It won't take long, and I'll send you on to the waxworks in a police car."

"*Gosh!*" Charlie's eyes shone. "Scotland Yard and a ride in a police car? That's *much* better than waxworks. Almost as good as the zoo."

"Wait till you see the Chamber of Horrors," said Belinda. "At least, Mummy wouldn't let me go in, but Derek raved about it."

Daisy came in, looking sleepy. After a chorus of "good morning," Alec said, "All right, you three. If you've finished your breakfast, go and get your coats. I want a word with Daisy."

"That sounds ominous," said Daisy as the children trooped out. "Just coffee and toast, please, Elsie."

"Just a question I would have asked last night if I hadn't been half asleep. What's the name of the person who remarked on Devenish's pursuit of the girl?"

"It was Fenella's husband, Fenella being Phillip's sister. Kerston is her married name. Elliot Kerston."

"Did anyone respond?"

"Yes. The girl sitting next to him said she didn't think Teddy was ever besotted with anyone."

"What's her name?"

"Heavens, darling, I haven't the foggiest. Introductions were sketchy and the noise was appalling."

"I'll have to start with Kerston, then."

"For pity's sake, don't let him know I was the spy in the ointment."

"I'll do my best. Might be better if Mackinnon tackles him, too. He managed nicely with Lucy, it seems. He said he went all Scottish on her and it worked a treat."

"Did she tell him about the Russian prince? I never got round to it."

"Yes, but as she didn't know his name, it's going to be difficult to find him. Even if we had a name, these Russian émigrés tend to suffer from a persecution complex. They move often, frequently without leaving a forwarding address. Also, there's no record of a breach of promise suit against Devenish; that's been checked. So far, the Russian remains a mystery. And speaking of mysteries, are you going with the children to Maskelyne's?"

"I wasn't going to. They can't come to any harm, can they? They've promised to be home by six."

"I don't suppose so. But what do you bet, if they want a volunteer to be sawed in half, Charlie will be the first on stage."

Daisy laughed. "Undoubtedly."

Charlie's voice came from the hall, "*Do* hurry *up*, or Uncle Alec might go without us!"

"So much for my second cup of coffee." Alec pushed back his chair and stood. "You've done your bit, Daisy. I'll see that someone follows up with Miss Fanshawe and Elliot Kerston. No more nightclub investigating, please. And resist the temptation to pay solo calls on suspects, especially at midnight."

She wore her most innocent look again, but he couldn't guess whether because she had every intention of disregarding his plea or she had some other "helpful" ploy up her sleeve.

The door opened a couple of inches and a penetrating whisper issued through the gap: "Uncle Alec, have you finished having a word with Aunt Daisy yet?"

"I'm coming, I'm coming! I'll be home for dinner, love, with any luck."

"I should hope so, after being away for a whole week. The twins kept asking for Daddy."

"Miranda said she missed me. She's getting very articulate."

"Yes, it's high time she went to school. Governesses are so old-fashioned. We've got to talk about Nanny Gilpin."

"Not now!" said Alec, escaping.

THIRTEEN

After a visit to the nursery, during which she was told all about Daddy coming home, Daisy went reluctantly to visit Mrs. Gilpin. She was still angry at the nanny for abandoning her charges, apparently on a whim. However, the woman was suffering and—for good or ill—Daisy was still her employer.

To her relief, Nanny Gilpin was asleep. On a small table was a tray with the remains of breakfast for two. Mrs. Tring, in an old rocking chair, knitted placidly.

"How is she?" Daisy asked in a low voice.

"Doing nicely, Mrs. Fletcher. She's in her right mind and got her appetite back, though she still don't remember a thing that happened after she went off to the ladies'."

"Is the doctor calling again today?"

"Yes, he said he'd drop in this morning after his surgery. Unless things change, she won't need me no more. 'Less you want me to stay, I'll pop off home and see how my Tom's doing without me."

"Of course, Mrs. Tring. It's been very kind of you to help out, and I wouldn't dream of keeping you. I'll talk to the doctor after he's seen Nanny."

She went down to her office, bracing herself for the next unpleasant task. A letter from Angela Devenish had been among her post at the breakfast table. She hadn't opened it, but she couldn't put it off any longer. Worse, in the circumstances she'd have to write back right away.

Angela was her usual brusque self. She was coming up to town immediately. She would stay at Teddy's flat and ring up Daisy when she arrived.

Daisy's first thought was that at least she didn't have to answer the letter. Expressing her sympathy would be easier in person. She hoped. Her second thought was to wonder whether the police would let Angela stay in her brother's flat. Though it wasn't exactly a crime scene, they might reasonably expect to find information there that would suggest where to look for the murderer.

After the long train ride from Yorkshire, the poor woman would be in no condition to go hunting for a hotel, even if she had enough money. Despite a legacy from the great-aunt who had left the bulk of her large fortune to Teddy, Angela was always pinching pennies to scrape together the funds for her dog refuge.

Daisy groaned as she realised where that train of thought was leading. Like it or not—and Alec for one was not going to like it—she'd have to offer Angela a bed, if only for the first night.

She picked up the telephone receiver and asked the operator for New Scotland Yard. Surely just this once Alec would thank her for ringing him at work.

Alec was out, and so was Mackinnon. Daisy was put through to DS Piper. She had known him since he was newly promoted to the detective branch, as long as she had known Alec.

"Good morning, Ernie. Left behind to mind the shop?"

"As usual, Mrs. Fletcher. Keeping track of the details. They do let me out now and then."

"It's what comes of being best at the job."

"Flattery will get you a long way. What can I do for you?"

"With your head for details, you probably remember Teddy Devenish's sister Angela?"

"Dogs."

"Exactly. She's arriving this afternoon—"

"With dogs?"

"I shouldn't be surprised. The thing is, she wrote that she's going to stay at her brother's flat. I'd hate her to turn up, perhaps with dogs in tow, and find a guard at the door. Are you—the police—finished with it?"

"Yes. We had his solicitor in and with his permission carted off anything that looked hopeful. But I've just been through it for the second time without much luck. He hardly kept any papers. Secretive sort of bloke."

"Judging by what I've heard, he had a lot to be secretive about. So it's all right for Angela to move in to the flat?"

"From our point of view. She'd better get in touch with the solicitor pretty quick, though. He's in charge there at present. Cranford, Quentin Cranford, of Lincoln's Inn."

"Thanks, Ernie. I'll let her know."

"I'll have to tell the Chief she's coming."

"Try to keep my name out of it."

"I'll do me best, Mrs. Fletcher. No promises."

"Of course. I take it their parents are in town? Angela and Teddy's, that is."

"Lady Devenish is staying at Brown's, prostrated with grief. Sir James came up for a day, officially identified the deceased, and went back to Leicestershire to supervise the drainage of some field or other. No love lost between father and son, I gather, but the Chief doesn't reckon him for filicide."

Daisy hooted with laughter. "Even if he'd wanted to do his son in, the thought of Sir James dressing up as a nanny . . . No, too outré for words."

"I daresay, Mrs. Fletcher. If there's nothing else, I'd best get back to work. By the way, that young lad Ben—Miss Bel's cousin, is he?—he's a marvel with a map. No end of help narrowing down the search. DI Mackinnon was thinking he'd somehow have to get hold of dozens more men. He's gone off happy, I can tell you."

"I bet Ben's cock-a-hoop."

"Pleased as Punch with himself, right enough."

"Are the children still at the Yard?"

"I sent 'em off to the waxworks in one of our cars just a few minutes ago."

"Thank you." Ringing off, Daisy instantly thought of lots more questions she should have asked while Ernie was being communicative. Just as well she hadn't, though. She didn't want to get him into trouble.

She was struggling with her reply to Violet's letter, trying to avoid any mention of the events in the Crystal Palace, which would only upset her sensitive sister, when Elsie came in to tell her Dr. Ransome was ready to see her. Daisy welcomed him with open arms and a cup of coffee from the pot the parlour-maid had brought in a few minutes earlier.

The young doctor, who had recently taken over the practice, was cheerful. "Another day or two of peace and quiet and Mrs. Gilpin should be quite restored to health."

"In body *and* mind?" Daisy asked hopefully.

"Well, no. That is, I'm no expert when it comes to memory loss occasioned by trauma, but I've been reading up about it. There doesn't seem to be any cure, or even any widely accepted treatment. Sometimes the memory comes back, and sometimes it doesn't. Of course, if you want to call in a brain specialist . . ."

"No, I've heard the same from other people."

"You could take her back to where she was the last thing she remembers before the gap. However, there's always a risk that the shock might do more damage."

"That's out, then."

"In fact, I recommend that she go away to somewhere quiet, the country perhaps. Not that it's likely to help her fill in the gap, but a complete rest can't but do her good. As long as she's at her place of employment, she's bound to feel she ought to be busy, quite apart from worrying about the memory loss."

"She has a married sister in Somerset. Unless it's Dorset. If she can't go there, I'm sure my cousin Lord Dalrymple would take her in for as long as she needs to convalesce. I'll see what I can arrange. Thank you, Doctor."

"I popped in to see Oliver and Miranda," he mentioned. "They seem to be as healthy and happy as ever without their nanny, ungrateful creatures! The nursery maid is a sensible girl. You needn't worry about the twins."

He finished his coffee and left. Abandoning her letter to Vi in midstream, Daisy hunted through her address book for Mrs. Gilpin's sister and wrote her a note. There was no point troubling Nanny about it before she knew whether the woman agreed to the visit.

With several letters to post, Daisy and Bertha walked the twins and Nana to the letter box in Well Walk. Both Miranda and Oliver were endlessly fascinated by the lion and the unicorn fighting for the crown on the royal coat of arms. Miranda liked to be lifted up to put the letters in the slot, but Oliver wasn't convinced the box wouldn't swallow his hand along with the letters, and then pull the rest of him in after it.

Daisy had much the same feeling an hour or so later, as she stepped from Regent Street into the Café Royal with Sakari.

The huge room was dingier than ever, its proliferating gilt tarnished, the green pillars dulled by smoke, though the many mirrors were well polished. They reflected a clientele that varied from the famous—Daisy recognised Hugh Walpole and Jacob Epstein—to the would-be famous to smart onlookers, and a coterie of obvious foreigners.

Though once a denizen of Chelsea, she had little frequented Bohemian circles since her marriage, and not at all since the birth of the twins. As a journalist, she had little in common with the literary and political writers who flocked to this mecca along with artists and musicians of all stripes. Add the fact that she had come in search of a murderer, and it was hardly surprising that she felt like a fish out of water.

Not so Sakari. The head waiter hurried to her and she

followed him into the cacophonous throng and swirling tobacco smoke as if into her natural element.

He led them towards one of the small marble-topped tables
set along the walls. On the way, three or four people waved in
casual greeting to Sakari, then a woman with a thick greying
braid tossed over her shoulder called, "Mrs. Prasad, won't you
join us? And your friend, of course."

Sakari glanced back at Daisy, a mischievous look in her eyes.
Daisy nodded. It was just what she had hoped for.

They joined a group at a long table. Several people squeezed
together to make room for them, while others greeted Sakari as
an old friend. Two men were arguing vigorously at one end. One
of them, a youngish man with a vast ginger beard that would
have done a Victorian pater familias proud, broke off to say,
"Miss Dalrymple, isn't it? We were neighbours a few years ago."

Daisy searched her mental files. "Mr. Purdue. You sculpted,
I think?"

The bald man who had been arguing with him said, "And
still does, or so he claims."

A burst of laughter greeted this feeble sally. Unruffled, Purdue remarked sadly, "The avant-garde is always misunderstood."

"So is the rear guard."

"And Futurism is utterly passé."

"Neo-Romanticism is coming back."

"Neo-Neo-Romanticism?"

"Modernism, whatever that means in modern terms."

"Look at this!" A newcomer dropped a newspaper in the
middle of the table, an early edition of an evening paper. CRYS-
TAL PALACE CORPSE IDENTIFIED, blared the lead headline, with
a blurred, virtually unidentifiable photo below it. "Guess who!"

As people shuffled up again to make room for him, the
woman with the braid—whose name Daisy hadn't caught in a
hurried introduction—seized the paper.

"Teddy Devenish! 'Only son and heir of the notable hunting baronet.' Well, well, well, some general benefactor nailed
the bastard at last."

"Don't be so bitter, Judith," said a thin dark girl who looked as if she painted watercolours of fairies.

"She has every reason," the bald man said hotly.

"She's not the only one," said someone else, "not by a long chalk."

Daisy's head swivelled back and forth as she tried to make mental notes of all those who agreed with Judith.

"But none of us is a homicidal maniac," protested a man with a Crippen moustache. "The artistic temperament precludes physical violence."

"That's debatable."

"That's tommyrot!"

The argument swirled away from the personal to the abstract and Daisy's attention strayed. A couple more people came in with newspapers, but nowhere else did she see the same degree of reaction.

Waiters came and went. Daisy found herself with a drink she hadn't ordered, which she sipped cautiously, wondering whom to thank for it. She did manage to order and pay for her own food, choosing a bowl of chicken and vegetable soup. The menu had some strange foreign dishes on it, but how far could one go wrong with chicken soup?

The newspaper lay forgotten on the table, headline uppermost. Though she would have liked to see what it said, Daisy didn't want to draw attention to her interest.

The arrival of two bearded men caught her eye. The younger wore a long, belted shirt over tight-cuffed trousers, a round, peakless cap on his head; the other was very point-device in a dark suit of Continental cut, with a bow tie and a bowler hat. The latter waved a newpaper and was speaking animatedly in a language abounding in rolling Rs that Daisy was pretty sure was Russian. Or Ukrainian: She recalled the anger of a certain Ukrainian singer who had repeatedly been referred to as Russian.

But it was Russians who had been involved with Teddy Devenish, so wishful thinking insisted that these were Russians. Even, perhaps, the Russians she was interested in.

Certainly, they were wrought up over the newspaper. As they passed close by on the way to the far side of the room, Daisy noted that it was definitely the front page that excited them. She watched them join a group—all men—in a corner at the back. By then, as far as she could tell, the paper had disappeared into a coat pocket and the pair had calmed down. Fascinated, she saw them exchange kisses of greeting with their friends.

"Daisy? Are you with us?"

"Uh . . . Sorry, darling, I was thinking."

"Judith has invited us to go and see her studio. Do you wish to come or have you another engagement?"

How tactful of Sakari to present a possible excuse—as if she didn't know Daisy would like nothing better. "Oh yes, I'd love to see your work, Miss . . . Judith."

FOURTEEN

Judith, whose surname turned out to be Winter, had a studio occupying the entire space behind a small terrace house in Chalk Farm. As they entered, an enormous marmalade cat came to meet them, meowing loudly. Daisy stooped to stroke it but it slipped past her and out of the door.

"He's very much 'the cat that walked by himself,'" Judith explained. "He's not mine, though he occasionally condescends to visit. I don't think he belongs to anyone."

The room was stone-flagged, the walls whitewashed. Into it were crammed a large central table covered with red-checked American cloth, a workbench, a cupboard, shelves, a sink, and a massive kiln. Judith Winter was a sculptor.

On the bench were several objects ranging from a few inches to a couple of feet in height and width, all draped with random pieces of cloth. A larger mound sat in the middle of the table. The shelves bore finished pieces, from beautifully glazed bowls and vases ("My bread and butter," Judith said ruefully) to small bronzes.

At a glance, Daisy decided to buy a bowl or two, both because she liked them and for the sake of goodwill. She moved on to examine the sculptures, wondering the while how she was going to reintroduce the subject of Teddy Devenish.

Some of the bronzes were abstract, some semi-abstract. Their outlines were sleek, but a myriad of very fine grooves gave them texture and somehow suggested more complex shapes. Daisy wanted to stroke them. She didn't understand them all and didn't know the proper terms to describe them, but of a few she could say honestly, "They're beautiful!"

"My best are in galleries," said the creator. "At least, the ones the gallery owners think are the best. Will you have a cup of tea? The kettle is just on the boil."

She had a gas ring by the kiln. Sakari had found a seat on a tall stool by the table and was pouring milk from a bottle into mugs—made by their owner, by the look of them.

"Yes, please."

"You'll find another stool under the table. Sorry there isn't anything more comfortable." She brought over the full teapot, also apparently her own work. "I hope you don't mind mugs."

"Not at all. They're very attractive, and I love your bowls. I was thinking I might write an article about artists' studios in London, the ones that don't mind visits from the public. It would be something a bit different for tourists to do. I'll have to see if my American editor likes the idea."

"You're a journalist, aren't you? I thought I recognised the name. Is that why you're interested in Teddy's death?"

"Oh no, I'm not that sort of journalist, not a reporter. What makes you think I'm interested?"

"It was obvious, back there at the café. You're not a scandal writer, like Teddy?"

"Good gracious, nothing like that!"

"You didn't seem that sort. He was a horror. We didn't cotton on to it for ages and he was always made welcome because he pretended to admire our work and occasionally bought something expensive. Then he'd write something nasty in his beastly column—you couldn't call it scandal. Horrible, snide remarks, not about us but about our creations. He went for performers, too, actors, musicians, singers. Even ballet dancers."

"How mean-spirited!" Sakari exclaimed.

"Of course, in general creative people care far more about what's said of their work than of themselves. I don't know that he did much harm. People who appreciate the arts don't go to gossip columnists for serious criticism."

"One can't help wondering what he had against creative people," Daisy mused.

"Sour grapes," said Judith succinctly. In response to their questioning looks, she elaborated. "I've heard he had aspirations to be a second Lord Berners. He found out he has no talent in *any* direction."

"So he takes it out on those of you who do. Not nice. All the same, you say his words broke no bones, which doesn't sound bad enough to make people actually pleased to hear of his death."

Judith flushed. "I didn't mean . . . I suppose it was rather a brutal thing to say, though I didn't mean I was glad he's dead. But if you knew what he did!"

"Tell me."

"People say, 'Oh, it's just a practical joke.' Until it happens to them. When it's your livelihood, it's about as unfunny as it could be. I had a commission; they're few and far between, I can tell you. A bronze, about thirty inches tall, lots of fiddly bits. I spent ages on the clay model. It was all but ready to make the mould, just a few last touches, when that bastard came to call. He wanted me to coach him in walking like a woman for some amateur theatrical affair. Idiotic, when I've got barely room to move in here."

"Amateur theatricals?" Sakari forestalled Daisy. "He enjoyed amateur acting?"

"So he said. Don't ask me, I've never had time for that sort of thing."

"Displacement," said Sakari profoundly. "Having failed to

become a second Lord Berners, he played at acting, pretending—and perhaps convincing himself—that his ambition was never serious."

"At any rate, he minced about, declaiming some sort of rubbish and making sweeping gestures, until he managed to knock my model to the floor. Of course it was wrecked. I could have killed him! I really might have if I'd done it right away, on the spur of the moment." She looked down at her clenched fists and carefully opened them. "You can't kill anyone with a wooden scraper."

"Are you sure it wasn't an accident?" Daisy asked.

"Dead certain. He claimed it was, of course, and apologised, but the look on his face . . ." Words failed her. "Even so, I might have thought I was mistaken if I'd been the only one."

"He made a habit of such 'accidents'?"

"Never quite the same thing. He bought coals for Mon—for a friend of mine, saying her room was far too cold to write in, and then used a manuscript to start the fire. That was really bad, but there was petty stuff, too: arranging a meeting at an address that didn't exist, for instance, or making an appointment to buy something and sending a note hours later to say he'd bought something else instead."

"But didn't—"

"I'd rather drop the subject, if you don't mind. I'm sorry I spoke like that about Teddy, but I can't pretend I shall be sorry never to see him again. More tea? I can easily boil some more water."

"No, thanks."

"No, thank you," said Sakari. "We ought to be going, Daisy."

"Yes, but I would like to buy some bowls. They *are* for sale?" Daisy slipped down from the stool and stepped over to the shelves.

Judith brightened. "Oh yes. One must eat. Which, in particular?"

"The blue with lavender swirls and the green with yellow. They'd make lovely fruit bowls."

The transaction concluded, Judith asked, "If you're not a reporter, what *is* your interest in Teddy?"

"His sister is a friend of mine," Daisy told her disingenuously. "She's coming down from Yorkshire, and I'll be seeing her later today."

"You're not going to tell her what I've said about him!"

"I wouldn't dream of it."

"I shouldn't have spouted off. I talk too much. It's one of the perils of spending a good deal of time alone. I even talk to the cat when he pops in."

Daisy and Sakari took their leave, Daisy carrying her bowls, well wrapped in newspaper and stuffed into a sturdy brown paper bag. Kesin was waiting for them. He relieved Daisy of the package, nodding gravely when she warned him it was fragile, and handed them into the big car.

"Ah, that's better," said Sakari, sinking back on the seat. "I have not the figure to perch on a stool. That was interesting, was it not? I am sorry my friend was so badly treated by the corpse. I cannot believe she was responsible for his transition to the next world."

"It does seem unlikely." Daisy frowned. "I can't see her plotting revenge, and she wouldn't have joined Teddy in his prank just for fun after what he did."

"The murder must have been plotted, must it not? Anyone who hated him enough to kill him would not wish to support him in such a childish exploit."

"True, unless he did or said something unforgivable when they were already in the ladies'."

"Such as?"

"Oh, I don't know. I'm sure Teddy could think of something really insulting if he put his mind to it."

"Why should he do such a thing?"

"On a whim. He doesn't appear to have needed a reason for being unpleasant. Or he planned it for a time when the murderer was extremely unlikely to resort to fisticuffs in retaliation. It's all pure speculation."

"No, Daisy, it is theorising. To return to facts, shall you tell Alec all that you have discovered?"

"It'll be difficult to pretend I didn't hope for results from going to the Café Royal, when he knows Lucy told me Teddy frequented the artistic set. But he never told me not to, just not to go to nightclubs. All the same, I'm going to offer the information to DI Mackinnon, if possible, not Alec. You never know, perhaps he'll be able to investigate further without telling Alec where it comes from."

Sakari laughed. "You may be lucky."

"I've been lucky so far, in meeting people with a grudge against Teddy. Which reminds me, did you notice the two men who came in together shortly before we left the café? They looked like foreigners. Not as foreign as you, darling, except that you're British and they looked like Russians. Or Ukrainians. Eastern Europe, anyway."

"I didn't notice them. Why?"

"Because they had the same paper as was on our table, and they were frightfully excited about the front page, where the news and picture of Teddy were. I told you, Lucy said he was involved with some Russians."

"Daisy, you will not go looking for these Russians? It is not a good idea."

"Why not? I've done very well so far."

"To be sure, though you yourself admit you have been lucky. The Russians are a different kettle of fish." Sakari looked pleased with her venture into idiom. "For a start, their experiences with the police of their own country have made them apprehensive. 'Jumpy' is the word. An attempt to find out about their relations with Teddy Devenish might well be dangerous."

"I wasn't going to go and ask if they had anything to do with his death."

"You couldn't if you wanted to, Daisy. You don't speak Russian."

"They must speak some English, surely. Not that it matters,

since I haven't the foggiest how to find them. Aren't you acquainted with any Russians?"

"Only in the way of business. The jeweller who set my rubies was Russian."

"Darling, I adore you! I'd quite forgotten, Lucy said something about the father selling off jewels. Your jeweller probably knows him, being in the business. All I have to do is visit him and ask about resetting something—I know, Great-Aunt Gertrude's aquamarines! The setting is hideous, too frightfully Victorian. I hardly ever wear jewelry so I've never got round to having them redone. And there's one missing, so I can enquire about replacing it and get the name of the prince—would-be or actual—who's selling stuff."

"Ingenious."

"What was your jeweller's name?"

"I remember that the name of the business begins with a Z, is quite short, and has two Vs in unlikely places. Let me think."

"Lots of Russian names end in V," Daisy said helpfully.

"Hush! I am trying to picture it. Zzzzz . . . Zvvv . . ."

"ZV? Surely not!"

"Zv . . . Zvirov, that's it. Or Zverev."

"Zzz-verov. As Lucy said, unpronounceable. It shouldn't be difficult to find in the directory. Um . . . The other thing Alec said was that I wasn't to go and talk to people on my own. I don't suppose you'd come with me, darling? After all, you have already met the man."

"As a matter of fact, I never met him. His daughter does the designing, so it was with her I consulted."

"Zverev has a daughter? I bet he's the one I'm after, then, and she's the one Teddy made promises to."

"It is possible. She is very pretty. Handsome, rather, if I correctly understand the distinction."

"That makes it practically certain, given the rumour of a breach of promise suit. When would it be convenient for you to go with me? Soon, or the police will get there first."

"Shall you tell them about the Zverevs?"

"Good question. I wonder whether Lucy mentioned the jewelry business. If so, they'll have found him by now."

"And if not?"

"I don't know for certain that the Zverevs are involved. Alec would say it's pure speculation. I suspect the Russian aspect isn't a high priority for the police, since it turned out there's no record of a breach of promise suit. And it's not as if I don't have a perfectly good excuse for going."

"Great-Aunt Gertrude's aquamarines? If I were Alec, I should wonder why resetting them has suddenly become an urgent concern."

"Let him wonder." Inspiration struck. "My interest was sparked by seeing all the beautiful jewelry at the Kit-Cat. So when shall we go?"

Sakari sighed. "I hope Alec will not blame me for leading you astray."

"Not a chance. I'm the one he'll blame for leading *you* astray. He'll be grateful to you for coming with me."

"You are very determined. Yet you did not like Teddy Devenish. Why are you so keen to find his killer?"

Daisy hadn't really considered the question, let alone put her reasons into words. "Not just because I found him, though that did arouse my curiosity. Partly for his sister's sake. Mostly because of Mrs. Gilpin. I wish her memory would return!"

"Do you think she would recognise the murderer?"

"Who knows? She was closest to her—or him. He might believe she could."

"So she is in danger?"

"It's possible, though I can't imagine how he'd find out who she is or where she lives. The other concern is whether the police suspect her of being somehow involved, other than being a witness, that is. Not Alec—I hope!—but Mr. Mackinnon. He can't avoid it. She was pretty much the only suspect available to him. It's not as if he had a houseful of people on hand ready to be investigated. And there's only the children's evidence that the third nanny ever existed."

"You don't doubt her existence, though."

"No, but I know the children. Charlie has a wild imagination, admittedly. The other two are as reliable as any adult, and more reliable than most. I'm certain there was a third person in nurse's uniform. I'll be happier once Nurse Gilpin's gone to stay with her sister."

"And in the meantime, suspects must be sought, and you are hot on the trail. Tomorrow morning we shall tackle the Russians. This afternoon, I shall put up my feet. I am quite exhausted."

"Darling, I'm sorry! Here I am dragging you all over town—"

"Nonsense, Daisy. You are very well aware that I would not miss the fun for anything. I shall pick you up at half past ten tomorrow morning."

FIFTEEN

Meanwhile, Alec had accompanied Mackinnon back to the Crystal Palace to present the searchers with Ben's map. He had visited as a child and remembered how huge it had seemed, but places generally appear to shrink when one revisits in adulthood. He was taken by surprise by the massive scale of the building and the extent of the park.

"I see why you're so happy to have the boy's help. Talk about a needle in a haystack."

"Even with this, I'll be astonished if we find the weapon, even if we drag all the lakes and fountains. We know it was something very slender, probably a hat pin. All he—or she—had to do was plunge it into one of the damned flowerpots, or even into the ground outside, and press it well in. A gardener may find it in a few years. The handbag's a different story. We ought to get that pretty quick now."

Alec listened in as Mackinnon explained the amended map to the sergeant in charge of the search team. As they walked back to his car, Alec said, "Remember, there's no reason to suppose Elliot Kerston knows any more about the victim's death than what he may have read in the papers."

"Got it, sir. All we want from him is the names of any of Devenish's friends or associates he may be aware of."

"Or enemies."

"Och aye." The Scot was stony-faced.

"Sorry, Inspector. I didn't mean to teach you your job. Perhaps I ought to explain that Kerston is the brother-in-law of a childhood friend of my wife."

Mackinnon grinned. "Verra weel, sir. I'll tread on eggshells."

"Thanks." Alec was irritated with himself. He had believed he'd long since moved past his jealousy of Petrie and his discomfort with Daisy's aristocratic background and her surviving links to that world. Just a passing twinge, he assured himself. He pulled himself together. "Is it late enough to call on a cabaret performer without disturbing her beauty sleep?"

"That'd be the one Mrs. Fletcher found?" Mackinnon asked slyly, getting his own back. "I'm not well acquainted with the habits of showgirls."

"I was going to give her to you, as well as Kerston, but you have enough on your hands. I'll risk her not being up yet. I can't hang about waiting, though. Heaven knows there's plenty of paperwork waiting back at the Yard."

"Anything is better than paperwork, even the horrors of rousing a showgirl in her pyjamas."

"A terrifying prospect. Charing Cross suit you?"

"Nicely, thank you."

Alec dropped the inspector at the station, where he had a choice of underground lines, and drove on to the East End. With a combination of luck and neat detective work, Ernie Piper had in less than fifteen minutes discovered Fay Fanshawe's real name—Florence Phipps—and the address where she lived with her parents.

Their street was typical of the area, little wider than an alley with smoke-grimed brick terraces of cramped houses. It was atypical in having preserved its self-respect through all vicissitudes. Clean windows were hung with bleached-white net curtains, matching the spotless stone doorsteps. Litter was at a minimum, even outside the inevitable pub on the corner—the Silk Weaver—and hopeful daffodils struggled for life in two or three window boxes.

A reasonably respectable-looking man in a sailor's pea jacket was lounging against the pub wall, waiting for opening time. Alec pulled his car in as close to the wall as possible, barely fitting between two doorsteps, and offered the lounger a couple of bob to keep an eye on it.

"Aye, cap'n. Rozzer, are you?"

"That obvious, is it?"

He shrugged. "In these parts . . ."

"Well, don't broadcast the fact. I don't want to embarrass the people I'm calling on, who are *not* under suspicion."

"Got it, cap'n. Me lips is sealed."

Alec found the number he wanted and knocked with the brightly polished brass lion's head. He was aware of the net curtain twitching on his right, but didn't glance towards it. The door opened on the chain, and a bright blue eye, crow's-feet at the corner, appeared in the crack. The hair above it was an improbable shade of red.

"Mrs. Phipps?"

"'Oo wants to know?"

A male voice demanded from within, "'Oo is it, ducks?"

"That's what I'm tryin' to find out, Bill. 'Old yer 'orses. Well?"

Alec passed his warrant card through the gap. "I'd like a word with Miss Phipps, please, madam. Nothing to worry about. I'm hoping she can give me some information."

"Our Florrie?" She held the card up to the grey light coming from outside. "It's a grasshopper, Bill. Plainclothes. 'E says not to worry."

"Better let 'im in afore Mrs. Snoop next door comes out on 'er doorstep to see what's 'appenin'. We got nothing to 'ide."

The door closed, and opened again without the chain. "Gotta be careful, 'aven't we," said Mrs. Phipps in a conversational tone. She was a short, thin woman, dressed in a flowery overall. "This ain't Mayfair. This is Mr. Fletcher, Bill. A chief inspector, 'e is, wou'jer believe it. 'E can't get up, 'e 'asn't put on 'is leg yet. I'll go see if our Florrie's up yet. She comes 'ome wiv the milkman, she does. In a manner of speakin', don't get me wrong."

Bill Phipps sat in a new-looking easy chair upholstered in green and red plaid plush, his one leg raised on a matching footstool. "Verdun," he said, with a gesture towards his pinned-up trouser leg. "But I don't need a foot to play the old squeeze box, though I can't sing out the old songs like I did, since swallerin' a lungful of the Kaiser's gas."

"Hard lines."

"Oh, there's many got it worse, not countin' them that didn't come back. I'm not complainin', 'specially since my girl bought this chair for me. Makes a bit of difference, that does! Bought it with 'er own bees, didn't she, earned fair and square. Buskers we are, and proud of it, but our Florrie got a reg'lar gig at a posh nightclub, pays nicely! It'd be summat to do with that you're int'rested in, eh?"

"There's a connection. I can't tell you more, I'm afraid."

During this interchange, Alec had heard Mrs. Phipps shouting up the stairs. Now came a flurry of footsteps. A mop of blond curls, natural by the look of them, poked round the door. A pair of bright blue eyes—just like her mother's—inspected him from head to toe and back again. Apparently he passed muster. A young girl bore her curls into the room—

No, not a young girl. A petite young woman who moved with the grace of an athlete.

With a touch of sarcasm, she said, "Not related to Mrs. Fletcher the writer, by any chance? If she reelly is that writer, not just a copper's nark."

"My wife," Alec confessed. "She really is that writer, and, trust me, the police would be delighted to find a way to curb her curiosity."

Miss Phipps/Fanshawe laughed. "Like that, eh? You're a toff, too, aincher! Too 'igh and mighty to come and talk in the kitchen? I don't want to disturb Pa."

"Not to worry, girl." Her father started to struggle to his foot, reaching for a crutch.

"Please, sir, don't move for my sake. I've no objection whatsoever to sitting in the kitchen."

He followed her through into a small, cheaply equipped, but clean and cheerful kitchen. Mrs. Phipps had put a kettle on the gas.

"I was just makin' a cuppa for everyone." She sounded anxious, in spite of Alec's attempt at reassurance.

"It's orright, Mum. I bet I know what Mr. Fletcher wants to ask about. I'll make the tea and bring you and Pa a cup. You go take a load off your feet."

She left reluctantly, not quite closing the door behind her. "Our Florrie" stepped over to gently shut it. Alec gave her an approving nod and took a seat at the table. After checking the kettle with her hand—a sign of nervousness despite her apparent coolness, as it couldn't possibly be hot enough yet—she produced four cups and saucers from a cupboard. They were pretty, flowered china, unexpected in the surroundings.

"Petticoat Lane," she said defensively.

"Nice." He was annoyed with himself for showing his surprise.

"Pa'll complain 'e wants 'is big cup, but 'e can just suffer for once. It's about Teddy Devenish, right?"

"Right. We're trying to reach all the people who knew him. Well, not all, I expect, but as many as we can."

"I didn't reelly know 'im. Not hardly at all, reelly."

"You didn't . . . keep company with him?"

"Not likely! I got more sense. Just the once, for a bit of supper." The kettle boiled and she made the tea. "Not that I didn't like 'im, at first. I expect Mrs. Fletcher told you the mean trick 'e played."

"She did."

"I was ever so angry. If I'd seen 'im right away I'd've slapped 'is face for 'im. But 'e wasn't worth hangin' for."

"I doubt anyone is. Was he on good terms with the other performers, male or female?"

"Not as I know of. I never saw 'im talkin' to them, and nobody's said nuffin'. 'Course, they wouldn't now 'e's dead, would they? But not before, neether."

"Fair enough. What about his companions, those who visited the Kit-Cat with him. Did you recognise any of them?"

"Not to put a name to," she said doubtfully, pouring tea. "He didn't mention any names. I'm too busy on stage to take much notice of the audience, even if it wasn't for the spotlight in me eyes. Not that I would if I could. Hang on 'alf a tick." She took two cups through to her parents.

Alec sipped his tea, very strong, with both milk and sugar stirred in as a matter of course.

When Florence returned, again closing the door behind her, she said, "See, Mum and Pa are happy I got the job but they don't want me hanging about with them sorts of people, not the patrons nor the kind that work there. They're not our sort and they don't trust 'em. They said there'd be trouble if I let Teddy take me to supper. Look where it's got me, chattin' to a copper about a corpse!"

Alec laughed. "It hasn't been such a terrible experience, has it?"

She grinned. "I've 'ad worser."

"Then just a couple more questions for the present. First, you didn't see his companions to 'put a name to.' Would you recognise them if you saw them again?"

"I dunno. I might."

"But you at least saw how many, and whether they were men or women?"

"Only after the first time 'e came backstage to talk to me. Before, 'e was just a face in the crowd, if 'e was there at all. After, I noticed 'im. It was always different, though, two or three people or a bigger group, both ladies and gentlemen. Once, 'e came with just a lady. If you ask me, he wanted to make me jealous, which 'e didn't, seeing I didn't care one way or the other."

"You're a hard nut to crack, Miss Phipps. I congratulate you. By the way, where were you on Wednesday morning?"

"I wondered when you'd get round to that. I worked Tuesday night so I got up late, like today. Then I washed me 'air, like I do every Wednesday and Sunday. That took the rest of the morning, seeing we 'as to boil kettles. Mum was 'ere 'elping. Pa went down the pub to get out of the way."

And both would lie through their teeth to protect their Florrie. "Thank you. That will do for now, though I may have more questions for you later."

"I've told you all I know, honest."

"I'm sure you think you have, but you will probably remember more details when you've had time to think. If so, I'd like you to get in touch with me. Ring me up at Scotland Yard and I'll see that you're reimbursed for the call. In any case, I'll come and see you again, or send one of my men. I'll make sure it's someone who won't give you a 'terrible experience.'"

For the first time, she looked vulnerable. "I can't stop you, can I."

"No. A man has been killed. He may not have been a good man or a pleasant man, but it's my job to find whoever murdered him and bring that person to justice."

What a pompous ass he sounded, he thought as he took his leave. Yet people often had to be reminded that he wasn't harassing them because he enjoyed it.

SIXTEEN

Back at the Yard, Alec dictated a brief report of his interview with Florence Phipps. He hadn't learnt much, but he'd satisfied himself that the young woman was an unlikely murderer. She appeared to have her head screwed on far too firmly.

DS Piper was battling a towering heap of reports. A myriad constables had trudged all over the city tracking down visitors to the Crystal Palace on that fatal morning. They were a small proportion of those who had bought tickets, as many had left before Mackinnon's men arrived to take names and addresses.

"So far there's a dozen or so that ought to be called on again, Chief. Fourteen, to be precise. Households, that is, not individuals. It's mostly family parties go there. Each of these includes someone who thinks they saw an overabundance of nursery nurses." Ernie looked moderately pleased with himself. He had taken Tom Tring's advice and studied to improve his vocabulary. "I'm about halfway through what I've got," he continued, "but there's more coming all the time."

Even as he spoke, a runner came in with a bulging folder and dropped it on his desk.

"So I see," said Alec. "Any that I or Mr. Mackinnon ought to see?"

"Not at this stage."

"Who's available?"

Ernie handed him a list of detective constables not specifically assigned to other cases. "I've heard that Angela Devenish, sister of the deceased, is arriving this afternoon and intends to stay at her brother's flat."

"Now I wonder how you heard that? Could it possibly be from my wife?"

"Er, as a matter of fact, yes, Chief. Mrs. Fletcher rang up just after you left this morning."

Alec groaned. "What's up?"

"Mrs. Fletcher wanted to know if it was all right for Miss Devenish to stay at the flat. I told her we'd finished there but Miss Devenish ought to get in touch with the solicitor."

"Damn!"

"Should I have—"

"No, no. It's just that I'm afraid she'll encourage Daisy to meddle. Perhaps she can tell us who his friends were. She was inexplicably fond of her brother, I seem to recall."

"That was my impression, too. And he of her, looks like. I talked Mr. Cranford, the solicitor, into disgorging the will. Deceased left everything, lock, stock, and barrel, to Miss Angela."

"Did he, now! I'll have to see her. Did Daisy say what time she's arriving in London?"

"She didn't know. I've looked up trains from Yorkshire but there are several, and I don't know what town she'll have started from. We've got her address, of course, but it's a tiny village in the depths of the country, about equidistant from Leeds, York, and Harrogate. We've got the telephone number of the flat, though, so we can ring up and find out if she's there before you go."

"That's something. Have someone ring every half hour or so from noon onwards. If possible, I want to speak to her before Daisy gets hold of her."

"Right, Chief." Piper was too used to Daisy's interference to blink.

"No word from Mr. Mackinnon?"

"Just that he's following up a couple of names Kerston suggested. The least likely, he said, but they may have further suggestions. He'll talk with you before the rest."

Alec nodded. Studying the first list Ernie had given him, he saw that his invaluable sergeant had grouped them by areas of London and provided a brief note of why he considered each worth a second visit. Checking the list of available constables, he chose three and sent for them.

Ernie was already deep in his reports again. No sound in the room would break his concentration unless his name was spoken.

The men came in, received Alec's instructions, and left. More reports landed on Ernie's desk. Alec turned reluctantly to the accumulation of papers on his own desk. It was a sobering thought that if he was promoted to superintendent he'd spend more time dealing with paper and less out on the job.

Then Mackinnon's sergeant telephoned from the Crystal Palace. "We found a handbag, sir. In one of the lakes close to the path we were told they took."

"Excellent. Anything useful in it? Keys, cheque book, letters, even a monogrammed handkerchief?"

"Nothing at all, sir. Not a sausage."

"Damnation! We'll hope for fingerprints. Your men haven't handled it, have they?"

"Just with gloves, sir, and carefully. I've wrapped it up. Should I send it straight up to the Yard?"

"Straight here, please, Sergeant. I'm expecting Mr. Mackinnon any minute. We'll get it to the dabs experts at once."

These days, only the stupidest of criminals made no effort to avoid leaving fingerprints. However, the circumstances surrounding the death of Devenish were so bizarre that Alec would have been astonished if the murderer's dabs were on file. The handbag might be smothered in prints for all the good it would do them until they had already nabbed the culprit.

And at present they had all too many leads to follow up with no solid suspects.

As Alec sent off the last two DCs presently under his command, Mackinnon arrived. He brought yet more names to add to the list.

"Toffs," he said. "Landed gentry, mostly, not peerage. I called at two houses and spoke to the ladies as neither husband was at home. Both elderly, with no young people in the household. We're agreed the murderer is probably under thirty or so, aren't we, sir? I can't see anyone much older going in for such a prank."

"Yes, with reservations. Go on."

"Both couples are friends of Sir James and Lady Devenish. That is, the ladies are friends, at least. That's the only reason they invited the deceased to their houses, or so they claim. They had heard rumours that he 'wasn't quite the thing,' but hadn't personally witnessed any behaviour that would make them ostracise the son of friends, not to mention a personable and usefully unattached man."

"Did you get anything of interest from them?" Alec asked impatiently.

"The names of hostesses at whose houses they recalled meeting him, and which have young people. And a fair bit of gossip, some of it possibly helpful."

"Let's have a look before you write it up."

Piper joined in as they discussed their results to date. Mackinnon took an even gloomier view of the usefulness of the handbag.

"Even if they find the fingerprints of a villain all over it, chances are it'll turn out to be a well-known sneak thief," he pointed out. "The light-fingered mob swarm to the Crystal Palace, especially on race and game days. They're good at lifting stuff but mostly not bright enough to remember fingerprints. I bet the bag was nicked, emptied, and dumped."

"They wouldn't remove every scrap of paper," Piper argued. "Women always—" The telephone bell cut him off. He lifted the receiver and listened. "Right . . . Right. D'you want to speak to him? . . . OK, mate." He hung up and turned to Mackinnon. "Your man at the Palace, Inspector. They've found the nurse's get-up, right down to the shoes and a wig, hidden under a bush near a gate—exit-only type, so no attendant—at the bottom of the park. Gives on to a busy street, the Penge Road, close to a three-way junction. Chief, he'd never have gone out to the street in his skivvies!"

After a blank moment, Alec proposed, "Athletic gear under his frock?"

"Ah," said Ernie, sounding exactly like Tom Tring as he uttered the ex-Sergeant's favourite monosyllable. "Shoes?"

"He could tie a pair of plimsolls round his waist under the cloak," Mackinnon proposed. "They probably have athletes training in the park all the time. Nice place to run. No one would take a second look."

"Leaving a car parked nearby," suggested Alec. "Near any of the gates, it wouldn't matter if he could run back through the park."

"*He*, or *they*?" Mackinnon queried. "Was the victim also in running garb?"

"No," said Ernie, the answer to any question of fact at his fingertips as usual, like his invariably well-sharpened pencils. "Which means . . ." He hesitated.

"Premeditation," Mackinnon said grimly. "The victim expected to walk out in the nurse's uniform and the murderer didn't."

Alec raised his hand. "Hold on. Maybe Devenish simply had more faith in his ability to depart in a dignified fashion. We can be almost certain his was the moving spirit, after all, judging by what we've heard of his character. But, strictly speaking, premeditation is a question for the courts, not us, except as character impinges on our hunt for the murderer. Besides, I only speculated that he might have changed into athletic clothing. *She* could have been wearing a second frock under the uniform."

"Or maybe," Ernie speculated in his turn, "they stashed a change of clothes in the park and the murderer took the victim's with him. Or her."

"Probably him. A woman could have worn a light frock under the uniform. Let's stick to 'him' unless to make a point. And let's get away from the subject of the clothes until they've been properly examined. They should tell us the size of the wearer, if nothing more. Mr. Mackinnon, you'd better write up your report and decide on priorities for interviewing the people on your list. Let Piper know where the top few are to be found. He'll work out the most efficient way for the three of us to get round to as many as possible this afternoon. Or . . . Is your sergeant as good at interviewing as he is at finding shoes and handbags?"

"He'd be all right with Sergeant Piper's lot. I wouldn't set him on to this uppercrust lot." He waved his notebook.

"Good enough. I'm going to try to clear my desk so that I can concentrate on this case. Ernie, if any of the reports coming in from the DCs seem urgent, tell me at once. Otherwise, no interruptions."

"Right, Chief."

The paperwork, a mixture of reports from recent investigations and administrative bumf, went faster than Alec had expected. Finishing well before lunchtime, he decided to escape, before the next flood arrived, and have lunch out.

"I'll ring up between interviews to find out if Miss Devenish has arrived yet," he told Piper. "She has first priority. Make sure whoever makes the calls assures her I'll be there very shortly and asks her to wait."

He had a frustrating afternoon. Many of those he wanted to see were not at home. Of those who were, none admitted to a close acquaintance with Teddy Devenish, far less friendship. Alec received a general impression that no one had much liked him or even approved of him, though it seemed he had saved his nastier tricks for those who couldn't fight back. He hadn't wanted to be banned from the society of his peers.

Two or three people—all ladies—made glancing references to a Russian scandal, but when pressed they were vague about details. It was just gossip, a rumour. Not one of them admitted to recalling who had told her.

He finished a particularly trying interview shortly before four o'clock. The butler of the house kindly allowed him to use the telephone to ring up the Yard, and the duty sergeant at last told him Miss Devenish had arrived at her brother's flat. Checking the address, he found that the ever efficient Piper's suggested route had kept him within easy reach.

Leaving his car, he walked there in a few minutes. The modern block of service flats was six storeys high and Devenish lived on the top floor. He would, Alec thought, then entered the marble-floored lobby and spotted a lift. His relief was tempered by dismay: Not so long ago, he would have taken all those stairs in his stride. Was it an argument for accepting the superintendent position, if offered, or ought he to try to get more exercise?

The approach of a uniformed porter put an end to the internal debate not a moment too soon. His inspection of Alec's credentials was blasé.

"We've 'ad a lot of you gentlemen from Scotland Yard the last couple of days. And the press, my word! But there's a lady just took up residence, the deceased gentleman's sister, so I better ring up." He retreated to his cubby, where he could be seen through the glass taking up his telephone.

Half a minute later, he reemerged, thumbs up. "Miss'll be happy to see you, sir."

"Happy" to see him? Making for the lift, one of the new automatic kind, Alec wondered whether the word came from Angela Devenish or was a gloss added by the porter.

At the top, a narrow but carpeted passage gave access to four flats, two each way. Devenish's was the second to the right. Alec rang the bell.

Daisy opened the door.

"Darling, that was quick. We didn't expect you for at least twenty minutes."

"What the deuce are you doing here, Daisy?"

"Angela is a friend of mine, the only one she has in town, really. She rang me the moment she arrived, before she even took off her . . . Down, Mr. Fisher!"

The scruffy dog thus admonished stopped jumping at Alec's knees but continued to bark.

"Mr. Fisher?"

"Doesn't he look sort of like a frog? His face, I mean. Anyway, Angela thinks so. She's making tea—the kettle just boiled. You're not going to try to make me leave, are you? Because she wants me to stay and I want my tea. Come in here."

Alec wasn't going to try to make her leave because he had strong doubts as to his success. He followed her into a spacious sitting room, Mr. Fisher sniffing suspiciously—but silently at last—at his trouser turn ups. A large, south-facing window provided plenty of light, even on this grey day. It revealed an expansive view over the lower buildings of Knightsbridge and Chelsea and even, between taller buildings, a glimpse of the river and Battersea beyond. Teddy had obviously done well from his great-aunt's will.

The furnishings were modern, with a good deal of chrome. Alec was surprised, until he remembered this was not Angela's environment but her brother's, though presumably the lease would belong to her once the will was proved. Avant-garde paintings on the walls, several small bronze sculptures, and a couple of African-looking wood carvings testified to his artistic tastes.

Angela came in carrying a tray. A lean woman in her late thirties, she bore its laden weight with ease. Her hair was tousled, her face weatherbeaten; she wore country tweeds and heavy walking shoes. Mr. Fisher rushed to her with delighted yips and danced round her. "Down, Mr. Fisher, or you may get a teapot on your head. Down! Hello, Mr. Fletcher. Or should I call you Chief Inspector?" She set down the tray and shook hands, her clasp firm and dry.

"Mister will do very well, Miss Devenish."

"Do sit down. These awful chairs are slightly more comfortable than they look. How can I help you?" she asked bluntly.

"Tell me about your brother."

Angela took a deep breath and blurted out, "I didn't like him. I loved him, of course. Sort of. One has to love family, doesn't one? Or at least stand by them. But I couldn't be *fond* of him after he kicked Mrs. Tiggywinkle."

"A hedgehog? No, one of your dogs, I take it."

"She was in whelp. All the pups were born dead and she was in pain for months."

"Oh no!" Daisy breathed in sympathy. Alec gave her a look, but Angela didn't seem to have heard her.

"I haven't seen Teddy since."

"I'm sorry. How long ago was that, Miss Devenish?"

"A year ago," she said vaguely. "Two years? I remember it was November, because we had the first snow just a few days later."

"You're sure it wasn't last November?"

"It might— No, it couldn't have been because then Mrs. T would have only just recovered. She's been all right for ages. In fact, I thought she was going to have another litter, but she didn't, thank goodness. There are too many unwanted dogs already. We try to keep the bitches confined when they're on heat. Some of them are real Houdinis, though. We had one—"

"'We'?" Alec interrupted. "You're not running it alone?"

"Gosh no, I couldn't manage it on my own. I couldn't have left them to come to London, could I! I've got a hired man, whose wife keeps house for me, and people in the village help out when they can. This week's the Easter hols so the kids from the manor come every day. The dogs adore them."

"They were there every day this week? You're sure?"

Angela seemed surprised at his insistence. "Absolutely. They'd come before breakfast if their parents would let them, and they often bring a picnic lunch. The dogs usually get quite a bit of it," she admitted gruffly.

"How old are they?"

"Nine and eleven. Or is it twelve? Sorry, I'm not awfully good at that sort of thing." Mr. Fisher laid a consoling head in her lap and she fondled his ears. "Does it matter?"

"Close enough." Alec glanced at Daisy. She was obviously pleased that Angela had provided herself with an alibi that could easily be checked, even if Angela herself was oblivious. Angela was equally oblivious of the tea tray, so Daisy took it upon herself to pour and hand round cups.

Alec took down the children's parents' names and address, and the hired man's for good measure. "Did your brother ever talk about his friends and acquaintances?" he asked next.

"That was pretty much his only interest," she said dryly. "I let it flow past my ears. Any names I heard, I've forgotten long since."

"Pity."

"I can give you a general idea of what he said about them, though, if that's any use to you. I couldn't help hearing some of it."

"I never know what will be useful. Please go ahead."

Angela hesitated. "I suppose I'd better go back to when we were growing up. You see, Teddy was always the favourite, naturally, because he was the only boy. He was always indulged."

"Spoiled rotten," Daisy murmured. Alec shot her a repressive frown. He was amazed she hadn't opened her mouth more often.

"As a result," Angela went on with a faraway expression, "if he was ever thwarted, he was convinced he was being picked on and, if he could, he retaliated. He usually got away with it." She stopped, dismayed at where her thoughts were leading.

Alec decided to press her. "With no repercussions, he came

to enjoy the mean tricks he played on people? He started to indulge his taste even without provocation, real or imagined?"

"Ye-es. Yes, I'm afraid so. He was such a nice little boy! Last time I saw him, he seemed to positively delight in scoring off people, even artists and writers and people like that whose work he admired."

Daisy's inarticulate mutter sounded like agreement. Alec shot her another glare, but she wasn't looking, being busy stroking Mr. Fisher's head. Not that it would have deterred her if she had seen it.

Again, Angela didn't appear to have heard her. "It was horrible to listen to his gloating. He revelled in telling me how clever he'd been, so that they could never be sure whatever he'd done wasn't an accident. He couldn't fool me that he kicked Mrs. Tiggywinkle by accident! He told me he tripped over her, but I saw him do it, absolutely deliberately. I'll never forgive him. I'm sorry he's dead, but all the same . . . Was he killed by someone he'd provoked?"

"Probably, given the circumstances."

"The circumstances?" She sounded puzzled. "Was there something odd about it?"

"You haven't read the papers."

"Lord no, I never read them. What . . . What happened?"

Apparently Daisy had funked the explanation, and Alec couldn't blame her. If there was a delicate way to tell a woman her brother had been murdered in a ladies' room while dressed as a nursery nurse, he couldn't think of it. He was glad someone else had had to break the news to Teddy's parents.

He had to be blunt. Though he tried to be gentle, his words made Angela flinch.

After a moment, she said, "He always did like dressing up, amateur theatricals, that sort of thing. And the ladies' room—just the sort of prank he would get involved in just for kicks. Or a dare, perhaps. He never could resist a dare."

Judging by Mr. Fisher, she was more upset than was obvious. The dog returned to her, laid his head in her lap, and licked her hand lavishly.

Alec sipped his tea, recognising the distinctive flavour of lapsang souchong. Teddy's taste, not Angela's, of course. It was lukewarm, so he hurriedly swigged down the rest. "Did your brother ever want to go on the stage professionally, Miss Devenish?"

"Not that I recall, but I didn't pay much heed. My father would have cut him off without a shilling. He considers all actors effeminate, and besides, it would have been 'betraying his class.' As I do, in his eyes. He'd approve if I kept any number of hounds and dashed about the countryside killing innocent animals, but rescuing hurt and abandoned dogs is beyond the pale. Not that I care," she finished defiantly.

"No, why should you? How long do you expect to stay in town?"

"As short a time as possible. London's a horrible place. I'll have to stay a few days, though. Teddy's solicitor wrote that I'm co-executor of his will. I've no idea what that entails but with any luck Mr. Cranford will do it all."

"Do you know how he's left his assets?"

"Not a clue. Father will be livid if Aunt Eva's money doesn't revert to the Devenish estate, even though most of it came from her husband. I daresay it will. What else would Teddy do with it?"

Alec was as certain as he could be that she was not aware of being her brother's sole legatee. If Teddy had revealed the fact, he would have been badgered to change his will. It would come as a nasty shock to Sir James, which was undoubtedly just what the baronet's undutiful son had planned.

SEVENTEEN

"*Thank you* for the lift, darling," said Daisy, as Alec let in the clutch and the Austin Twelve moved smoothly away from the curb, "but if you think I don't realise you just wanted to get me away from Angela, you've got another think coming."

"I know you far too well to suppose anything of the sort. However, I was sorry to see how disconsolate she was to lose your company, and I'm not at all sure there's any need to keep you apart, though we do need to check her alibi."

"It looks good, doesn't it?"

"Excellent. In any case, that was not my sole motive. I'm quite certain you haven't wasted your day. Tell me what you've been up to, besides beating me to Angela."

"I do have quite a bit of news." Daisy frowned in thought, casting back her mind. "Where shall I start?"

"Only you can decide."

"I'd better tell you about Mrs. Gilpin first."

Alec's relaxed grip on the steering wheel tightened. "She remembers?"

"No, and don't get your hopes up. Dr. Ransome still says it's quite possible she never will."

"Damn!"

"She's worrying about it, which doesn't help and may hinder, for all he knows. He thinks she should go away for a rest, so I wrote to her sister, to see if she could go there for a week or two. What do you think?"

"If we haven't solved this by other means in a week . . . ! It can't hurt. She's no help as she is. Yes, let her go, assuming she's willing."

"I haven't asked her yet. I wanted to hear from her sister before I suggest it. I hope she's not going to make a fuss about leaving the twins with Bertha."

"She can hardly do that, when she left them to Bertha at the Crystal Palace."

"I wish I knew why! Well, never mind. I went out to lunch with Sakari."

"She said in a portentous voice. Where?"

"The Café Royal. We met friends of Sakari's there. You know her thirst for knowledge. She likes to talk to artists and writers."

"And there's nothing writers and artists like better than to talk about themselves. Did they also talk about Teddy Devenish?"

"Only briefly. Someone came in with a newspaper that gave the identity of the 'Crystal Palace Corpse.' No one had heard before who it was."

"No, we didn't release it to the press till just in time for the noon editions."

"Several people made comments on the lines of 'good riddance to bad rubbish,' though not quite so crassly. We were all crammed together at a large table so I'm afraid I couldn't very well ask Sakari who they were. The only person I recognised was a would-be sculptor called Purdue, who was a neighbour when Lucy and I lived in Chelsea. I don't think he said anything at that point. He was too busy arguing with another chap."

"That's a fat lot of use! Whence the portentous tone?"

"Patience, darling, patience. You're always telling me to start at the beginning and not to wander."

"Also to cut the cackle and come to the horses. Never mind, go your own sweet way."

"I will! They didn't talk about Teddy for very long, really it was only those few remarks on hearing the news. If anyone said anything complimentary or sorrowful, I didn't hear it. The next thing was two foreigners came in. One was holding the same paper, with the headline about Teddy, and they both seemed all a-flutter over it. I'm sure they were Russians. Of course, I couldn't understand a word they said." In view of her proposed expedition to see the Zverevs next day, Daisy moved hastily on. "We left a few minutes later."

"You were able then to ask Mrs. Prasad the names of Devenish's detractors?"

"No, we weren't alone. One of her friends invited us to see her studio." She described the visit to Judith Winter. "I didn't get any names from her either. She was very discreet. But I bought two very pretty bowls."

"Bronze?" Alec asked absently.

"No, china."

"But you said Miss Winter works in bronze."

"Both."

"I wonder whether those bronzes in Teddy's flat are—"

"Three of them are. It's a pattern. Did I tell you about Lord Berners?"

"Lord Berners! Where the deuce does he come in?"

"He's a successful composer and involved in all sorts of other artistic endeavours—writing and painting for a start. Sakari has a theory that Teddy aspired to be a second Berners. When no one took him seriously, he'd be bound to blame anything and anyone other than his own lack of talent. It would explain his animus towards all sorts of artists. Especially good ones."

Alec grinned. "Mrs. Prasad is as bad as you for wild speculation, if not worse. When you say 'it's a pattern,' what exactly do you mean?"

"If you're going to scoff . . ."

"Only if I can't see this pattern of yours."

"Oh, all right," Daisy sighed, giving in. "It seems to me he had a genuine appreciation of the arts. He not only admired and bought, he displayed what he'd bought. Then he became jealous of the creator's talent, and that's when the nastiness surfaced. It happened over and over again; that's where the pattern comes in."

"It's a reasonable interpretation," Alec agreed. "Another would be that he bought in order to win the artists' trust, so that when he turned on them it would come as a shock and be that much more painful to them, amusing to him. Alternatively, if they regarded him as a patron and friend, he could more easily pass off his tricks as accidental."

"Or perhaps all three, at different times. He was rather pathetic, wasn't he?"

"Not to his victims."

"No." One had been upset enough to do him in. "What I can't fathom is his reason for inviting or coercing one of them to dress up and go to the Crystal Palace with him. If they were unmasked, he'd be equally humiliated, or in equal trouble. Is it against the law for a man to masquerade as a woman and enter the ladies'?"

"That's a good point. I've no idea. As for his purpose, I don't suppose we'll ever know. He surely wouldn't have revealed it to his companion."

"Probably not, though you can't be sure."

"All right, we've covered your gleanings from the Café Royal." Alec turned into Constable Circle, circled the communal garden, and pulled up in front of the house. "What about Angela, before I arrived on the scene? Did she say anything of interest?"

"Not a thing."

He opened the car door for her. "If I hadn't kidnapped you, were you going to keep all this to yourself?"

"Of course not, darling! I was going to ring up the Yard and

149

spill the beans to Mr. Mackinnon or Ernie. If you weren't there," she added quickly. "Will you be home for dinner? Half an hour early, remember, because of the children."

"I expect so. I'll ring if not. Thanks for the leads. We had no starting place for delving into the artistic community. Oh, by the way, I called on your friend Fay Fanshawe. Alias Florrie Phipps—"

"No!"

"Yes. You'll be glad to hear she's a respectable young woman, living with her parents, and low on my list of suspects. All the same, I suppose I have to thank you for discovering her, too, though I'm *not* happy about your wandering round backstage at the Kit-Cat. The Café Royal was a good idea—an innocuous place on the whole. I'm glad you had Mrs. Prasad with you, especially when you visited the sculptor. But *please*, Daisy, no more investigating!"

A sudden flurry of rain gave Daisy an excuse to dash up the steps without answering. She waved from the shelter of the porch and went into the house.

The dog came scampering down the stairs to greet her.

"Nana!" Belinda called from the landing. "Sorry, Mummy, I *told* Charlie to shut the door."

Charlie was close behind Nana. Ben and Belinda followed.

"As long as she's clean and dry, no harm done." Daisy let the little dog sniff her hands, which undoubtedly smelled of Mr. Fisher.

"She is, Aunt Daisy," Charlie promised. "We just got home so we haven't had time to take her out. We went to Madame Tussaud's. It was . . . it was *specacular*!"

"Spec*t*acular," Bel corrected.

"And there was lots of history, too," said Ben more soberly.

"In history, they used to cut people's heads off. There was a big fat king, his name was Henry, and he had lots of wives and he cut off their heads, like in the *Arabian Nights*."

"Not nearly so many," said Ben.

"Eight. That's lots, isn't it, Aunt Daisy?"

"Six. Far too many wives, but he only cut off the heads of two, you bloodthirsty creature."

"Then we went to a magic place—"

"Maskelyne's."

"And Mr. Maskelyne cut a lady in half!"

"What fun," Daisy said dryly.

"She was all right," Charlie assured her. "It was magic. She came out and bowed afterwards and we clapped."

"I'm glad to hear it. Have you had tea?"

"I saved enough for penny buns," said Belinda. "We ate them on the bus."

"With currants," Ben elaborated, "and icing. They were good but they made me thirsty."

"Go and ask Mrs. Dobson for a drink."

"And then may we take Nana out, Mummy?"

"Yes, but take umbrellas and be back in time to tidy yourselves for dinner. Daddy said he'd probably be home in time."

"Oh, goody! He's always in a rush at breakfast."

Daisy went upstairs rather wearily. She popped into the nursery to find the twins with their mouths full of fishcake and surrounded by milk moustaches.

"Are you managing all right, Bertha?"

"Oh yes, madam, very nicely. They're such good children, aren't you, my poppets? I wondered, madam, seeing you're here, if you fancied helping bath them? Not that I can't manage," she added hastily, "but I 'member you once asked to and Mrs. Gilpin was ever so—didn't think it was a good idea."

"I'd love to. I'll go and change."

"And I'll lend you one of my aprons, madam."

Daisy had such fun splashing with the twins and washing their little faces, she wished she'd put down her foot long ago. Then she helped to put them to bed, heard their prayers, and read them a story, watching their eyes close as they drifted off to sleep. How much of their childhood she had missed because of Nurse Gilpin's rigid ideas! Yet Oliver and Miranda were happy and healthy . . .

Unless the woman had absolutely no excuse for her behaviour at the Crystal Palace, Daisy would give her an excellent reference and recommend her to Lucy. Lady Gerald Bincombe was unlikely to want to bathe her baby, and if by some remote chance she did, she was quite high-handed enough to overrule Mrs. Gilpin.

Dinner was enjoyable too. The older children took Alec's mind off his case with their chatter about waxworks and magic. At last Elsie removed the scant remains of the rhubarb tart, what little was preserved from the insatiable appetites of growing boys.

The three youngsters went off to play Happy Families, if Bel could find the cards. Alec and Daisy settled down to coffee in the small sitting room.

Daisy badly wanted to find out whether there were any developments in the investigation, but she didn't want to disturb a rare peaceful evening. Nor did she want to open the possibility of questions about Russians.

However, not many minutes past before he remarked, "You're like a cat on hot bricks. Give me a small brandy and I'll spill the beans."

"Why do I sense a quid pro quo?" Daisy poured a small tot. "Water? Soda?"

"Neat, thanks. Because there is one. A quid pro quo. Not that I expect any objections: I want to pick your brains."

"Darling!" She fanned herself with her hand. "I was beginning to think you didn't think I had any!"

"I know you do. Sometimes you're very good at hiding them."

"Well, thanks for the compliment. If that's what it is. What can I do for you?"

"It's about the handbag. Mackinnon's team found it—pretty much where Ben and Charlie between them said it would be, by the way. Bright boys, both of them."

"That's my impression. What about the handbag?"

"It's black patent leather, just about the perfect surface for fingerprints, and the dabs people found plenty in spite of a couple of days' immersion. Too many, in fact, both male and female."

"And nothing inside to identify it by?"

"It was empty. Not so much as a matchbox. It took Ernie's sharp eyes to notice the label of Angels, the theatrical costumier, sewn in to the lining at the bottom. Then the clothes were checked, both the discarded bundle and those Devenish was wearing, and unsurprisingly they too had Angels labels."

"They must have recorded the name of the hirer, of course. I'd bet it was Teddy."

"You'd win."

"So you're no further forward. Why do you think I might be able to help? Not, I trust, just because I'm female?"

"Well, yes," he admitted. "How is a mere man to understand the female attitude towards handbags?"

"They're a nuisance to carry, but I'd as soon abandon mine as you would empty your pockets and abandon the contents."

Reflexively, Alec reached into a pocket and produced his pipe and tobacco pouch as he queried, "Even if it were an empty prop?"

"I can't conceive of carrying an empty handbag. If I did, I expect I would hang on to it by instinct."

"That's what I suspected. I'm more and more persuaded that the assailant of Devenish and Mrs. Gilpin is a man."

"The more I find out about Teddy's character, the more I'm convinced of it. There would be no earthly point in his taking a woman with him into the ladies'. She'd have every right to be there, even in hired plumage."

EIGHTEEN

Kesin came alone to pick up Daisy next day. "The memsahib send excuses, madam," he told her. "She very busy this morning." For a moment Daisy was afraid she would have to call off the expedition. She really didn't want to tackle the Russians on her own. But the chauffeur continued, "We drive back now to fetch her."

It was a chilly day, and he tucked a tartan rug round her knees before they whizzed down Hampstead Hill to St. John's Wood. The Prasads occupied one of the larger detached houses, Sakari's husband being an important official at the India Office. It was a late Georgian building standing square and solid in a good-sized walled garden. Kesin jumped out to open the wrought-iron gates, then drove in between beds of multicoloured wallflowers, their scent overwhelming the ever-present fumes of petrol.

He pulled up at the bottom of a wide flight of steps. "I go see if memsahib ready, madam. You wait or prefer come in?"

"I'll wait while you see how long she'll be."

"Very good, madam." He ran up the steps, to return a couple of minutes later with Sakari leaning on his arm. She was always a bit unsteady coming down steps, because—as she was wont to explain—she couldn't see her feet.

Kesin handed her in beside Daisy and swathed her in two rugs. After years in England, she still felt the cold, and her insistence on wearing saris didn't help, even with a coat on top. There was no such thing as a warm woollen sari.

"I am sorry to be late, Daisy. A minor domestic crisis. You brought your aquamarines?"

"Yes." Daisy patted her handbag. "If they're used to dealing with diamonds and rubies and emeralds, they're going to think these pretty paltry, but the stones are quite nice. They do definitely need a new setting to show them off."

It didn't take long to reach the narrow shop in the maze of alleys, closes, passages, and mews in the vicinity of Soho Square. There were three other shops in the alley, selling antiques, wine and spirits, and books respectively. The sign above the jeweller's door read simply Зверев-г3бепеб. Green blinds were down in the half-glass door and the window, but a card hanging between blind and door pronounced the place open.

The Sunbeam was almost as wide as the alley. Daisy had to slide across the leather seat and get out on the driver's side after Sakari.

Sakari spoke to Kesin in Hindi. He salaamed and got back into the car, while she turned to Daisy and said, "He will leave the car in the square under the nose of a policeman and return to wait at the door. Let us go in."

A bell jangled harshly as she pushed open the door. The interior, wider than it was deep, was murky, lit by a single bulb over the counter that divided the small space lengthwise roughly in half. Behind the age-blackened counter was a bare, white-washed wall with a rectangle of matte brown tile that suggested a closed-off fireplace. In one corner was a doorway masked by a velvet curtain, a startlingly vivid royal blue in the otherwise featureless room. It was warm, though there was no visible source of heat.

Three plain cane-bottomed chairs stood stiffly against one

155

wall. Above them hung a small oval painting of the Virgin and Child in an ornate gilt frame. Two tall stools were positioned before the counter. Sakari at once hitched herself up onto one of the latter, as if it might escape her should she give it the opportunity.

The curtain swayed. A beringed feminine hand held it aside and a tall woman came through.

"*Mesdames*, what can I do for you?" She flicked a switch behind the counter, turning on a brighter electric light. It revealed an elegant figure in a black frock of heavy silk, a patterned cashmere shawl over her shoulders. Her abundant dark hair was done up in coiled braids on top of her head. She looked nearer thirty than twenty, older than Daisy had—for no particular reason—expected. "Ah, it is Madame Prasad, *n'est-ce pas?*"

"*Namaste*, mademoiselle. This is my friend, Mrs. Fletcher, who wishes to have some gems reset in the modern style."

"*Bienvenue*, madame. I am Zvereva, Zinaïda Stepanovna. Certainly we can help you. You have brought the gems?"

"*Les voici*, mademoiselle." Daisy placed the tissue-wrapped package on the counter.

"*Vous parlez français, madame?*"

"*Un peu seulement.*"

"Then we will speak English. I had an English *gouvernante* as a child."

"And I a French governess, but little practice," Daisy said with a smile.

Miss Zverev—Zvereva?—returned a slight smile. "*Bien*. Before I look at what you have brought, I wish you to examine my hands." She laid them flat on the counter. "As you see, I wear a number of rings. Those on my left hand are in the old fashion. Those on my right are more modern. Before I begin a design, I must be sure I understand what you want."

Daisy pored over the gleaming rings, noting the slender, well-kept hands they adorned. The massive older settings emphasised the left hand's elegance but seemed to weigh it down;

the contemporary rings, much more delicate, made the hand that bore them look strong and capable in contrast. Much more appropriate for a modern woman who had no intention of spending her life languishing on a chaise longue, Daisy thought. She herself rarely wore anything other than her wedding ring. They always seemed to catch on things, so she reserved even her engagement sapphire for special occasions.

"I prefer these," she said, indicating the right hand, "but I don't want rings."

"Let me look at your jewels." The young woman unwrapped the heavy, ornate aquamarine necklace, earrings, and bracelet. "Ah, sapphires . . . *Mais non*, these are aquamarines. One sees not often such fine dark blue." She held up the necklace and looked at Daisy through the arc. "One is missing, I see. This colour will be difficult to match if you wish to replace. If not, I can make design without."

"Yes, no need to try to find one to match."

"The colour of the stones is perfect for you, madame, matching your eyes, but the settings—*non, non, non*. You are wise to desire a change."

"Is this not exactly what Mr. Devenish told you, Daisy?" Sakari put in.

"Teddy? Good heavens no," said Daisy, surprised. Then she realised she had momentarily lost sight of the real purpose of the visit to the Zverev establishment in the interest of the ostensible purpose. She had to admire Sakari's deft introduction of the name. "No, I didn't know him well enough for that, though I believe his artistic judgement was good, whatever his faults."

Miss Zvereva's hands had balled into fists. She leaned forward over the counter and said in a low but intense voice, "You are friends of Teddy Devenish?"

"No." Daisy explained: "Mrs. Prasad never met him, did you, darling? I was acquainted with him very slightly, only because he was the cousin of a friend of mine."

"Is true he is dead?"

"It's true."

She straightened with a sigh, apparently of relief, and murmured something that sounded like "Horror show," but presumably meant something else in Russian.

"You knew him?" Daisy asked.

"Yes." With a backward glance, she went on, still in a hushed voice, "My father wished me to marry him." She shrugged. "He is—He was English and rich, and one day title."

"You didn't want to?"

"Never! And this is not what you say 'sour grapes,' like Aesop. I heard stories about Teddy. He pretend to love me but I did not trust him. Was not surprise to me when he . . . he jilt me. Was shock to Papa. Blamed me for not encouragement." Her fractured English bore witness to her emotional state.

However, Daisy couldn't be sure of the reason for her agitation. Quite possibly being jilted upset her more than she would admit. Or did she suspect her father of having a hand in Teddy's death? If not the murderer, he might conceivably be the instigator.

It depended whether he viewed Teddy as a reluctant suitor to be wooed or a trickster who had never seriously intended to wed his daughter. Did he have a son who might have decided or been persuaded to avenge his sister? How could she find out?

"I hope others in your family support you, mademoiselle," said Sakari, commiserating, as if she had read Daisy's mind.

"We are only two, my father and I. I do not like to disobey, but I tell him, we are now in England. Daughters are not oblige to marry man chosen by father."

"Absolutely not," Daisy said warmly. "You had a narrow escape from Teddy Devenish. He wasn't at all a nice man."

"I think not. I cannot be sorry he is dead. Alas, my father now encourages a second Englishman. He—" She broke off abruptly as the blue velvet was thrust back with a rattle of curtain rings.

The man who entered looked to be in his late thirties. Like the Russian Daisy had seen at the Café Royal, he was dressed in a long, belted shirt worn over his trousers. Bareheaded, he was clean-shaven and wore his dark hair clipped short. He was stocky, about the same height as Zinaïda. Daisy decided he could have passed for a rather stout woman.

In a deep voice, he spoke in Russian to Miss Zverev, addressing her as Zinaïda Stepanovna and saying something about "Stepan Vladimirovich." Or rather, that was what Daisy thought she heard. Russian names were extraordinarily complex, as she knew from having once attempted to tackle a translation of *War and Peace*, only to give up because she never knew who was talking to whom.

Miss Zverev answered in Russian, then turned back to Daisy. "Madame, the prince my father wishes to see the jewels before I agree to make design for them. He is very particular about my work. I would like to make for you, but in this I will do as he decides. They will be quite safe with my father and Vasily Ivanovich. You do not object?"

"Not at all," said Daisy, hoping that her stones came up to scratch. She didn't care so much about them in themselves, though she was more interested than she had been. What she wanted was an excuse to come again.

On a pretty silver tray from beneath the counter, the aquamarines disappeared beyond the curtain.

"Vasily Ivanovich is a skilled gold- and silversmith," said Sakari. "Has he been with you for many years?"

"All my life. His grandfather was a serf in the household of my grandfather. My father obtained for him an apprenticeship in the workshop of Fabergé."

"The Fabergé who made the Imperial Easter eggs?" Daisy asked. "I've seen pictures. Not surprising that he's good, then. One of my editors might like an article about the eggs. I wonder where they are now."

"The Soviet thieves have some," said Zinaïda contemptuously, "and most of the rest are in the hands of American millionaires." Her contempt for American millionaires sounded not much less than for the Soviet thieves. "The rest—who knows?

They are lost. Stolen by the rabble and broken up to be sold bit by bit, probably."

"That would be a great pity."

The goldsmith returned with the aquamarines, closing the curtain behind him. He set the small tray on the counter and spoke to Zinaïda. When she demurred at whatever he said, he urged the point, addressing her—Daisy thought—as "Zinochka." She shrugged.

"My father has some very fine small diamonds. He suggests a setting that will surround the largest aquamarine with these brilliants."

Daisy foresaw what was supposed to be a minor expenditure for the sake of sleuthing ballooning into a financial disaster. "Oh no, I don't really . . ."

Zinaïda lowered her voice. "This is not what you want. Would make again heavy, elaborate, old-fashion pieces such as you do not wear. Leave to me, I will make what suits you. I draw two, three, four different designs, and if you like none, I draw again. You pay small deposit, commits you to nothing."

Daisy glanced at Sakari, who nodded. "Thank you, that is perfect."

"Bah, it is good business. My father is prince, does not understand how to do business."

Again consulting Sakari, Daisy wrote a cheque for the five pounds. It seemed like a lot for some drawings that might prove worthless, but she had no experience of jewellers and she supposed that those who dealt in precious gems had their own scale of values. Sakari certainly knew what she was doing.

Zinaïda gave her a receipt. "Now I must make sketch and photograph of stones. *Mesdames* may wait or go away to drink coffee or look at hats, return in half hour, one hour."

Outside the door, Kesin was waiting. Sakari asked something in Hindi and the chauffeur responded with a gesture down the alley to the left. "He reminds me that there is a respectable coffee room round the corner. I take it you do not choose to look at hats?"

"How well you know me! Thank you, darling, for introducing Teddy's name so neatly. You must have been reading my mind. I couldn't think how to bring him into the conversation. Also, to tell the truth, I'd momentarily forgotten him."

"The different styles of Miss Zvereva's rings are interesting, are they not?"

"Yes, but not as interesting as what she had to say about Teddy." Daisy dropped the subject momentarily as they stepped into a cosy coffee shop just round the corner. Coffee served, along with a selection of pastries that Sakari insisted on ordering, she asked, "Do you think he was ever truly attracted to her? She's very elegant. She might even be beautiful if she smiled more."

"I have read much about Russian culture. It is not their custom to smile often. It is why they tend always to look solemn, but when they do smile it is very meaningful."

Daisy laughed. "Not like what's-his-name in Hamlet."

"King Claudius. 'One may smile and smile and be a villain.'"

"Did you find out about their names in your studies? They seem very complicated."

"The names themselves are not difficult once you know the rules, but the usage is complicated. The first name and patronymic—"

"Don't bother to explain, darling! Just tell me: Women add 'a' at the end of the surname?"

"Yes, so Zinaïda is Miss—or Mademoiselle—Zvereva. Another thing I learned is that before the revolution the aristocracy mostly spoke French among themselves."

"And she speaks it; so her father may really have been a prince."

"Let us say rather that it is not impossible. A member of high society, at least."

"Hmm, and the story about the goldsmith's grandfather being his serf could be true, not 'merely corroborative detail.'"

"Household serfs were not given land when emancipated. Many continued to depend on their masters for their livelihoods, therefore they were likely to remain loyal, like your old family retainers and ours, in India."

"The plot thickens! Suppose he—Vasily Ivanovich, was it?—managed to steal some Imperial Easter eggs from the Fabergé workshops."

"Or perhaps lesser eggs. The Czar had some made to give as presents to his court, and other bejewelled knickknacks, and jewelry for wearing, too."

"Those might be easier to steal than the Imperial eggs. Might his loyalty to the family be strong enough make him take the loot to the prince?"

"Who knows? If they had been particularly generous to *his* family. But this is a fairy tale, Daisy. Why should not the jewels Zverev is selling be family property alone?"

"They probably are," Daisy admitted with a sigh, "you killer of fairy tales. On the other hand, if they are from the imperial workshops, and somehow Teddy found out, he could threaten to inform the Soviets if the old man didn't support his pursuit of Zinaïda."

"Wealth and title seem to me sufficient motive for that."

"It's a good motive for wanting him dead, though."

"And so is the insult offered by the jilting of Miss Zvereva."

"A plethora of motives. I'm going to have to tell Alec."

"Daisy! Were you seriously considering not telling him?"

"Not really, I suppose. I hate to think what he's going to say. How long have we been here? Let's go back to the shop. I want to ask her about the second suitor she mentioned. Did he appear before or after Teddy's defection?"

"Not to mention, who is he?"

"That too, of course. How can I find out without seeming frightfully nosy?"

"Impossible," said Sakari, laughing, "but I will try to provide an opening as I did with Teddy. She talked so freely about him that I suspect she is in need of a sympathetic confidante."

"She must be acquainted with some Russian women, don't you think?"

"I daresay, but perhaps they are not sympathetic."

"Perhaps." Daisy frowned. "They may be right. Perhaps the Zverevs *would* be safer if she married an Englishman."

"This is not your concern, Daisy. You cannot solve all the world's problems. Concentrate on sympathising with Mademoiselle Zvereva."

Daisy had no immediate opportunity to follow the excellent advice. Looking back at Sakari as she reached the shop door, she wasn't concentrating on pushing it open. The bell gave a single soft *ting* and swung only a few inches. The gap was wide enough, however, for the sound of raised voices to reach her ears.

Maddeningly, though not surprisingly, they were shouting in Russian. She recognised Zinaïda's and Vasily's voices. The third was a gravelly bass she assumed to be the prince.

Two against one, and if so, which two and which one? Or was it a three-way quarrel? No way to tell. She and Sakari exchanged raised eyebrows, then she gave the door a good shove.

The jangle covered the voices. By the time it ceased, so had they.

"Oh blast!" muttered Daisy. Zinaïda was not going to be in any mood to answer nosy questions.

NINETEEN

"*You what?*" Alec asked absently as they settled with their coffee that evening.

"I took Aunt Gertrude's aquamarines to be reset."

"Why? You never wear them."

"Darling, that's why, as well as one being missing. What happened to your keen analytical brain? If they had a more up-to-date setting, I would wear them."

"Good." His keen analytical brain drifted again and he started stuffing tobacco into his pipe in a meditative way.

Daisy persevered. "Seeing all the beautiful jewelry at the Kit-Cat Club made me realise they're going to waste. I took them to a jeweller's Sakari recommended."

"Mrs. Prasad has excellent taste. In an exotic Indian fashion . . ."

"The jewelry people aren't Indian, they're Russians."

"Whatever their nationality, I hope you'll find them satis—Daisy! Russians? You're poking your nose in again."

"I didn't know they were going to turn out to be the ones Lucy mentioned. Have you been looking for them?"

"Of course. We asked all divisions for information about

Russian families that include young women of marriageable age. We keep pretty close tabs on the émigrés because of the anarchist threat and the monarchist-communist conflict, but not in that sort of detail. I'm sure reports have come in. Ernie hasn't had time to collate them yet."

"Not the highest priority, then," said Daisy, relieved that her forgetting to mention the jewelry connection had not held them back.

"No. Should it have been? You look like the cat that ate the cream. What have you found out?"

"As it happens, quite by chance—"

"Of course. You wouldn't walk in and deliberately start asking nosy questions," Alec said ironically.

"Well, I didn't. Miss Zvereva—"

"Their surname is Zvereva? Spell it."

"No, it's Zverev—Z-V-E-R-E-V. It looks like three-B-E-P-E-B in the Russian alphabet. The feminine version is Zvereva."

Alec groaned. "Isn't life complicated enough? All right, go on."

"She was showing me different styles of jewelry, and she said the new designs would suit me much better than the Victorian. And Sakari said wasn't that what Teddy Devenish had advised. *I* didn't introduce the subject."

"I'm glad you had the sense not to go alone but I deplore your inveigling Mrs. Prasad into joining your snooping."

"Inveigle nothing! I didn't prompt her to say it, it was entirely off her own bat."

"And I suppose you didn't ask her to go with you fully intending to—"

"Sakari has been there before. In fact it was she who told me about them. Darling, do you or don't you want to know what we found out?"

"Sorry. Go ahead."

Daisy recounted everything Zinaïda had said about Teddy, studiously avoiding her own speculations. "That's everything of interest, I think. Sakari and I went to have a cup of coffee while she sketched Aunt Gertrude's jewels. When we got back they were having a row, all three of them. In Russian. If it had been French, I might have caught a few words. As it was, not a hope. I haven't the foggiest what they were rowing about."

"You mean you actually didn't come right out and ask?"

"I hope I'm not quite so ill mannered. I did say I hope the men weren't upset by anything we'd said, but Zinaïda was very short, civil but a bit snappish, if you know what I mean."

"Pity. I can only be glad you didn't press her, though. That's our job. Not that your whole encounter isn't properly our job!"

"But . . ." Daisy said encouragingly.

"But?"

"But what's done is done and . . ."

Alec sighed. "What's done is done, and you have probably saved us considerable time and trouble. And for pity's sake keep out of it from now on! Come here, you sleuth-hound, you." Setting aside his pipe, he pulled her onto his knees.

As a deterrent to sleuthing, Daisy thought as she returned his kiss with enthusiasm, it was a tactic doomed to failure.

The following day, Ben and Charlie were going home to Fairacres. Cousin Geraldine and their sisters were to pick them up, staying to lunch before driving on to Worcestershire.

When Daisy went down to breakfast, the boys were already on their way out of the door for a last walk on the Heath with Bel and Nana.

"There's packing to be done," Daisy warned.

"We won't be long, Aunt Daisy," said Ben. "We can't waste such a ripping day."

"The baby ducks may have hatched," Charlie reminded her. "We want to see them before we go home."

Daisy forbore to point out that there would be plenty of ducklings on the Severn at Fairacres. It would be his first spring there. Let him have a delightful surprise.

They dashed off. Alec had already left. She turned to the post and found a letter from Mrs. Gilpin's sister Myrtle. She would be ever so pleased, she said, to have dear Ivy come and stay for her convalescence. She would get a room ready right away.

Ivy? Daisy had quite forgotten Nanny's christian name. Somehow it made her more sympathetic, less adversarial.

The parlourmaid came in with fresh toast and tea.

"Thank you, Elsie. Would you fetch me the *Bradshaw* from my desk, please. And I'd better have my notebook and a pencil. Mrs. Gilpin is going to stay with her sister to recuperate."

"Oh, that's good, madam. Bertha told me Nurse is very keen to go if convenient. It's a healthy part of the country, by what I've heard. I'll get the book."

She should have known her proposal couldn't be kept secret from her household.

Armed with tea, toast, and timetables, Daisy quickly worked out the best way for a semi-invalid to travel, with the fewest changes and the shortest waits. After a second cup of tea and a glance through the rest of her post, she went to the office, took five pound notes from a locked drawer in Alec's desk, and put them in an envelope with the proposed train schedule torn from her notebook.

This she slipped into her pocket. She had no intention of presenting it baldly to poor Mrs. Gilpin with a suggestion amounting to an order that she depart on the next train.

She went upstairs and knocked on the sick-room door. The weak voice that responded was nothing like the nanny's usually inflexible tone. Going in, Daisy found her sitting in an easy chair by the window, in a pink flannel dressing gown, her face pallid. She started to rise.

"Please don't get up, Nurse." Daisy perched on the bed. "How are you this morning?"

"Very well in body, madam, but not easy in my mind." Her hands clenched on a sheet of notepaper.

"Naturally you're worried about your lost memories. Have you recovered nothing at all?"

"Not a thing, madam, between telling Bertha she was in

charge of the twins for a few minutes and waking up with a terrible headache. The twins— They're doing all right?"

Daisy realised she didn't really want to hear that Oliver and Miranda were perfectly happy without her. "Bertha takes good care of them," she said. "You've taught her well." Hastily she moved on: "I've heard from your sister."

"So have I, madam." She held up the letter she had crushed in her fist, then carefully smoothed it on her knee. Head bent over it, she said in a low voice, "She thinks a rest in the country will be good for me, like you and the doctor."

"You don't want to go?" Daisy asked uneasily.

After a heavy silence, Mrs. Gilpin conceded, "I might as well, I suppose."

"I'm sure you'll feel better for a little peace and quiet and good country air. I've written out a train schedule for you, not the fastest but one that I hope you will find restful." She handed over the envelope. "Of course, I don't mean to bundle you off today if you don't feel up to it. When you're ready, I'll drive you to Paddington or ring for a taxi. There's cash in with the timetable to pay for a porter, and a taxi when you arrive, and for refreshments en route."

"I'm sure it's very good of you, madam." She looked at the schedule. "I've got just time to get dressed and packed, so I might as well be off right now. Perhaps you wouldn't mind sending Myrtle a telegram to say I'm on my way?"

"Of course," said Daisy, feeling guiltily that she'd rather bundled the woman off despite her fine words. "Would you like Elsie to give you a hand?"

"Oh no, madam, I can take care of myself, and I know there's the young gentlemen's packing to be done." She hesitated. "Is it all right if I say good-bye to the twins?"

"I'll leave it up to you, Mrs. Gilpin. I expect you know better than I whether it's likely to upset them."

And that, Daisy thought sadly, more or less encapsulated their relationship. Though she was closer to Miranda and Oliver than her mother had been to her and Violet and Gervaise, their nanny was closer still, yet Daisy always had the final say. No wonder each resented the other.

Daisy sighed. Being a modern woman and a modern mother was in some ways not much more satisfactory than being the old-fashioned sort who left everything to Nurse and never thought twice about it.

She went to the bedroom telephone—the one that rang at inconvenient hours to send Alec haring to the outer reaches of the kingdom—and ordered a car from the local garage to take Mrs. Gilpin to the station.

Then, reminded of the boys' packing, she went to their bedroom to see what needed to be done. Remembering the usual state of Gervaise's room, she was not at all surprised to find their belongings scattered over every surface, including the floor. The children came back from the Heath as Daisy and Elsie started tidying up, sorting, and folding.

Ben was apologetic. "You don't need to do that, Aunt Daisy. We'll just put everything in the suitcases."

Elsie was outraged. "If you think I'll let one of her ladyship's maids unpack a regular jumble thrown together anyhow, Master Ben, you've got another think coming."

"Where's my new pencil box?" Charlie demanded.

It turned out that somehow their belongings, plus the souvenirs of their visit acquired in the past week, had migrated all over the house from attic to basement. One shoe of Charlie's two pairs was found in the scullery, and Ben's Latin primer, which he was supposed to have been studying, had somehow made its way to the mantelpiece in the nursery. The pencil box, full of extremely sticky peppermint bull's-eyes, was discovered on the terrace behind the house; a swarm of ants had discovered it first.

Once peppermints and ants had been disposed of and everything known to be missing assembled in the bedroom, it was obvious that the boys' suitcases could not possibly hold all their acquisitions. A raid on the box room was indicated.

Belinda, Ben, and Charlie went off to look for an appropriate receptacle, while Daisy left Elsie to get on with folding clothes and disposing them neatly in the suitcases. She went down to the kitchen to check on preparations for lunch.

"You look a bit frazzled, madam," said Mrs. Dobson. "Sit yourself down and have a cuppa. I was just going to have one meself. Everything's under control here."

"And smells delicious." Daisy subsided onto a chair at the kitchen table.

The cook-housekeeper set a cup of tea in front of her and sat down. "We're going to miss them two boys, that's for sure. Charmers, they are, and that Master Charlie's quite a chatterbox. Could talk the hind leg off a donkey, he could."

"I bet they've scrounged a lot more cake and biscuits from you than I'm aware of!"

"Now that'd be telling, madam." Mrs. Dobson took a meditative sip. "Quite a tale those two'll have to tell to their schoolfriends when they get back."

"Oh dear, yes, I hadn't thought of that. I suppose it wouldn't be the least use ordering Charlie not to talk about it."

"Likely they'll think he's romancing, that age," said Mrs. Dobson comfortably. "It'll be nice to see Mr. Truscott again. Quite the gentleman though he is a chauffeur."

"I hope you've set aside something good for his lunch."

"Don't you worry, madam. I wouldn't want him going back to Fairacres and saying we don't eat as good as his lordship. He'll have to eat the same time as the company, seeing they have to get on after, but Elsie and me'll eat later so don't you worry about the service at table."

"I don't know what I'd do without you."

Mrs. Dobson looked as if she didn't either but was too tactful to say so.

The telephone bell rang. Daisy gulped her tea and hurried up to the hall to answer it.

"Daisy, it's Lucy. Darling, you simply must come to tea."

"Why? What's up?"

"Angela has invited herself. It's too utterly devastating!"

"Angela Devenish?" asked Daisy, disbelieving.

"Yes, dear Cousin Angela. Plus dog. I haven't the foggiest what she wants. Promise you'll—"

"Hold on." She was facing the staircase, and she saw Mrs. Gilpin coming slowly down, holding the rail, followed by Elsie carrying a large carpetbag. "Let me ring you back in just a minute, darling."

She hung up on Lucy's "But I'm—"

Lengthy farewells were forestalled by the driver's knock on the front door. The nanny had one parting question, imparted in an anxious whisper: "Are the police going to come bothering me at my sister's?"

"I hope not. I can't promise. I'll tell you what, why don't you send me a postcard every day saying simply 'No change.' Unless, of course, there is a change. In that case they'll want to see you, whether you stay there or come back to talk to them."

"Oh, all right, madam. I'll do that. Myrtle would be ever so upset if the police came round."

"Let's hope they won't need to."

The car rolled away down the Circle and Daisy felt a weight roll off her mind. Not that the problem of Nanny Gilpin was solved, but it was no longer right on top of her, so to speak. Mrs. Gilpin was a sensible woman. If she regained her memory, she'd report right away.

Wouldn't she?

TWENTY

Having seen Mrs. Gilpin off, Daisy reluctantly returned to the telephone to ring Lucy back. She liked Angela and was sorry for her. Lucy had been her best friend since early schooldays. But she did not feel it was up to her to mediate between them. They were cousins, after all, though there was no love lost between them.

She couldn't help wondering what on earth Angela wanted of Lucy.

Picking up the receiver, she gave the operator Lucy's number.

"Lord Gerald Bincombe's residence," said the butler's resonant voice.

"Galloway? This is Mrs. Fletcher. Lady Gerald is expecting my call."

"Indeed, madam. I fear her ladyship is presently unable to come to the instrument."

"Not another attack of you-know-what, Galloway? I thought she was over that."

"So I believe, madam. I understand her ladyship is—ah—indulging in a mud mask."

Daisy went off into peals of laughter. "Not really? I thought those were for ancient dowagers."

"I believe not, madam. The idea, I understand, is to preserve the youthful suppleness of the complexion so as not to suffer the ravages of age. Or so her ladyship's maid informs me. But I must not keep you, madam. Do you wish to leave a message?"

"No, thanks." Once she had seen Cousin Geraldine and her brood on their way, she'd have time to consider at leisure whether she wanted to embroil herself in what promised to be a decidedly fraught tea party.

The luncheon party, at least, went well. Lady Dalrymple and her two adopted daughters had enjoyed their stay in London as thoroughly as had her two sons. Amidst the chatter, Daisy was surprised that neither Ben nor Charlie mentioned the subject that absorbed her thoughts. They had plenty to talk about without the adventure at the Crystal Palace. She could only be glad that the proximity to murder so easily slipped from their minds.

It took a reminder of the time relayed by Elsie from Truscott to move the departing family. At last everything and everyone was packed into the Wolseley. Daisy and Belinda stood on the front steps waving until the car turned into Well Walk and disappeared from sight.

"The house will seem awfully quiet and empty," said Belinda, sighing.

"What are you going to do this afternoon? Get together with some of your local friends? Deva's probably well enough by now, and you haven't seen Lizzie in ages."

"No, I'll see them at school all term. I want to play with the twins and go for a walk with them and Nana. Then I'll read. I've got *two* set books I haven't even opened yet."

"All right, darling. I may have to go to tea with Aunt Lucy, but I'll be home till then."

"Mayn't I go with you?" Bel asked eagerly. "I wouldn't get in the way, promise, and Aunt Lucy has the best cakes—Oh! Don't tell Mrs. Dobson I said so. And after tea I could go down and look at the stuff in the dark room. I wouldn't touch."

Daisy was tempted. Belinda would be an added buffer between Lucy and Angela, and she was reaching the age when such visits would be acceptable. But the very fact that her first thought was the cakes showed that she hadn't quite reached that age.

Besides, she really shouldn't risk Bel being caught in the crossfire. "Not this time, I think, darling. Aunt Lucy wants to discuss something that's on her mind. I'll tell her you'd like to see her one of these days."

"Oh well, at least I can get started on those books."

Daisy rang Lucy again only to be told she was taking a nap, as recommended by her doctor. She left a reluctant message that she would be there at four o'clock.

She had a busy afternoon catching up with letters and household matters that she'd put off while the boys were staying, even though Belinda had taken most of the entertaining off her hands.

Forgetting to watch the time, she found it was too late to change into a tea frock. The grey-blue costume she was wearing would do for Lucy and Angela, she decided, dashing upstairs to fetch a coat and her handbag and powder her nose. She popped into the nursery to give the twins a kiss each and stuck her head into Belinda's room, finding her lost in *Jane Eyre*.

"I'm off, darling. I expect I'll be home by six, but if by any chance I'm delayed and Daddy isn't home, go ahead and have your supper. You can have a tray or eat with Bertha or in the kitchen, as you prefer."

"All right, Mummy. Jane's aunt was perfectly *beastly* to her. It makes me realise Granny wasn't so bad after all. Have a nice time and give my love to Aunt Lucy."

Pulling on her gloves, Daisy descended the stairs. She had just reached the hall when the doorbell rang.

"Oh botheration, who can that be? Just see who it is, Elsie," she added as the parlourmaid appeared, setting her cap straight. "I've got to get away."

Daisy hung back as Elsie opened the door. She saw the figures on the doorstep as silhouettes but she'd recognise the voice that asked for her anywhere.

"Phillip! What . . . Oh, hello Fenella. How nice to see you, how nice of you to call, but I'm afraid I'm just on my way out and already running late."

Phillip shot her a desperate look. "Daisy, I—we have to talk to you."

Fenella seemed ready to burst into tears. But Lucy—Daisy reminded herself—had sounded as desperate as they appeared.

"Honestly, darling, I can't stop. Can you come back this evening?"

"Will Fletcher be home?"

"Possibly. Probably."

"Please, Daisy," cried the woebegone young matron. "I simply must talk to you now or I'll burst!"

"Then you'll have to come with me and tell me in the car."

"I'll drive you," offered Phillip, turning towards his new Rolls-Royce sports tourer.

"Phil, it's a two-seater. That's mine." She pointed at her sky-blue Gwynne Eight. "Elsie brought it round—"

"Elsie? Your maid?" The car fanatic was interested.

"Yes, she wanted to learn so I taught her."

"Did she—"

"Phi-i-illip!" wailed his sister, climbing into the front passenger seat of the Gwynne.

Daisy went to the driver's side, opened the door, pulled the seat forward, and stood back to let Phillip squeeze into the back seat. He started to protest. Both the women glared at him and he shut up. With considerable wriggling he crammed his long legs into the narrow space. Even slewed sideways, his knees were under his chin.

"You call this a four-seater?" he snorted.

"For a young family," Daisy defended her beloved car.

"An infantile family! Don't tell me Fletcher squashes himself in here."

"He drives it sometimes."

"With his knees?"

They bickered amiably as Daisy drove round the Circle and down Hampstead Hill. Fenella kept trying to get a word in, and Daisy gathered she wanted to talk about her husband. Why she imagined Daisy had any interest in let alone influence upon Elliot Kerston, Daisy could not fathom. She was happy to encourage Phillip's chatter.

It wasn't until she stopped in front of Lucy's house that the name of Fay Fanshawe emerged from the babble. Her interest in Fenella's marital difficulties suddenly doubled—or rather, suddenly came into being, as it had been virtually zero before.

"I'm sorry, Fenella, Lady Gerald is expecting me." She got out and leaned in to suggest, "I do wish you'd have Phil bring you round this evening. Even if Alec's home, he doesn't have to sit in. If that's no good, come for coffee tomorrow morning."

"But Daisy—"

"Phil, you'd better take my car back to pick up yours, if you think you can steer with your knees. I'll take a cab home, or the underground."

"We'll take a cab," said Phillip, extricating himself with difficulty. "And I'll bring her round this evening. You can skip the party, Fen. Come along."

"But Phil—"

Daisy ascended the steps, leaving them to wrangle it out.

Or so she intended. As Galloway opened the door, she heard footsteps behind her.

"Daisy!"

"Mrs. Fletcher." The butler bowed, and looked past her. "Mrs.—er—Kerston, I believe."

"Yes," said Fenella breathlessly. "I came with Mrs. Fletcher."

"So I see, madam."

"Fenella, for pity's sake—" her brother entreated.

"And Mr. Petrie." Galloway, omniscient, was manifestly enjoying himself. "Please come in."

Phillip uttered a last heartfelt plea: "Fenella!"

His sister ignored him and followed Daisy into the hall, with Phillip, scarlet-faced at this blatant disregard of etiquette, close at her heels. Daisy unfortunately caught Galloway's eye and had to suppress a fit of somewhat hysterical giggles.

With stately tread, the butler showed them up to the drawing room. On the way he murmured discreetly to Daisy, "Her ladyship and Miss Devenish are in her ladyship's sitting room. I shall inform her of your arrival."

Obviously, as Daisy had expected, Lucy had intended a private meeting with Daisy and Angela, not a drawing-room tea to which any callers were welcome. On the other hand, if she'd been alone with Angela and Mr. Fisher for a while, she might be ready, even desperate, for an interruption.

As soon as Galloway closed the drawing-room door behind him, Fenella dropped into a chair and burst into tears. Phillip stood over her and scolded, which only made her cry harder.

"Phil, there's a tantalus over there. Go and get yourself a drink. I'll make it all right with Lucy. And stay there, or go and look out of the window or something. Anything! But stay away from your sister till she's calmed down."

"All right," Phillip said meekly, and fled.

Daisy thrust a handkerchief into Fenella's hand. "All right, that's quite enough, Fenella. You'll make yourself ill. You've only got a minute to tell me what's wrong before Lucy and her other guest come in. For pity's sake, pull yourself together and keep it short."

Fenella sniffed, dabbed at her eyes, and blurted out, "It's Elliot."

"So I gathered." Daisy struggled to sound patient. "What's he done? And what makes you think I can help you?"

The story was punctuated with sobs, sniffs, and gasps. "You went to see Fay Fanshawe backstage, Daisy, I know you did. And Elliot was watching her and talking about her with that horrid Albert Bagley. I heard them say her name. And then the police came to talk to him—Elliot, not Bagley. Well, perhaps they talked to Bagley too, I wouldn't know. And Sophie, my maid, said Hibbert—he's our butler—said he heard that woman's name mentioned. Between Elliot and the policeman, I mean. And Elliot won't tell me what the policeman wanted, though he usually tells me everything. So!"

"So you jumped to the conclusion that he's having an affair with her. I'm sure he's not. She's a very respectable young woman who lives at home with her mum and dad. I have it on the best authority. Elliot was watching her because she's a performer. She's paid to be watched. Weren't you watching her, too? As for the horrid Bagley and the policeman, those conversations were about something else altogether. Miss Fanshawe was merely peripheral."

Fenella's brow furrowed. "Per-iff . . . ?"

"Unimportant. Irrelevant. Beside the point."

"Oh." She giggled. "I was never any good at English. Phil! It's all right. It was all a mistake."

"I told you Daisy would sort it all out."

"So now we can go."

"Go? Of course we can't go! Lady Gerald—"

"Yes, Mr. Petrie?" Lucy, at her most languid and sarcastic, stood in the doorway. "You wanted to see me?"

"Oh! No, not at all," Phillip stuttered. "Dash it, I mean, that is, we just called. My sister and I. In a friendly way, don't you know."

"Indeed." Her raised eyebrows gave the same effect as a dowager's lorgnette.

"Come off it, darling. You've known Phillip for donkey's years. Why shouldn't he bring his sister to call?"

"His sister? Oh, I beg your pardon, Mrs. . . . Kerston. I didn't notice you in that corner there. Good afternoon. May I offer you a cup of tea, since it seems to be the proper hour?"

"Yes . . . no . . . that is . . ." Fenella shot an appealing glance at Daisy. "Thank you, that would be very nice, Lady Gerald."

As Lucy stepped into the room, Mr. Fisher peered round her sheer silk ankles and Angela appeared on the threshold behind her.

"I say, Daisy, what luck. Just who I wanted to see. D'you have a moment?"

"Not at present, Angela. Do you know Mrs. Kerston? And this is her brother, Phillip Petrie. The Petries are our neighbours in Worcestershire. Miss Devenish is a cousin of Lucy's, Fenella."

"How do you do, Miss Devenish, is that your darling doggie? May I stroke him?"

"He won't bite you," Angela said gruffly, "but be very gentle. He's been mistreated and he's nervous."

"Oh, the poor little thing," Fenella crooned.

Daisy left Angela explaining the facts of canine life to Fenella and turned back to Lucy and Phillip. She was just in time to stop Phillip pouring the stiff drink Lucy requested.

"Darling, should you?"

Lucy glared at her. "The doctor said after eight weeks—"

"I bet he didn't say you could start drinking cocktails at teatime."

The gin bottle hovered over the glass.

After a moment, Lucy said, "Oh, all right. Make it a drop of brandy and plenty of soda, Phillip."

With obvious relief, Phillip complied, saying, "I'm really most frightfully sorry to have barged in like this, Lady Gerald."

"So you said."

"Fenella was absolutely determined to talk to Daisy, you see. I couldn't stop her. Now Daisy's set her mind at rest, I can take her away."

Lucy glanced at Angela and Fenella, still fussing over Mr. Fisher. For a moment Daisy thought she was going to invite Phillip to carry out his suggestion. Good manners prevailed by a hairsbreadth—unless it was the realisation that he couldn't carry off her cousin as well as his sister.

"Do stay to tea," she invited in far from cordial tones.

Phillip looked uneasy, but providentially Galloway and a maid came in with tea things. Lucy set down her drink and became a gracious hostess. The rest responded like properly brought up guests. For a while, peace reigned. Angela, with an absent frown, munched steadily through an entire plateful of bread and butter, feeding an occasional scrap to Mr. Fisher, who sat in front of her, his eyes never deviating from her face.

The rest made polite conversation. As often happened in Phillip's presence, they ended up discussing motorcars, though Daisy acquitted him of deliberately steering the others in that direction. At least he avoided the more technical aspects of the subject.

Daisy refused a second cup of tea, feeling she had devoted quite enough time to Lucy's and Fenella's problems. She had reckoned without Angela, who roused from her bread-and-butter fuelled reverie as Daisy was about to make her escape.

"Don't go, Daisy. I want to ask you something." She looked from Fenella to Phillip, her expression making it absolutely clear that their absence was desired.

Even Phillip, never the swiftest to catch on, realised that it was time to go. Once again he profusely apologised to Lucy. Lucy responded with a languid, dismissive wave.

While Fenella bade her involuntary hostess good-bye, Phillip came over to Daisy. "I spent the evening at my club last night," he said in a low voice. "Some of the fellows were talking about you-know-who. All right if I drop in this evening? Fletcher may be interested, too, if he's there."

"Good for you, Phil. Come about half past nine."

"Without Fenella. Thanks for setting her mind at rest, by the way."

"I'm glad I was able to."

He took Fenella away and Daisy turned to Angela.

"Lucy says Teddy was involved with a Russian girl and you know all about her." No beating about the bush with Angela.

"I said," Lucy protested, "I'd *heard* Teddy was involved with a Russian girl and you *might* know *something* about it, Daisy."

"I do know a bit," Daisy said cautiously.

"All I want to know is: Did he make her pregnant?"

"Oh! No."

"Good. I hoped I wasn't going to have to cope with a squalling brat." She stood up. "Thanks, Daisy. Thanks for the tea,

Lucy. I'm going home tomorrow. Can't leave the dogs any longer. Come along, Mr. Fisher, old chap."

Lucy stared after them, shaking her head. "I always thought my aunt and uncle were relatively sane—"

"Pun intended?"

"What? Oh. No. How did they manage to produce two such children as Angela and Teddy?"

"And your parents are dears. How did they manage to produce you? Darling, you were abominable!"

Lucy shrugged. "Self-defence against the invasion. I gave them tea, didn't I? What on earth possessed you to bring them with you?"

"Fenella hopped into my car before I could stop her, and I didn't feel like wrestling her out. I could have not come, but you sounded desperate."

"I was. I was feeling particularly foul when I rang you."

"Not morning sickness again?"

"Not nausea, no. Just utter exhaustion striking in the middle of the morning. I had to lie down and relax for the facial treatment and that set me right."

Daisy scrutinised her face. "You have beautiful skin. I can't see that you need mud masks, apart from an excuse for a lie-down."

"But if I didn't have them, I'd need them. You ought to try it. London air is so filthy." Lucy studied her critically. "Though I must admit you don't seem to need it. I hadn't noticed before that your freckles have completely faded away."

"Yes, thank goodness!"

"Congratulations. Now tell me about the Russian girl. Did she kill dear cousin Teddy?"

"I don't believe so. She might have if she'd cared about him. She has the temperament, I should think—dark flashing eyes and I heard her rowing passionately with her father. But she told us—Sakari and me—that she didn't give a hoot for Teddy."

"Or so she says, darling, so she says!"

TWENTY-ONE

"*Remember to* try to avoid using my name, Ernie," said Alec, stopping for a moment to regard the façade of the small shop. With its blinds drawn, it had a secretive look that the unadorned, unrevealing sign did nothing to dispel. Only the OPEN card in the door was remotely welcoming.

DS Piper grinned. "Right, Chief. It wouldn't do for them to put two and two together and realise Mrs. Fletcher put us on to them. She's a wonder, is Mrs. Fletcher. Comes up trumps every time."

"Not quite every time. All right, you go first."

Gently, slowly, Piper pushed the door open. No more than a soft *tink* came from the bell intended to announce the arrival of customers. Treading with care, Alec followed him into the dimly lit shop.

After a swift glance around, Piper crossed the room with steps as light as a cat's, towards the corner where a velvet curtain hung. He leaned over the counter towards it. For a minute he listened intently. Then he shook his head, returned to Alec, and whispered, "They're talking foreign. Not French; prob'ly Russian."

Alec turned back to open and close the door vigorously, making the bell jangle.

The curtain stirred. A woman's hand laden with rings drew it back. She came through and let it drop behind her. "Good evening, messieurs. What may I do for you?"

She turned on an electric light and the shop brightened, though the décor was still on the gloomy side. Alec noted that the light was directed downward at the counter. Enough spilled elsewhere for him to note also that the young woman—about thirty, at a guess—was elegantly dressed, though with a somewhat old-fashioned air. Perhaps it was her abundant dark hair that lent that impression. Her features suggested too much strength of character for conventional prettiness, at least of an English kind.

She could be formidable—in the English sense, not the French—if she felt the need, Alec guessed. He wondered what had attracted Teddy Devenish to her.

While he studied her, Ernie had presented his warrant card. "Detective Sergeant Piper, madam. My chief and I would like to ask you a few questions."

"You are police? You have not the uniforms."

"Plainclothes branch, madam. You are Miss Zerverev?"

"Zvereva," she corrected him, "but I do not expect the English to pronounce it properly. What is it that you wish to know?"

"I understand Edward Devenish was a friend of yours?"

"Ed—Ah, Teddy. Yes, Teddy was a customer who became a friend . . . of sorts. This is the proper expression, I think."

"'Of sorts'? Would you care to explain?"

"Teddy came first to shop to have ruby set as tie pin. Was beautiful stone from brooch of his aunt deceased, too large, too beautiful for gentleman. I tell him better several small stones. I am designer. This is my work, yes?"

"So I've heard, madam."

"This is my . . . my professional judgement. I know what is proper. He is annoyed that I contradict." She shrugged expressively. "He insisted. I was not pleased. Ruby is ost . . . ost . . ."

"Ostentatious?"

"Ostentatious, yes. The English do not like ostentatious. It is not good taste, though this I do not say to Teddy. But you have proverb: The customer is always right. I must earn living, no?"

"Of course, madam," Ernie said stolidly.

"So, I promised to make very nice design pin to show off big ruby. I tell Teddy come back next day to see sketch. He comes, oh yes, he comes, and he brings flowers, big bouquet carnations. Is apology, he says, for not taking advice. He never listens to advice and never cares for opinion of other people. I discover later, this is truth."

"You accepted his apology?"

"I cannot refuse. He brings perhaps more work."

"Did he bring more work?"

"Yes, and he brings friends." Miss Zvereva frowned. "Not friends. They do not like him, I think, and they do not wish to give work to me. He makes them come, against their wish. I do not know how."

Alec saw Piper's ears prick up, metaphorically.

"That's very interesting, madam. Can you remember the names of any of these people?"

She hesitated. "You will not tell them? Some have give us more work though first they came unhappy. I do not want to spoil this."

"I can't promise, but it's very unlikely we'll need to tell them the source of the information."

"All right," she agreed, still hesitant. "I cannot easily recall these English names but I will recognise if I read in order book. I will make list for you."

"That would be helpful, madam."

"However, will not include those who did not order."

"Never mind. It sounds as if Mr. Devenish was pretty helpful to your business?"

"Yes. My father was very grateful."

"And you?"

"I also, of course," she said too quickly.

184

Piper glanced at Alec. He had done very well so far but now he seemed uncertain how to proceed.

Alec stepped into the breach. "It's difficult to be grateful to someone who demands gratitude, isn't it, Miss Zvereva?"

"Impossible! But I must pretend or my father grows angry. The flowers, you comprehend. He believes Teddy is in love with me. He finds out from his . . . his good friends, Russian friends—"

"Cronies?"

"That is the word! Papa finds out that Teddy is rich. Not just one ruby he owns, but much money. Is good. Also, he finds out that Teddy is of nobility. He will be baron—no, not baron—baronet, yes?"

"Yes, when his father dies. Not quite nobility, but aristocratic."

"Never will Papa let me marry to one who is not of good family. Russian nobility is best, but we are in England. With English aristocrat in family, we are safe. So my father believes."

"And you, Miss Zvereva? You agree?"

Again her shoulders lifted in that so expressive shrug. "Perhaps. But when I marry it will be for love, not for money or safety."

"Are you thinking of getting married?"

"What young woman is not? But I did not even like Teddy."

"Why?"

"Why does one like one person and not another? To me, he was conceited and arrogant, always expected—no, 'assumed' is the correct word?"

"Your vocabulary is excellent."

"My grammar not so," she said ruefully. "No matter, if I am understood. Teddy assumed I will be always grateful and delighted by his courtship. To my father, he was too agreeable. Papa saw only good manners and deference. To Vasily Ivanovich, he—"

"Vasily Ivanovich?" Alec queried.

"Our gold- and silversmith. The person who makes from my designs."

"D'you mind spelling that, madam?" Piper begged.

She obliged, then advised him, "Not everyone transcribes Cyrillic alphabet to Latin exactly same way. This is one possible. Surname is Petrov. You can spell?"

"Petrov. Yes, thanks."

"Vasily Ivanovich is first class fine craftsman. Teddy treated him like servant." Her contemptuous tone was clearly aimed at Devenish's bad manners, not at Petrov, Alec thought.

"You told your father you didn't care to marry Devenish?" he asked.

"I told him I did not believe he really wanted to marry me. I have heard stories. Teddy likes to . . . I do not know words."

"Raise expectations?" Alec said dryly. "With no prospect of their fulfilment?"

"Yes!"

"We have heard such stories, too."

"Stepan Vladimirovich—my father—refused to listen. He said an English gentleman would not behave so. He remind me I am thirty, may be last chance for husband."

"Never give up," said Piper staunchly. He was courting a young woman of about the same age.

Miss Zvereva flashed him a smile, the first they had seen. It transformed her face. If she smiled more often, she'd have no trouble attracting suitors, Alec decided. Whether any would be acceptable to both her and her autocratic papa was another matter.

"Did you give in to your father?" he asked.

"He is old man, not well. If I say 'never will I marry Teddy,' will be much argument, not good for him. And tiring for me! I did not agree to accept Teddy if he asked me. I tell Papa only, I will not . . . rebuff him. When Teddy jilt me, as I expect always, he blames me for not encourage enough."

"He was angry with you, as well as with Devenish."

"With me. Not so much with Teddy."

"I've heard rumours of a breach of promise suit."

"Rumours only. Teddy made no promise and wrote no letters. Lawyer tells my father, is no grounds for suit."

"Which, I should think, just made him angrier."

"Monsieur, if you believe my father killed Teddy, you will take one look and know it is not possible," she said calmly. "I have answered many questions. I have been frank. Now I cannot spare you more time. I have much work to be done."

"Just one more question: Where were you last Wednesday morning?"

"Here, as I am every morning except Sunday. I cannot risk losing customers because is no one to attend."

"Did any customers in fact come in?"

"I do not remember Wednesday in particular but I can check in ledger. Will be noted—if we do business."

"Very good. Thank you for your cooperation, Miss Zvereva. I appreciate your frankness." Though he was dubious about parts of it. "We won't keep you from your work any longer. I should like a few words with your father now."

"Stepan Vladimirovich speaks very little English. You speak not Russian, I think? French?"

"Very little, I'm afraid. I'll have to ask you to interpret for us. I'm sorry to keep you longer from your work."

She frowned, leaning forward with her hands flat on the counter. "And if I refuse?"

"Then we'll have to invite Mr. Zverev to accompany us to Scotland Yard where we can send for a Russian interpreter."

For a moment she stared silently down at her hands. When she raised her head, Alec read anxiety in her eyes. "Very well. You leave me no choice. You will remember that the prince is old and in poor health. I shall go and prepare him." She swept out through the curtained doorway.

"Quick," said Alec in a low voice, turning to Piper, "refresh my memory about Russian princes."

The DS grinned. "For a start, they're not nearly as rare or important as British princes. They're more like our dukes in some ways, except all their children are also called prince or princess."

"Leading to a vast proliferation!"

"For sure. Prob'ly got rid of a lot in the revolution," Piper said callously.

"No doubt. So Miss Zvereva is a princess?"

"If her dad's really a prince, yes. It'd take a bit of nerve, though, to use the title serving in a shop."

"However, her father may expect his, since he seems to stay behind the scenes. How do you think I should address him? I don't want to antagonise him unnecessarily."

"Just 'prince,' I think, Chief. No 'my lord' or anything."

"That's a relief. Thanks, Ernie. Good job I told you to find out just in case."

"Here she comes, Chief."

Alec swung round as curtain rings rattled. Miss Zvereva drew the drapery to one side and opened the gate in the counter to usher them through.

"Please come this way, messieurs." She stood back to let them pass.

Alec noted that the door usually concealed by the curtain was steel, with a top-quality heavy lock.

The room behind the curtain was a surprise. He had expected it to match the shop, cramped, ill lit, bare. Instead, although the same width as the shop, it was much deeper and had large windows as well as a glazed door. They looked out onto a small paved courtyard with high walls of dingy, soot-stained London brick to left and right. The far side was filled wall to wall by a two-storey outbuilding, probably once a mews. Evergreen shrubs in large terra-cotta pots struggled to survive the lack of sunshine and the smoky atmosphere.

Indoors, Alec's quick scan took in the main features: a sloped drawing table, angled to catch the light from the windows, a camera on a tripod, a small but solid safe, and a couple of cabinets. A curious apparatus on a small table he recognised as a samovar. On the right-hand wall hung half a dozen icons and several pencil drawings. A staircase occupied the left-hand wall, with the usual cupboard under it.

Against the fourth wall, shared with the shop, was a huge

tiled stove, radiating heat. Beside it, leaning on a stick, stood the prince. Once tall, he was stooped, white-haired and -moustached, his unhealthily plump, sallow face creased. He was heavily built, flabby. The thought of his having masqueraded as a nanny was ludicrous. That didn't mean he hadn't had someone else to exact his revenge for him.

And there was one obvious person.

Alec offered the prince a slight bow, seeing from the corner of his eye Piper clumsily emulating the gesture. Zverev, expressionless, responded with a curt nod.

The sergeant might as well take over. They were not likely to get much information out of the father with his daughter as interpreter. Alec might learn more by watching closely.

He gestured to Piper, who stepped forward, saying slowly and clearly, "Detective Sergeant Piper, sir, from Scotland Yard, and this is my chief inspector. I have a few questions to put to you. First, may I have your full name for the record?"

Zverev showed no sign that Alec could detect of understanding anything but the words "Scotland Yard," at which he blinked.

Miss Zvereva said something full of rolling Rs, then turned to Piper. "My father's title is *knyaz*, usually translated as 'prince'. His name is Stepan Vladimirovich Zverev." She spelled it out.

"I don't want to keep you standing, sir. Please be seated."

The suggestion, translated, first met with a refusal, but Miss Zvereva pressed her father and he subsided into his chair with a grunt.

"You were acquainted with Edward Devenish, sir?"

The prince caught the name and a volley of bitter denunciation ensued.

"Yes," said his daughter. Piper just looked at her with raised eyebrows. "He was snake in chest," she added reluctantly.

Piper looked blank.

"Viper in bosom," Alec told him sotto voce.

"Ah! Where was Mr.—the prince—on . . ." he started to ask Miss Zvereva. Correcting himself, he addressed the man himself. "I mean, where were you, sir, last Wednesday morning?"

This time, she didn't translate. "Here at home," she said coldly. "Where he is every day except Sunday, when we with much difficulty take him to our church and then to Russian café to meet friends. Cronies. Please do not upset by remind him he is cripple."

"'We'?"

"Please?"

"Who's 'we'? Who helps you take your father out?"

"One of the servants."

Alec was sure she was holding something back. Piper also picked up on it, or perhaps simply doubted that she and a single servant could manage the heavy old man between them.

"And? Who else helps?"

"Vasya—Vasily Ivanovich," she muttered sulkily. "Last name Petrov."

"The goldsmith," said Piper with satisfaction.

"We shall see him next," said Alec. "He's in the workshop out there?" He pointed at the outbuilding beyond the courtyard.

"How you know this?"

"Good guess. While we are talking to him, please prepare a list of the names of your father's friends."

"Already you want Wednesday customers list! I have work to do." She gestured at the drawing table.

"If it's more convenient, Miss Zverev, you may bring the lists to Scotland Yard tomorrow. Does Mr. Petrov speak English?"

"Very little. Almost none."

"Enough, I expect. Come along, Sergeant."

They went out. She said something to her father, then followed, catching up as they reached the door of the building.

"I will interpret—"

"I wouldn't dream of keeping you from your work. I'm sure we'll manage. If not, I'll send DS Piper to fetch you."

Her dark eyes widened, apprehensive. Alec turned away. He heard her footsteps on the stone flags, retreating, as the door opened in response to Piper's knock.

TWENTY-TWO

"*Mr. Vasily* Ivanovich Petrov?" Piper asked, consulting his notebook.

"*Da.* Yes. You are police."

"How did you know?"

"Stepan Vladimirovich told me with speaking tube. Come in, please."

His grasp of English seemed quite adequate, his accent possibly better than Miss Zvereva's. Alec wondered about his calling the prince by his first and second names. Did it suggest that they were on terms of close friendship, not just employer and employee, or was it just a quirk of Russian usage?

Stepping over the threshold, he was met by a blast of hot air, its source a small gas furnace in a firebrick-walled corner. A safe matching the one in the shop's back room stood in another corner. Two tables, one topped with zinc, occupied much of the room, and Alec recognised a machine on a shelf at the back as a wire-drawing apparatus. Other shelves bore moulds and a variety of tools of the goldsmith's trade. The rear wall had neither door nor windows. The building might share a wall with one in the next alley.

The smith himself was a dark man of about Alec's own age. Clean-shaven and short-haired, shorter than Piper who had barely passed the minimum height for the police, in a wig and nanny's outfit he could at a pinch have passed for a woman.

Alec couldn't conceive of any reason for him to take part in Devenish's prank, but Devenish was notoriously persuasive, by fair means or foul.

While he was studying the room and the man, Piper had introduced both of them, again neatly avoiding giving Alec's name. "We have a few questions to put to you, sir," he continued.

"About Mr. Devenish, yes." He checked the temperature gauge on the furnace. "I can leave furnace for short time. Is cooler upstairs. You come?"

Whatever its original use, the first floor was now a small flat. Petrov had furnished it plainly but comfortably. Sash windows overlooking a narrow alley were wide open, letting out some of the heat that rose palpably from the floor.

Petrov offered tea. After a glance at Alec, Piper accepted. If— for whatever reason—the natives chose to appear friendly, there was no harm in responding in a friendly manner.

While he fiddled with his samovar, Piper asked a couple of preliminary questions, confirming for the record his name and address and profession. Alec went over to a shelf of books. Most were in Russian, but there were a couple in English and a two-way dictionary. Clearly Petrov had made a serious effort to improve his English skills. So what had Miss Zvereva meant by saying he spoke almost none?

And whatever her reason, had she intended to make some sort of sign to him to speak only Russian?

Petrov poured small amounts of already made tea, very dark brown, from a silver teapot into glasses with intricately wrought silver holders, then added hot water.

"Your work, Mr. Petrov?" Alec asked, holding his glass up to get a good look at the glass-holder's interwoven flowering vines. The tea itself, milkless, was a beautiful clear amber, very different from muddy English tea.

"My work. Zina—Zinaïda Stepanovna's design."

"Very attractive."

Piper regarded his brew with suspicion. Petrov regarded him with amusement.

"You like sugar, Mr. Piper?"

"Yes, please!"

Alec accepted a slice of lemon in his.

"You have questions, sir?" Petrov asked him.

"I do. You knew Edward Devenish."

"Only because he was friend of Stepan Vladimirovich."

"You didn't consider him a friend of yours?"

"He was nobleman. No, aristocrat, not nobleman. But I—I am craftsman. Prince not consider suitable friendship for me. He employer of me. Also, I not liked—disliked Mr. Devenish. He was not genuine. I know bad man from good as I know fourteen-carat gold from eighteen-carat."

"A useful skill. You didn't see much of him, then?"

"As little as possible. I meet sometimes by chance in house."

"Did he admire your work?"

He shrugged. "Admired Miss Zvereva's drawings. She bring him to workshop where is made from drawing beautiful jewelry. He has only contemp'. He says any ordinary goldsmith can do this. I, who was apprentice in Fabergé workshop, thanks to Stepan Vladimirovich, I am not ordinary goldsmith! He knows nothing."

"You must have been angry."

He shrugged again and laughed, but there was an edge to his laughter. "Opinion of ignorant is nothing to me. Also, I know he wants only to make Miss Zvereva think he is very clever. If he praises my work like hers, she think he praises always what he sees, so his praise of drawings of her is not so . . . so . . ."

"Meaningful?"

"Da, is good word. I tell you what I think?"

"Please do."

"This man is what you call nuts. He has flying mice in the bell tower. You understand?"

193

Alec managed to hold back a smile but a muffled snort came from Piper and his mouth twitched.

Petrov looked at him and smiled. "This is funny? An Englishman tell me anyone will understand what is meaning."

"And so anyone will, sir, but if you don't mind me saying so, he was pulling your leg."

"*Tak!* To make fun of foreigner is joke in Russia also. Please, what is correct expression?"

"Bats in the belfry, sir. Bat—that's sort of a flying mouse; belfry is same as bell tower. So you weren't that far out."

"In your opinion, then, Mr. Petrov," Alec brought them back to order, "Devenish was not wholly sane?"

"Holy sane? England has same 'holy fools' like in Russian? I have not seen. Mr. Devenish was not such."

Alec groaned silently as Piper enquired and Petrov explained. Developing rapport with a suspect sometimes proved useful, he reminded himself.

Piper himself returned to relevance. "What exactly made you think he was nuts, sir?"

"I try to explain. For man to court young lady, change mind, jilt—this happens, da? But Devenish, to me seems he courts Miss Zvereva with intending from start to jilt. This not normal."

Normal for Devenish, Alec thought. He asked, "Was she very distressed when he jilted her?"

"Not at all. She did not like him."

"What about her father? He must have been angry."

"Stepan Vladimirovich is old man and cripple. He is angry; he curse; he shout; but is nothing he can do."

"Did he suggest that you should do something as he could not?"

"I am not servant to do such for him. I am grateful he obtain for me apprentice with Fabergé. I am happy for good job. But to commit crime—this, no!"

Alec was pretty certain he was speaking the truth, possibly nothing but the truth, but probably not the whole truth. However, he decided not to press him immediately. He wanted to hear Ernie's impressions. Besides, they had a great many people who hadn't yet had preliminary interviews. The Russians looked most promising so far, but there was a long way to go.

"Do you think any friends of the Prince might have acted for him, Mr. Petrov?"

"Most are old men. Not able for what I read in papers."

"Do you know of any other friends, acquaintances, or enemies of Devenish?"

"I have not met any such."

"Where were you last Wednesday morning?"

"I not remember anything different about that day, so I was here, working. We do good work, Miss Zvereva and I. We are always busy."

"Us too!" said Piper.

"Now must go to furnace. Is wasting gas."

They left him to his gold. Crossing the courtyard, Alec said, "I wonder why Miss Z didn't want me to speak to him except through her."

"Dunno. He gave us damn all. A cagy customer."

"He was holding something back?"

"If you ask me."

"I agree. But I don't think he killed Devenish, and I doubt he has any idea who did."

As they entered the house, Alec saw that the prince was not in his cosy corner.

"Your visit upset Papa," Miss Zvereva said. "The servant and I helped him to go upstairs. It is not easy without help of Vasily Ivanovich, but he insisted."

"We won't disturb him," said Alec. "I'd like to see the servants, though."

"I will call them downstairs."

There were two English housemaids, young and giggly, and a Russian manservant with an impressive beard. Alec wrote them all off as possible nanny impersonators immediately. As sources of information they might be useful. He nodded to Piper, who wrote down their names. He needed Miss Zvereva's assistance with the man's, as he understood little English and spoke less.

Leaving his sergeant to continue the laborious attempt to wring information out of the Russian, as interpreted by the man's employer, Alec asked the girls to step through to the shop for a few minutes. At moments like this, he badly missed Tom Tring, who would have had them eating out of his hand in no time. Ernie would never have the same light touch.

Unsure which girl was which, he took their names again. "You remember Mr. Devenish?" he asked.

"Coo, yes," said Doris, the smaller and prettier of the two. "Ever so 'andsome 'e was, wasn't 'e, Nance."

"'Andsome is as 'andsome does."

"Go on! 'E was a good tipper, too. Is it true 'e was done in, sir, like what the papers say?"

"I'm afraid so. That's why I have to ask you a few questions. He was a friend of your master's, was he?"

They exchanged a glance.

"That's as may be," said Nancy. "They didn't 'ave much to say to each other, and what they did say was in foreign."

"French, it was, I think. Not Russian."

"'E was always welcome, any road."

"Only 'cause 'e was sweet on miss."

"And she was sweet on him?" Alec queried.

"Not 'ardly!"

"Come off it. 'Ow would you know? Maybe she was playing 'ard to get."

"I seen the look in 'er eyes, 'aven't I. She put up with 'im so's not to upset 'er dad, you take my word for it, sir."

Provisionally, he did, as it agreed with what he'd heard before. "What about Mr. Petrov? Was he a friend of Mr. Devenish?"

"I never seen 'em together."

"They never come upstairs at the same time."

"I think," said Nancy darkly, "'e stayed away when 'e knew Mr. D was 'ere."

"Did anyone else—anyone I haven't mentioned—visit upstairs while Mr. Devenish was here?"

"One evening 'e brought a bloke round."

"What was his name?"

"Can't remember. I only seen 'im once or twice."

"Clark. It was Clark."

"With an E or without?"

The girl looked blank.

"It wasn't Clark anyways," said the other. "It begun with R."

"It didn't, neither. Clark it was."

With or without an E, Clark was one of the commonest surnames in England, if it actually was the man's name. "Do you happen to know his christian name?"

The maids looked at each other and shook their heads.

"All I remember is, it was kind of funny. We 'ad a good giggle, didn't we, Nance?"

"Not John or Jim or Joe," the other agreed. "I just read it on 'is card once, when he first come here, and it went right out of my head."

A man possibly called Clark with an unusual first name: The police had more than enough leads to follow without starting that wild-goose chase unless as a last resort. Devenish might have lacked any intimate friends but he had had a damnably vast acquaintance.

Alec wondered how Piper was doing. It was time to move on. They could always come back. He thanked the girls and ushered them into the back room.

Miss Zvereva dismissed the servants upstairs.

"Did Mr. Clark give you any business?" Alec asked casually.

"Clarrrk? No. He was friend of Teddy."

"So he won't be in your order book. Do you happen to remember his first name?"

She shook her head. "Not at all. I have no interest. I will make list from order book and send to Scotland Yard, yes?"

"To Detective Sergeant Piper, if you please, madam."

197

"Very well. I hope you will not need to come again," she said as she showed them out through the shop.

"Can't promise," the sergeant said cheerfully.

The door closed behind them. "You sound pretty chipper," said Alec. "Don't tell me the Russian gave you something useful?"

"Not him. Not a word. He refused to speak English at all, and going by what Miss Zed said, which I had to, all he said in Russian was 'I don't know.' Did the maids have anything helpful to say?"

"A partial name, possibly misremembered, of yet another friend of Devenish, if anyone he ever associated with can be called a 'friend.' All we seem to be getting is an ever-growing list of names."

"We'll weed 'em out, Chief. Look, why don't you go home and see if Mrs. Fletcher's got any more names for us—"

"Just what we need!" Alec groused. "Not to mention that I told her not to do any more digging."

His insubordinate subordinate grinned. "And have a bit of dinner. You'll feel better after. I'll go do some digging of my own. If I find anything, I'll ring up. Otherwise, you could take the evening off for once."

"Who's the chief here? All the same, I think I will. I feel as if I'm coming down with something. I'll take you back to the Yard and have a word with Mackinnon if he's there."

Alec reached home just in time for dinner. The rest of the evening's interviews had been parcelled out between Mackinnon and another couple of men, and Piper was sorting out the reports that had come in during the day.

"I may have to go back to the Yard," he warned Daisy.

"Oh, darling! You've hardly had a moment to take a breath since you got back from Bristol. You look exhausted."

"You work too hard, Daddy," Belinda admonished.

"Persuade the crooks to lay off, pet, and I will too."

He felt much better after a good, peaceful meal, listening to Belinda's chatter about the shopping she and Daisy were going to do the next day in preparation for the beginning of the summer term.

"And tennis whites," she added to her mental list. "I'm getting quite good at tennis, Daddy. I do hope you'll be able to come for sports day this year."

"I do try, Scouts' honour."

"Perhaps this will be the lucky year."

If he were promoted to superintendent . . .

Belinda went off to bed and still no call had come from the Yard.

"Whisky?" asked Daisy.

"A small one. I'll get it. What would you like, love?"

"I'll have a Drambuie."

"The house seems very quiet without your young cousins."

"Doesn't it! So peaceful I keep wondering what they're up to. Cousin Edgar wired that they all arrived safely. I hope Mrs. Gilpin has, too. I expect her sister would have wired if she hadn't."

"She's gone?"

"Yes. You didn't want to see her before she left, did you?"

"Not really, assuming she had no returning memories to report."

"I wouldn't have sent her if she did. There was a wire from Phillip as well. He's had to rush off to deal with some emergency in the North—Sunderland's in the North, isn't it? A factory up there is having difficulties with a new kind of windshield glass that Mr. Arbuckle wants them to make."

"And why exactly did Petrie feel the necessity of informing you about his troubles with windshield glass? You weren't planning another nightclub outing, were you?"

"Of course not, darling. He was going to come round here this evening to tell you something he found out about Teddy."

"Don't tell me he's been sleuthing on his own!"

"Not deliberately. He was at his club, the RAC, last night—"

Alec groaned. "His club! Devenish was a member?"

"Apparently."

"I *must* be tired. I never even thought of checking for club membership. It would be a last resort, if I had thought. It's damn difficult to get them to disgorge any information whatever about their members, almost as bad as solicitors and doctors. What did Petrie find out?"

"I don't know. That's why he was going to drop in tonight. He just said everyone there was talking about Teddy but he didn't want to tell me on the telephone or in the presence of his sister and Lucy and Angela."

"Lucy and Angela? Teddy's sister Angela? Great Scott, Daisy, what the deuce did—"

"It's not really relevant, darling, and it was quite harrowing. I'd rather not go into details."

"All right, I'll trust your judgement."

"For once."

"When is Petrie coming back to give us the benefit of his discovery?"

"He managed to write a long telegram without ever mentioning that, nor how to get in touch with him."

"Heaven preserve us from amateur meddlers! Since I have no idea of the length of his absence nor the significance of his knowledge, I don't feel inclined to ask the Sunderland police to make the rounds of glass manufacturers hunting for him."

"Gosh no. He may turn up back in London tomorrow."

"He's driving?"

"Can you imagine that car fanatic taking the train?"

"Frankly, no. I daresay he'll be exceeding the speed limit all the way, and I'll be called upon to bail him out because he claims to have essential information I need." Alec set down his empty glass and stretched. "I think I'll get an early night while I can and get up bright and early in the morning. Ernie's not likely to ring so late. Coming up?"

Arm in arm they went upstairs.

TWENTY-THREE

Daisy and Belinda spent the next morning shopping for school clothes, then went to Maison Lyons for lunch, a favourite farewell treat before the start of the summer term. Their patisserie was a big draw for the back-to-school crowd. Daisy let Bel have both an éclair and a napoleon, and they bought a cream bun to take home for the twins to share.

"Because Nanny wouldn't let them eat cream buns, Mummy, but Bertha will."

"I hope it won't upset their tummies."

"It wasn't 'cause of that, she just didn't want the mess. Is Mrs. Gilpin coming back?"

"I'm not sure yet. It depends."

"Bertha's a perfectly good nurse and much nicer."

"Don't say nasty things about people who aren't present to defend themselves."

"Well, I would never say it to her face, Mummy."

"I'm glad to hear it. Better not to say it at all."

"Till I'm grown-up."

Daisy laughed. "Then you can judge the situation for yourself and whether there is any good purpose for voicing your opinion. Now, check your list one more time to make sure we've bought everything. I don't want to have to rush back to Oxford Street for last-minute stuff."

When they reached home, Elsie waylaid Daisy in the hall.

"There's a person to see you, madam." Elsie disapproved, and she was obviously going to make Daisy go through a game of twenty-questions.

"A person? Male or female?"

"Female, madam."

"Old or young?"

"Not old, madam, but not exactly young. She said you'd know her. Name of Phipps, she said."

"Phipps? I don't know any—Oh, wait! Faye Fanshawe."

"Phipps is the name, madam."

"Fanshawe is her stage name."

"She looks as if she might be a theatrical person, madam."

"An actress? Oh, Mummy, may I meet her?"

"Nightclub performer, darling, though quite a respectable one. I think not. Not just now, at any rate. I wonder what she wants. How long has she been waiting, Elsie?"

"Nearly two hours, madam. I put her in the small sitting room."

"Thank you."

Fay Fanshawe-Phipps jumped up as Daisy entered the room. "Oh, Mrs. Fletcher, I 'ope I done right to come. Only I telephoned Scotland Yard, like Mr. Fletcher said to do, and they wouldn't let me talk to 'im. And Pa said it'd be just the same if I went there, they wouldn't let me see 'im, and 'e said I wasn't to, it was just askin' for trouble. But I promised 'im and he was decent to me, and 'e said you was 'is wife, so I thought . . ." She faltered to a stop.

"That's quite all right, Miss Fanshawe. You can tell me anything he needs to know and I'll pass it on, or you can write it down and I'll see he gets it today."

"Oh no, I couldn't write it. It would take ever so long and I'd be bound to spell everythin' wrong."

"Tell me, then. It's about Edward Devenish, I presume?"

"Yeah. See, Mr. Fletcher wanted to know did I ever meet any of 'is friends. I didn't remember—it was a few months ago—it was 'im that interduced me to Ray Richmond. That wasn't 'is real name, mind. He had a stage name, same as me, only 'is was because 'e didn't want 'is posh pals to find out 'e was workin' wiv me."

"Posh pals? You said something before, at the Kit-Cat, about your partner being too high and mighty for the job."

"S'right. I can't hardly ever find one o' me own sort to work wiv. Not-so-good ain't good enough for the Kit-Cat. Them that's really up to it've got good jobs in the circus or the music hall, and they like that life, the comradry like they call it. No offence, but they're not comf'table wiv toffs. Now me, being as how us buskers work the theatre queues, we got to get on wiv all sorts. Busking's not a steady income, though, and I gotta think of Mum and Pa."

"Of course." Daisy couldn't see the relevance to Teddy, but she was interested in this glimpse into a way of life.

"Me first partner, Billy, was a bloke I known since I was a kid. 'Is family's circus, but 'e married a London gal that hated touring, so 'e gave it a try. We worked out the routine ourselves and proposed it to the management. Billy didn't like it. He was bored to death sitting about back stage and he missed the animals. So I put an advert in the paper. You coulda knocked me down with a feather when this young gentleman answered it!"

"I bet. Did he explain why?"

"The geegees, 'e said."

"His horse always came in last?"

"Ain't that the way of it? He was down to 'is uppers."

"You must have known he wasn't likely to stay long."

"Didn't 'ave much choice, did I. He was the only one that answered. He wasn't bad, took a while to learn the routine. 'Course, you 'ave to change it to suit what they're best at, and so the patrons don't get bored. But 'e'd been a gymnast at school and 'e played squash so 'e was pretty nippy. He stuck wiv it for a couple of months, till 'is quarterly allowance fell due. 'E wasn't a bad bloke, stayed till I'd found someone to take 'is place. The next was a friend, a busker that fell ill and couldn't work outside for a while. He stayed till 'e was well enough. Couldn't stand working indoors, 'im."

"I admire your persistence."

"Oh, I went through another two or three before 'im I was telling you about."

"The one who knew Teddy Devenish."

"Yeah. I told Teddy about having trouble keeping a partner and the sort of fella I needed. Next time 'e come round, 'e brought this bloke, friend of 'is that des'prately needed a job."

"Gymnast and squash player?"

"You got it. He lasted longer than most, but he wasn't 'appy, 'specially when Teddy wrote that bit in the paper I told you about. That was mean, that was."

"But it sounds as if it was aimed at the friend, not at you." Quite a stretch as a motive for murder, Daisy thought. "What was his name?"

"His stage name was Ray Richmond, like I said. He was ever so particular about never using 'is real name, and 'e shaved off his moustache and dyed 'is eyebrows so no one wouldn't reckernise 'im. Trouble is, seeing 'ow I never used 'is real name, I can't remember it, not for sure."

"What do you remember? It may help."

"His christian name was kind of funny and 'e had a hyphen in 'is surname. All I'm sure of is the last bit: Clark."

"Oh dear, that's not much, is it. Quite a common name, too. I'll pass it on to my husband, of course. You never know what the police can do with a tiny scrap of information."

"Tell 'im I'll try to remember the rest. Only it's been a while and I dunno . . ."

"He'll be grateful for your taking the trouble to come. I know he'd want me to reimburse your fare." Daisy had her purse on her, having just come in. She offered Miss Fanshawe a pound, but she wouldn't accept more than the actual fare to Hampstead and back.

She ushered the acrobat out and went to the office to ring the Yard.

For a wonder, Alec was in and the switchboard put her through after only a minute or two.

"What is it, Daisy?" he asked impatiently.

"Darling, you ought to know by now that I never ring you at work for nothing." She continued hurriedly before he could tell her to get on with it. "Fay Fanshawe—I've forgotten what her real name is—she came here. You told her to ring you up if she thought of anything—"

"I did."

"She tried and they wouldn't put her through."

"Indeed! I'll deal with that. Why the deuce did she go to you instead of coming here?"

Daisy explained about the father's prohibition. "You'd told her I was your wife, and I'd left her my card. She decided it was the best thing to do."

"For all the trouble she took, I hope she had something worthwhile to tell."

"That's for you to decide. You asked about Teddy's friends, I assume. She recalled that one of her partners in her act had been recommended by Teddy."

"An acrobat?"

"No, a squash player who had been a gymnast at school. He went by the stage name of Ray Richmond, but his own name was so posh as to have passed through her mind like water through a sieve. All she remembers is the bit after the hyphen: Clark."

"Clark!"

"It means something to you?"

"Does it ever! Did she mention with or without an E?"

"No, and I didn't think to ask. Sorry."

"Never mind. How many hyphen-Clarks can there be in London?

"So Mr. hyphen-Clark is a person of interest?"

"No more so than a dozen or more others. That's our trouble. Hold on half a tick." The distant sound of voices cut off as he put his hand over the receiver, then he said, "I must go, love. Thanks for hyphen-Clark. 'Bye."

Daisy hung up and turned to the second post, which Elsie had put on her desk. Among the bills, circulars, and letters from friends and relatives was a brief note from Mrs. Gilpin's sister.

"Dear Ivy" had arrived safe but "exosted," and was tucked up in bed. That was one worry off Daisy's mind.

She was dealing with the rest of the post when the telephone at her elbow rang.

"Sorry to disturb you, Mrs. Fletcher." It was Ernie Piper's cheerful voice. "Do you happen to know where we can find Miss Angela Devenish? She's not answering the telephone at the flat and the bobby we sent round can't get an answer at the door. Before we try the lawyer, DI Mackinnon wondered if she might be with you."

"No, but I know where she is. She was taking the train home today. She was anxious about her dogs. If she didn't tell you, I'm sure it was an oversight, not with evil intent."

"Ever so keen on them dogs, isn't she?"

"She is, but I don't believe for a moment that she did Teddy in because he once hurt one of them."

"That's as may be, Mrs. Fletcher. He left her a lot of money, and money's a powerful motive."

"Not for Angela." But how thrilled she had been when their aunt left her enough to start her dog refuge. How many dogs could be saved by adding Teddy's enormous share in that inheritance? Did they really suspect her? "Anyway, she would never run away and abandon the dogs. You'll always be able to get hold of her there."

No sooner had she hung up than the bell rang again. Mackinnon this time, perhaps? She was tempted to let Elsie answer but picked up the receiver.

"Daisy? Sakari here. Do you remember Judith Winter?"

"The sculptor? Yes, why?"

"She is here. May I bring her to talk to you?"

Daisy wanted to ask why, but she assumed Judith was near enough to hear. Otherwise Sakari would have told her. That in turn suggested that she wasn't likely to enjoy the conversation.

It was much easier to leave someone else's house than to evict someone from one's own house.

All this flashed through Daisy's mind and she said, "I'll pop over to your house, darling. Is Deva free? I'm sure Bel would like to see her. She's feeling a bit lost without her cousins."

"Very well." Sakari sounded amused, as if she had overheard the mental calculations. She lowered her voice. "The sooner the better."

"Oh dear! I'm on my way."

Belinda was busy showing off to Mrs. Dobson and Elsie the new afternoon frock they had picked up from the dressmaker. She was delighted to be able to show it off to Deva as well.

They drove down the hill and were ushered into Sakari's exotically furnished drawing room just after the arrival of the tea tray. Daisy was still full from their lunch extravaganza, but she welcomed the sight because the girls' presence at tea must surely postpone the incipient explosion she read in Miss Winter's face.

By the time Deva took Belinda off to her room, Daisy had recalled the gist, if not the precise words, of her previous meeting with the sculptor.

"I've just found out you're married to Detective Chief Inspector Fletcher," Miss Winter accused her, "who's in charge of investigating Teddy Devenish's murder. Why didn't you warn me?"

"I don't make a habit of proclaiming to new acquaintances the profession of my husband. In fact I don't believe I have ever done so. It would be a rather odd proceeding, don't you agree?"

"Well, yes, but in the circumstances—"

"Nor was I the first to mention Teddy. You recognised my name as that of a journalist and asked if my interest in him was due to my intention of writing about his murder. You merely guessed that I was interested after watching me at the Café Royal, not because of anything I said."

"This is true," said Sakari in a conciliatory tone. "The guess was correct, however. I, too, am interested in the murder of Teddy Devenish, though my husband is not a police officer and I do not wish to become a reporter. You see, Judith, both Daisy and I were at the Crystal Palace when it occurred. It is natural to be interested, I think."

"My children's nurse was also there. I expect you've read in the newspapers that the victim was disguised as a nanny?"

"And the murderer may have been, too. So your nanny is suspected?"

"It's more complicated than that, but I do want to find out what happened for her sake. Also, Teddy was related to two friends of mine, another reason to take an interest."

"You weren't working for the chief inspector?"

"No. He was pretty annoyed with me." Daisy hesitated. The sculptor had calmed down, but what she had to say might reignite her ire. Still, she couldn't avoid saying it. "I did pass on to Alec what you told us about Teddy's nasty tricks."

"I knew you must have set the police on to my friends!"

"Hold on! I didn't give him any names. You didn't mention any."

"Not one," Sakari confirmed.

"If you were married to a policeman, Miss Winter, you'd understand that when it's a case of murder it's not a good idea to withhold information. It's a cliché that someone who gets away with one murder is very likely to kill again, but after all, clichés become clichés because they're mostly true."

Miss Winter looked as if she were trying to come up with a counterargument and failing. "I daresay, but when it's your friends . . ."

"The sun is nearly over the yardarm," said Sakari with the pleasure she always took in using a colloquial expression. She rang the bell. "Time for a drop of sherry."

TWENTY-FOUR

"*I still* think it's fishy that Miss Devenish left town without informing us," said DI Mackinnon.

"If you'd met her," said Alec, "you'd realise that it would be much more fishy if she *had* notified us, because out of character."

"I want to meet her. I'd like to check her alibi in person. Who knows how competent the local bobby is? With respect, sir, I think you've dismissed her as a suspect too easily."

"I haven't dismissed her. She's just low on my list. She's a very earnest woman and the soul of candour, with no notion whatsoever of hiding her feelings."

"And she's inherited a fortune from the victim, with nothing to stop her devoting it to what she considers the best of all possible causes."

"All right, Mac, if you want to trek to darkest Yorkshire. We haven't a shadow of grounds for making her come back."

"I hope you like dogs, sir," Piper put in cheekily.

"I and my wife have two terriers, Sergeant, a Scottie and a Westie. Find the best train for me, please."

"Tomorrow," said Alec. "This evening I want your opinion

of the Russians. Ernie, we'll need a copy of the list Miss Zvereva sent over. And let my wife know I won't be home for dinner, would you?"

"Right, Chief. I'll tick off the duplicate names from other lists, the ones we've already vetted. Mr. Mackinnon, here's the last train tonight and the first in the morning, and all the changes."

"Already? You're a wonder-worker."

"I had it ready in case of need."

The sandy-haired Scot regarded him with approval. "Verra efficient."

The jeweller's shop was still open when Alec and Mackinnon reached it. At least, the sign still read OPEN and the door was unlocked. The jangle of the bell as they stepped in out of the chilly drizzle failed to bring anyone from the backroom, however.

The inspector looked round with interest. "That'll be the back o' the Russian stove?" he asked, indicating the tiled wall. "A fine thing that would be in a Scottish winter! Shall I knock on the door behind the curtain, sir?"

"You can try, but it's a heavy steel door. If it's closed, we'll have to try the doorbell again."

Mackinnon drew the curtain aside. The steel door was open, the room beyond empty.

Stepping through, Alec swung towards the safe. As far as he could see it was closed as it should be. He frowned. "I wonder what's going on. I hope—"

A clatter of footsteps rushing down the stairs cut him off. Petrov appeared, his hair in disarray. "*Kto*—? Eh, police! I go fetch taxi." He strode past Alec, but Mackinnon stood square and solid in the doorway.

"Where are you off to, sir, if I might ask?"

"I fetch taxi. Most oldest friend of Stepan Vladimirovich dies—is dying. He must go say farewell, *da?*"

"Whose friend?"

"The prince," said Alec. "Let him pass."

"*Spacibo, gospodin.*" Petrov dashed off.

"But sir, he may be doing a flit!"

"Possibly. What do you want: a knock-down fight, roll about on the floor and clap on the darbies? We haven't a ghost of a justification, you know. I never took you for an impetuous man."

"I'm not! I'm a dour, canny Scotsman. It just goes against the grain . . ."

"I know. That's life. Come along, we'll go up." He crossed to the stairs, treading softly.

He was halfway up the steep narrow flight, Mackinnon close behind, when an irate roar in Russian emanated from above. A firm response in a female voice indicated that two of their birds were still in the coop. The old man muttered fretfully. Alec wished he understood what was being said.

The door at the top was ajar. He knocked, producing a sudden silence within.

"*Kto*—Who is there?"

"Police." He pushed open the door and stepped into the hot, low-ceilinged room. "Good evening, Miss Zvereva, sir. I'm sorry to trouble you at this time—"

"Mr. Policeman, is good time! My father very agitating—agitated. Cannot talk to you. You help my father down the stairs, yes? He goes to visit dying friend. These stupid girls he not trusting and I am not strong enough to go down. Is more harder than up."

Alec gave in. As she said, the prince was in no state to answer questions. She was also correct about the difficulty of getting the hefty old man down the stairs. It was a struggle even for two reasonably fit coppers—given the manservant's lack of English, Alec helped Mackinnon. From the bottom of the steps it was easier. The prince, muttering what sounded like imprecations all the way, could walk after a fashion and needed only support on each side. A cab backed into the alley as they reached the street.

Petrov jumped out. Alec stepped back and let him and Mackinnon get Zverev into the back seat. That accomplished, Mackinnon was about to close the door when Miss Zvereva slipped past him to join her father in the taxi. Saying something to the driver that Alec didn't catch, she pulled the door out of the inspector's hand. It shut with a thud and they were off.

Mackinnon uttered something very Scottish that sounded blasphemous. "I thocht the lassie was biding here," he said.

"Never mind, Petrov didn't go with them." The goldsmith was standing in the middle of the alley, looking very much as if he wished he had departed with his employers. "Did you get the address?"

"The street. Not the number."

"We'll find the dying friend if we want him. Mr. Petrov, we'd like a few minutes of your time, if you please. I suggest we go indoors."

Without a word, he passed them and entered the shop. He held the door as they went in, then shut and locked it and turned the sign to CLOSED.

"Please to come in, *gospoda*," he said with an ironic bow, holding back the blue velvet curtain.

In the back room, he seemed as at-home as in his own quarters on the other side of the courtyard, going straight to the samovar. Like the kettles eternally on the hob in England, the Russian apparatus seemed to be kept ever-ready to supply tea.

"This is Detective Inspector Mackinnon, Mr. Petrov." Again Alec avoided mentioning his own name. "The inspector would like to ask you a few questions."

"How do you do, sir," said Mackinnon, accepting a glass of tea without any sign of misgivings. "Thank you. Let's start with everything you know about Edward Devenish."

"He was *diletant*. Is same word in English, da? He think he knows all, he criticise all, he makes—*nyet*, he *creates* nothing."

"You didn't like him."

"I despise him. He is not worth two thoughts."

" 'A second thought.' Your English is very good, sir. Do you meet many English people?"

"Vo-cab-u-lary is good. Grammar not so much, is difficult. I go to evening class to make better. Is not sense to live in country, not learn to speak language."

"Very true, sir. Miss Zvereva knows you take these English lessons?"

"*Konechno!* Of course. Is not secret."

"Yet when the chief inspector and DS Piper came to interview you, Miss Zvereva said your English was very poor and she was determined to interpret for you."

"She is interested—curious to hear, perhaps." He shrugged. "Who can understand what is in woman's mind?"

Or man's. Though calmly composed, to Alec he sounded evasive. It was hard to judge since his speech in general was deliberate, careful, halting, as he hunted for the right words in a foreign tongue.

"You have known Miss Zvereva a long time?"

"Since child. I grow up on estate of prince. My father was servant, my grandfather was serf. I live there until sent to be apprentice in Fabergé workshop."

A situation that might lead to eternal loyalty or to undying resentment, Alec thought, or to an uneasy mix of both. Loyalty to the prince and resentment of his daughter's privileged childhood? It certainly complicated the question of what motive Petrov might have for murdering Devenish.

"I understand Devenish didn't admire the skills you learned under Fabergé."

"If Mr. Chief Inspector tell you this, he say also that I care nothing for opinion of this *diletant* whose opinion is not worth to have."

"Naturally, sir, I've read DS Piper's report. You said Devenish was crazy."

"I have learn new word—egzentric. This better perhaps than crazy. But Zinaïda Stepanovna believe he court her with meaning from start to jilt, only because she dislike his wish for tiepin. But is not better reason we can guess. Is crazy, *nyet*?"

"Sounds pretty crazy to me. And very upsetting."

"For her, not. Was more relief. She did not like, and Stepan Vladimirovich wanted that she marry him."

"Stepan—oh, her father. The prince must have been angry."

"First angry with daughter that she did not encourage, then more angry with Mr. Devenish for insulting. Was insult to both. In Russia, would be duel. Here is legal matter, but Devenish did not write promise to marry, and Zinaïda Stepanovna will not swear he said this. She does not wish to marry. Prince can do nothing."

"Someone did something. Do you have any inkling who—"

"Excuse: 'inkling' is what?"

"Sorry. Do you have any idea—can you make a guess—who might have killed Devenish?"

"I? Why you think I have idea?" He sounded surprised, not at all agitated. "I meet him two-three times, not know who are his friends, who are his enemies."

"But you know he had enemies?"

"I see what he did to Zinaïda Stepanovna. He is . . . 'spiteful' is the proper word?"

"Spiteful would suit."

"Spiteful man is not likely only one time to do such thing. Make plenty enemies, *da*?"

"*Da*. Nicely argued, sir. You're right. We know of a number of people with no cause to love him. We're asking all of them the same questions, more or less. Including the most important, of course: Where were you last Wednesday morning?"

"Again!" Petrov sounded exasperated. "I have said already that I was at home, in my workshop, working. I checked order book; now I can tell you exactly what I made—what I was making and show you. This will prove nothing."

"Very true." Mackinnon glanced at Alec, who nodded. "I'd like to see, all the same."

"You come to workshop."

They crossed the courtyard in a light drizzle that made the paving stones slick. Alec noticed Petrov's knee-high boots, worn over his trousers, which appeared to be made of some sort of rough fabric.

"Your boots are Russian, Mr. Petrov?"

"Da. They are *valenki*, made of felt, like hats. Very comfortable."

"They look quite new."

"Made by Russian shoemaker in London. Plenty Russians here to buy."

Many, maybe most, émigrés stuck together with their fellow countrymen, a fact worth remembering when any of them became involved in an investigation.

Petrov unlocked the workshop door and ushered them in. Mackinnon looked round with interest. "Nice setup you have here, sir."

"Is good business. Would be stupid to risk for . . . little revenge. Is better word . . ."

"Petty revenge, we say."

"Petty, like French *petit*."

"You speak French?" Alec asked.

"A little. From Russia we go to China. China was not good place. Prince was badly beaten by thieves and princess very ill. When she died, we go to France. Was good, but Stepan Vladimirovich hear of old friend from Russia now living in England so we come here. Same old friend that he visits tonight."

"I've been meaning to ask how you happened to join the prince after the revolution."

"Was during revolution. Bolsheviki come to workshops, I run away, go to estate of prince, Bolsheviki come to estate, all run away. Some day when you not think I killed Devenish, you come drink vodka like friend, I tell you stories will make hair curl."

"Thank you." Oddly enough, Alec felt honoured by the exile's offer of friendship. "I hope that day will come. In the meantime, may we see your book with the record of last Wednesday?"

The order book was very neat, but of course it was written in Russian, in a tiny hand. No wonder Petrov hadn't balked at letting them see it. However, after poring over it for a few minutes, he and Mackinnon deciphered the dates and found the page they were pretty sure was last Wednesday's.

It had several small, rough sketches and a good deal of writing on it, at least as much as any other page, suggesting that as much work as usual had been accomplished. The writing was as firm and regular as the rest, without waverings that might have indicated unsettled emotions. All in all, as Petrov had pointed out, it didn't prove anything, but it certainly leaned towards indicating innocence.

On the other hand, a man who had survived hair-raising experiences, who retained his composure when suspected of murder, could conceivably have killed in the morning and worked late into the night with a steady hand.

"You wish to see also detail sketches of Zinaïda Stepanovna by which I work this piece?"

"That won't be necessary at present," said Alec.

"Thank you, sir, perhaps later," said Mackinnon. "Would I be correct in assuming this gives the name of the customer for whom you were working?"

After taking a moment to work out this convoluted question, Petrov shook his head. "*Nyet*. Number only. Is not need I know name. You can read in Zinaïda Stepanovna's book."

"You wouldn't know whether it was one of the people Devenish introduced to your work?"

"*Nyet*."

"Did you meet any of those customers?"

"*Nyet*. Is not my job to meet customers."

"Never?"

"*Nu*, now and then I meet by chance in shop if go to speak to Zina. Sometimes she introduce me. I do not remember names."

"You don't recall a man named Clark?"

216

"Clark? *Da*, him I remember. But he was not customer. Was friend of Devenish, but not rich, no jewelry."

"Do you remember his full name?" Mackinnon asked eagerly.

"*Nyet*. Was introduced as Mr. Clark."

"Can you describe him?"

"I saw one time only. Fair hair. Face not . . . rememberable. Like any young English gentleman. I would not recognise. His clothes I remember: good when new; now old, wore out."

"Tall? Short?"

"Not very tall. Perhaps more than me, is hard to be sure. Thinner, make to look taller."

"He sounds far from memorable," said Alec, "yet you remember him in spite of seeing him only once."

"He came many times, first with Devenish, then alone. Stepan Vladimirovich tell me always when they will come. Then he not need me to play *nardy*—is game like backgammon I play often with him. He does not want me to be there."

"That must have rankled," Mackinnon commented.

"Please?"

"It must have upset you."

Petrov shrugged. "I am not aristocrat. Is way of world."

"What about Clark, is he an aristocrat?"

"So I am told. He will be lord—and rich—when relative dies. This is what he says. Is true perhaps. Stepan Vladimirovich wishes to believe."

"Did they play backgammon together?" Alec wondered aloud. "I assume neither Devenish nor Clark speaks Russian and the prince doesn't speak English."

"He understands English. He will not speak for not wanting to make mistakes, look foolish. Zinaïda Stepanovna must always be there to interpret for him. She said to me he tells stories of old life in Russia, and sometimes they play cards because he will not learn English backgammon game."

The prince had not admitted to understanding English when

Alec spoke to him. Nor had Miss Zvereva admitted the fact. She had translated everything Alec and Piper said into Russian for him.

Whatever was going on, Petrov didn't seem to be part of it. He had freely admitted to speaking English, though Miss Zvereva had claimed he didn't. Whether her obfuscation had anything to do with Devenish's death was obscure. It would probably have to be sorted out sooner or later, but at present they had more than enough on their hands.

Mackinnon pulled him out of his reverie. "Any more questions for Mr. Petrov, sir?"

"Not just now. We'll probably have to come back, I'm afraid, Mr. Petrov. This is a complicated business."

Impassive, Petrov bowed without speaking. He ushered them out, across the courtyard and through the shop. Alec heard the shop door's heavy lock clunk behind them as they turned away.

"What do you think of that, Mac?"

"The soul o' candour wrapping a secret that may or may not hae aught to do wi' the case."

"I couldn't have put it better myself. If he knew, or suspected, that Miss Zvereva had killed Devenish, would he try to protect her, if only to preserve his own livelihood? Those customers whom she says she saw that morning will have to be thoroughly questioned. Would they even have noticed if someone—another woman with a Russian accent—had stood in for her? How often does one really notice someone serving in a shop? It's a pity she's out this evening."

"Ye won't want to disturb the deathbed, sir?"

"No. I can't see Miss Zvereva fleeing the coop with a cripple and no luggage. We'll catch her tomorrow, Piper and I, while you're in Yorkshire. Who's next on our list?"

"Desmond Mathieson. He's probably the author whose manuscript Devenish had used to light a fire, by Miss Winter's account. She didn't name him, mind you. Piper's narrowed it down from all the reports that have come in. Mathieson refused to talk to the DC who went to see him, but the lad says he's clean-shaven and not outlandishly tall to pass as a nanny. He writes thrillers, so there's a good chance he's studied a bit of anatomy."

"Mathieson it is." Alec sighed. He was going to miss the twins' bedtime again, and Bel was off to school in a couple of days. The superintendent's job looked more and more attractive.

TWENTY-FIVE

After dinner, Daisy and Belinda listened to a play on the wireless. When it ended, Alec had still not come home. Bel went reluctantly to bed. Daisy picked up a book, but her mind kept drifting to the mysterious hyphen-Clark. The name dredged from Fay Fanshawe's memory obviously meant something to Alec.

He had heard it from another suspect, she presumed. The question was, whom? He was investigating all sorts of people.

Though Miss Fanshawe regarded him as a toff, that might mean merely that he didn't drop his aitches. He could well be middle class. The police probably wouldn't waste time checking through *Debrett's*, a huge job when the initial letter was unknown, except as a last resort. Even if Daisy had a copy she wouldn't tackle it.

Easier than searching *Debrett's* would be asking Lucy, though even for her, identifying half a surname might present difficulties. Worth trying, perhaps. Was it too late to telephone?

She glanced at the clock on the mantelpiece. A bit on the late side, considering Lucy's condition. If she felt well, she'd be out at some dinner party. If not, she'd be asleep in bed. Besides,

Daisy was warm and comfortable in the big armchair by the fire. Why move? Especially as she had decided, after the awkward business with Judith Winter, that she was going to stop meddling—as Alec called it—in his cases. She was going to try to stop, at least.

Though with Nanny Gilpin involved . . .

Mrs. Gilpin had seen the second nanny, and had paid sufficient attention to her to notice something that induced her to follow the woman—or man—all through the building and down to the bottom of the park. Had she witnessed the murder? Surely in that case she would have notified the authorities, or asked the advice of ex–DS Tom Tring, or at least told Daisy, rather than put herself in danger by sleuth-hounding.

Had she seen the murderer's face? Would she recognise him if she saw him again? Or her, as the case might be. It hardly mattered as long as she couldn't remember. But he didn't know she had lost her memory. Was she still in danger?

He couldn't possibly know who she was, Daisy reassured herself, let alone trace her to her sister's in Dorset.

If she hadn't seen the murder, what had she seen? The question that most interested Daisy was whether the nurse had been justified in haring off without a word. And that question was, at present and perhaps forever, unanswerable.

"Wake up, Daisy!"

She blinked up at him. "I wasn't asleep, I was thinking."

"Deep thoughts," Alec teased.

"I just didn't hear you come in. Have you found Mr. hyphen-Clark?"

"Is that what you've been thinking about? I assume your thoughts were fruitless or you would have greeted me with the bit before the hyphen."

"Actually, I was thinking about Nanny."

"Don't, love. It only upsets you."

"I can't help it. Gosh, it's late. Shall I make cocoa? Have you made any progress?"

"Yes to cocoa." He took her hands and pulled her out of the

chair, into a hug. "No to progress, unless you count eliminating a lot of people."

"It counts as long as you haven't eliminated your whole list so you don't know where to turn." Daisy led the way down to the kitchen.

"It's not that bad. We still have hyphen-Clark in the offing, for one. So far, he's not much more than a rumour."

"You heard of him from someone else apart from what I passed on from Fay Fanshawe? If you see what I mean."

"We did, but I'm not telling you who. You haven't heard from Petrie, I take it?"

"Not so much as a telegram saying when he'll be back."

"Blast the man! Here, let me pour the milk. You're half asleep still. By the way, I've got to go in early tomorrow. Mackinnon won't be there to do his share of the organising. He's hopped it to Yorkshire."

"Not to hound poor Angela! Bad choice of words: Harass her, I mean."

"No, to ask her a few questions. He has a bit of a bee in his bonnet about her."

"You can't possibly suspect her!"

"You must see that she has to be on the list, love. She's a rich woman now. Look out, don't let the milk boil over!"

He refused to say another word about the case. But he did promise to be home for dinner the next day, to say good-bye to Bel.

In the morning, Alec left early, before Daisy looked at the post. The top envelope was meticulously addressed in a round schoolboy hand to Mr. and Mrs. A. Fletcher and Miss B. Fletcher. It contained two letters, a short one from Ben and a long one from Charlie.

Daisy read Ben's aloud to Belinda. " 'Dear Aunt Daisy, Uncle Alec, and Belinda,' " Ben's began. He thanked them for an enjoyable visit, which he had enjoyed very much. Only in the post script was any sign of his personality. "'I put Charlie's letter in the same envelope to save the stamp. It's awfully long. Please don't mind the spelling, he's always in a hurry.'"

"Let me see Charlie's spelling. Gosh, it is long. Shall I read it to you?"

"Just the best bits, darling. Here's one from Angela Devenish that I simply must read."

"'Dear Bell' with two Ls," Belinda read, "'and Ant Daysy'— D-A-Y—I rather like it that way—'and Uncle Alick,' with a crossed-out K. 'I had a fritefly good time at your house.' The spelling of 'frightfully' has to be seen to be believed! And then he writes about all the things we did, all spelled wrong." She giggled. "'So thank you very much and please can I come again one day lots of love from Charlie.'"

"Has he written about the Crystal Palace?"

"Yes, let me find that bit. Here it is: He just says he wishes he'd had time to look at the monsters properly."

"Nothing about chasing the nannies or the police?"

"He wrote something about hoping Mrs. Gilpin is feeling better. I only skimmed through because of you reading Miss Devenish's letter, but I think I would have noticed if he'd mentioned the police. Why?"

"I was a bit worried that he was more upset than he seemed here."

"I don't think so, Mummy. I'm sorry Mrs. Gilpin got hurt and Aunt Lucy's cousin got killed, but when it was happening it was just like a real live adventure story."

"That's all right, then." Daisy turned to Angela's letter.

After a normal salutation, Angela, never one for roundaboutation or social niceties, plunged headlong into the iniquity of Teddy's lawyer. Cranford not only refused to hand over her inheritance immediately, offering instead to advance a piddling sum pending legal formalities, he was trying to prevent her handing over the bulk of the fortune to the RSPCA as soon as she got her hands on it. He was a coldhearted, unfeeling brute, who had no compassion for the dogs and other animals who would suffer in the meantime.

Angela knew Daisy had the welfare of mistreated dogs at heart and she was sure Daisy must know how Cranford could be made to knuckle under. She counted on receiving her advice by return post.

Daisy decided the best advice she could give was to herself, not to get stuck between the obdurate lawyer and the unworldly Angela. She felt for both. Now that she was able to vote, she read the political news, and she knew that whatever the government said about negative inflation, prices kept rising. Angela might give away her money and find herself in a few years with no means of supporting her own rescued dogs. Whether she could be made to see things that way when her heart was bleeding for the immediate suffering . . .

But Daisy wasn't going to try to explain it to her. Should she advise her to consult the Devenish family lawyer? Her family's lack of sympathy made it unlikely that he'd approve of her plans.

No, she'd sic Angela onto Tommy Pearson. The Fletchers' lawyer was a family friend, stuffy at times but with an unconventional streak that just might make him able to appreciate her point of view. He had been very helpful and knowledgeable when it came to setting up a trust for the twins and Belinda, and a trust, come to think of it, might be the very thing for Angela's dogs.

That settled, Daisy turned her mind to the implications of Angela's urgent desire for instant cash.

Was DI Mackinnon right? Was it possible she had killed Freddy for the money? But why on earth would she have agreed to join him in such a pointless prank? She certainly wasn't the sort of person to find it funny or clever. Before the dog-kicking incident, she might have gone along to indulge him or to try to keep him out of trouble. Not now.

Daisy had a feeling she was caught in circular reasoning. It had always been one of her failings. She dismissed Angela temporarily from her mind and asked Belinda what she was going to do on her last day before the start of the summer term.

"Mostly pack," Bel said mournfully. "And take the twins and Nana to the Heath if it stops raining. Why does it always rain on the last day of the hols?"

Phillip telephoned at noon to invite Daisy to lunch. He had just got back to town and found several messages from Scotland Yard awaiting him at his hotel.

"Dashed if I'm poking my head into that hornets' nest," he told Daisy. "They'd probably keep me for hours answering questions and I've got to be on my way to Bristol. So I'll tell you and you can pass it on."

"Why don't you come here, Phil? It's Belinda's last day of the hols and I don't want to go out."

"Oh, all right."

Over lunch, Phillip was avuncular, asking Bel about school and answering her questions about life in America. When he and Daisy adjourned to the sitting room for coffee, he started telling about the new type of automobile glass being developed in Sunderland. "Think of it, curved windscreens!" he said rapturously.

"How nice."

"Nice! It's revolutionary. Think of—"

"Phil, you could spend the rest of the day explaining and I daresay I still wouldn't have a clue why you're excited about it. Remember 'nature study' was the only science we had at school."

"Nature study! That's not science. I suppose you were learning to pour tea properly instead. Yes, thanks, I'll have another cup. And boys' schools teach Latin and Greek instead of physics and chemistry. Just think how advanced we'd be if—"

"Please, Phil, another time. You claimed to be in a hurry to get to Bristol, and I'm dying to know what you found out at your club."

"Oh, well, it wasn't all that much, really. Some of the fellows were playing billiards and someone started talking about Teddy Devenish, wondering whether his heirs would be selling his car for a song, wanting to get rid of it."

"How callous!"

"It is the RAC, you know, old dear. All the fellows are frightfully keen on cars or they wouldn't be members, and Teddy's was a 1927 Mercedes-Benz S-Type Sportwagen with a supercharger clutch and—"

"Phil!"

"Oh, sorry. Anyway, they were calling him 'poor devil' so they weren't completely callous. Though none of them sounded as if they liked him much, I must say. He was always kicking up larks—Well," Phillip said tolerantly, "all young fellows do, and of course, it goes without saying, there were plenty to egg him on. No one ever proposed a bet he didn't accept, I gather. The thing is, he always managed to do it in a way that caused the most inconvenience to everyone else."

"Such as?"

"They were all laughing about the time he set loose half a dozen monkeys in Harrods. He put numbered collars on them, but left out number one, so even once they'd collared the lot, they thought one was missing."

"I did hear something about that, though I didn't know it was Teddy." Daisy tried not to giggle. "It must have been pretty funny."

"I daresay, if he hadn't picked the week before Christmas, when everyone's doing their Christmas shopping. Lots of customers left to shop elsewhere. It must have been quite a big loss for Harrods."

"All the same, if that's the worst they had to say—"

"Not by a long shot. One of the chaps blamed him for leading this other young fellow astray."

"Which young fellow?"

"Ricky, they called him. Not a member, I gathered. Not anyone I know. One of the chaps was a great pal of his older brother, Lord Somebody, it seems. And at one time Devenish used to bring him—the younger brother—to the club now and then, so several of them were acquainted with him."

"Ricky? Is that his surname?"

"I don't believe so. A lot of the young chaps call each other by ridiculous nicknames. I don't know what the world's coming to."

"If it never comes to anything worse than that," Daisy said pointedly, "it'll be in good shape. But what was Ricky's surname?"

"I never heard it, and I didn't care to ask. Thought Fletcher wouldn't be any too pleased with me if I let on I was interested."

"Nor his brother's title, I take it."

"I've forgotten," Phillip apologised. "It was something very ordinary and it didn't stick in my head."

"Too full of automotive glass, I suppose. Blast! Ricky sounds like a good candidate. Did they say in what way Teddy led Ricky astray?"

"It seems to have started with gambling. First the gees, then when he lost, lent him a bit and suggested he could pay it back by winning big on the illegal stuff."

"Of course he lost."

"Of course. All those games are rigged. Beats me how anyone can expect to beat the house. If he'd been a gentleman, Devenish would have told him to forget the debt and stay away from both the tables and the horses. Instead— Mind you, old thing, I'm just putting all this together from snippets I overheard. Don't go telling Fletcher it's gospel."

"I won't, Phil. But do go on, it's fascinating in a morbid sort of way and it fits to a T what I know of Teddy."

"It does? No wonder someone bumped him off."

"He must have had a down on poor Ricky for some slight, very likely imaginary. Getting even for things most people would barely notice seems to have been his modus operandi."

"I thought your education excluded Latin," Phillip said suspiciously, "as well as maths and science."

"It did. That's just one of those phrases one hears. Go on, about Teddy and Ricky."

227

"Ricky got to the point where he moved out of his rooms and into a cheap lodging house. Even so, he had to hock anything worth a few pounds, including his best clothes. He'd been a medical student, but he dropped out when he couldn't afford the fees, and without decent clothes he couldn't get a decent job. Devenish found him some sort of job to tide him over, so that he could redeem his togs and look about for something better."

"Did they happen to mention what the job was?"

"I gather Devenish was very secretive about it, wouldn't drop a hint."

"I suspect I know, then." By this time Daisy was convinced "Ricky" was Miss Fanshawe's Ray Richmond, alias Mr. hyphen-Clark. Richard something-Clark, she presumed. "I must say, Phil, you're making a beautifully dramatic story out of your few overheard snippets. I never knew you had such narrative skills."

"Yes, well, I was thinking about it on the drive up from Sunderland, putting it all together, because I knew you'd want to know as soon as I got back."

"How right you were, except that Alec wanted to know the day before yesterday. Did you gather whether Ricky appealed to his family for help?"

"No, but he'd worn out his welcome among his friends, having never repaid the odd fiver, so I daresay it was the same with the family."

"Very likely. Besides, if he was very down-at-heel, he was probably ashamed to go home or to approach his friends in person, and a begging letter never goes down well. I suppose with so much to gossip about, no one said anything about his being an athletic type."

"As a matter of fact, they did. One of the fellows said Ricky was hopeless at billiards, which was odd because he was a demon at squash."

"It all fits together." Daisy frowned in thought. "He's Mr. hyphen-Clark all right. But it doesn't answer the main question."

"Mr. what?" asked Phillip, baffled.

"Mr. hyphen-Clark. It's all we have—all Alec has of the name of a suspect. One of many, however. Still, it should help them find him. Do have some more shortbread and another cup of tea?"

"Yes please. Dash it, old girl, the fellow can't be a murderer. He's a gentleman even if he's on his uppers. He'll be a lord when his brother dies."

"Really, Phil, you are naïve!"

The comment provoked a childish squabble that took Daisy back to the days when Phillip was her big brother's best friend and tried to lord it over her on the basis of his five years' advantage.

TWENTY-SIX

Early as Alec reached Scotland Yard that morning, he found Ernie Piper already at work. He had prepared a list of people who ought to be interviewed a second time, neatly divided into groups according to their whereabouts, with suggestions as to which of the available sergeants should tackle each group.

"I wasn't sure, Chief, whether you'd want me to take on some of them or stay here and keep track of stuff as it comes in."

"On the whole, you're more valuable here, Ernie, but as DI Mackinnon has vanished into the wilds of Yorkshire, I want you to come with me to see the Russians again. We should catch them if we go just after lunch, don't you think? I'll brief the men now, and then I've got some thinking to do. Send for coffee, will you?"

"Right, Chief."

While waiting, he glanced through Ernie's lists of names, discussed a few with him, and approved his suggestions. Coffee and several detective sergeants arrived at the same moment.

"You all know by now what we're looking for," he said as Ernie distributed their lists, which included brief descriptions of what was known of all those on them. "All these people have been checked once and picked out for a second visit. If you receive any information you consider significant, report by telephone immediately after the interview. Speak to Piper if he's here—he and I will be out for a while but in his absence a shorthand typist will be on duty. Is anything not clear?"

He answered a couple of questions and sent them on their way, then settled at his desk with lukewarm coffee and copies of all Ernie's files. Knowing the way he worked, Ernie had sorted them into three sets, labelled "possible," "maybe," and "unlikely." The third was the most numerous, Alec was glad to see. He started going through those, hoping as always to knock suspects off his list.

Happily, he was able to set three-quarters aside and add a few from the second set, to be returned to as a last resort. He was halfway through the third pile when Ernie brought him a couple of sandwiches and yet another cup of coffee.

With a sigh, Alec pushed back his chair and stretched. "I don't believe I have ever in my life come across anyone who made so many people's blood boil."

"Dunno that I've ever come across anyone who seemingly set out on purpose to make people's blood boil."

"And was by all accounts hugely successful. No, no one over the age of fifteen or so. There are plenty who don't care whom they upset, but that's another matter. What's this?" He started unfolding waxed paper. "The canteen's best cheese and pickle?"

"I sent out, Chief. Best roast beef and plenty of it. It's still raining. Shall I order a car to go to the Russkis?"

"If you brought your raincoat, we'll walk. It's not far and I need to stretch my legs."

When they reached the shop, the OPEN sign was in the window. They stepped inside out of the rain, the bell announcing their arrival.

Its clangour went unanswered.

231

For a nasty moment, Alec thought he had guessed wrong and the Zverevs, with or without Petrov, had skipped. They could hope to submerge themselves in the reclusive community of Russian exiles, or even go abroad where they undoubtedly had friends. Their pockets full of gems, they would be welcomed anywhere.

On the other hand, with an elderly invalid travel would be difficult at best, perhaps impossible, and they must realise that if they lay low in England the police would find them sooner or later. Besides, they would hardly have hung out the OPEN sign and left the door unlocked if they had fled.

They waited a few minutes, then, at a nod from Alec, Ernie opened and closed the door again, setting off the summons of the bell.

This time it had immediate effect. One of the maidservants instantly popped through the curtained doorway. "I'm ever so sorry to keep you waiting, sir," she said breathlessly. "Miss called me upstairs for a minute just when the bell rung the first time and I didn't know which to answer so I goes up and tells 'er and she sends me down and then you rung again. I been watching the shop, see, 'cause Miss is looking after the master, poor ol' man! His friend died last night and 'e's took to 'is bed with the doctor."

"I'm sorry to hear that."

"Oh, he was ever so old, even older than the master. Wait half a mo'. I forgot to switch on the light. Be forgetting me own 'ead next! There, that's better. Oh, it's you, sir! The copper what come round before."

"It's Nancy, isn't it?"

"That's right. I'm to ask what you want and go tell Miss."

"I want to talk to her. And Sergeant Piper here wants to talk to you, so you can stay here and have a word with him while I go up to Miss Zvereva. I'd rather not ask her to come down when she's busy." Without further ado, Alec went through to the back room.

It was in a state of chaos that suggested the prince's confinement to his bed had been seized on as an opportunity for spring cleaning. Nancy had not been idle while waiting for the bell to ring. Alec stepped over a rolled rug and made for the stairs.

Miss Zvereva stood on the small landing at the top of the flight, her back to the light. He couldn't make out her expression, but her voice enlightened him as to her feelings.

"Again you! What you want now? You know my father ill?"

"Nancy told me. I'm sorry."

"Bah!"

"I shall not disturb him." He recalled the difficulty of getting the cripple up and down stairs. "His bedroom is on this floor? Come down and talk to me below."

" 'Talk to me.' Always 'talk to me.' Everything I have said already."

"No, you haven't. You are concealing something. Come down."

" 'Concealing'?"

"Hiding."

"I have tell you all that is your business."

"You will have to let me be the judge of that." Alec turned and descended the stairs. Behind him, he heard slow, reluctant footsteps.

At the bottom, he waited to hand her down the last step. She almost refused the courteous gesture but at the last moment thought better of it and laid her hand lightly on his arm, for just a second. Then she swept past him and went to the ever-steaming samovar.

"You will drink tea."

"Thank you."

She was an extraordinary creature, tall, elegant, self-possessed. Alec found it hard to believe that, barely out of girl-hood, she had undergone the terrible flight from Russia and the harrowing odyssey from country to country with an ailing father, losing her mother en route.

Her survival proved her strength of mind. Whether the experience had hardened her—to the point of committing murder without turning a hair—he couldn't be sure.

Her back to him, she said, "What you want to ask me?"

"Please come and sit down." He retrieved a couple of seat cushions from a corner and replaced them on the recently brushed-down chairs.

"One moment."

The samovar gurgled. Outside, rain gurgled in the gutters and pattered on the paving. Through the gloom shone the lights in the goldsmith's workshop. Petrov was at home. He was, of course, the next target.

Miss Zvereva handed him a glass of tea and waved him to a chair. She hesitated before seating herself in the other. "I am ready."

"Tell me about Teddy Devenish."

Exasperation exploded from her. "I have told all I know! And more—I have told what I think about him."

"Tell me again. From the moment you met him. No, let's start before that. Had you ever heard his name mentioned?"

"If I hear, I not remembered."

"All right, your first meeting."

She repeated the story of the tiepin and her unwillingness to set the large stone he wanted. "I do not say is vulgar. One does not speak so to customer. I tell him is not fashion in present, and he say he will set fashion. He does—did—not appear angry, but now I believe was then he decide to pretend he is in love."

"Why? What makes you think he was not sincere right from the beginning?"

She shrugged. "'Intution' is word?"

"Intuition."

"*Da*. I feel it. Also, later is no reason for change. Fall in love, fall out love, is possible. To change from love to . . . to . . ."

"Spite."

"To spite, this is not natural."

Alec was far from certain that it was not natural for Teddy Devenish. If apparently genuine admiration could turn to spite, why not love? He found it hard to fathom a mind that could spend a good deal of money on works of art and then turn on the artists and wreck their current work.

However, his job was to fathom that mind only to the extent that it suggested the proximate motive of his murderer. Even that was not essential to the case, but it was necessary to an investigation more often than not.

Motive was not hard to find in this investigation, however. The wonder was that no one had bumped Teddy off sooner. The trouble was that too many people had motives.

Alec's brief silence while he pondered did not stampede Miss Zvereva into inconsidered speech.

"How did you feel when you realised his courtship was a sham, a pretence?"

"Much relief, like I tell you before. I dislike. Father wants me to marry. Is not so easy in Russian culture for daughter to disobey father's wish. So I am happy that Teddy does not want to marry me."

"And your father?"

"He is blaming me more than Teddy. If you ask hundred times, will be always same answer, because is truth."

"All right." Alec dropped that line for the present. "Tell me about Mr. Clark. He was a friend of Teddy Devenish?"

"Clark?" She was startled. "Teddy introduce him. He comes . . . came again with Teddy, only one time more, I think."

"He came only twice? Two times?"

"Only twice with Teddy. Then Teddy stop to come. Mr. Clark came few more times."

"You didn't mention this before."

"I forget. Is not memorable person."

Petrov had used the same word, Alec recalled. "His last name is Clark. With or without a final E, do you know?"

She shook her head. "Never I see in writing."

"His other names?"

"Always I call him Mr. Clark. My maid announce him as Mr. Clark and Teddy call him Clark."

What on earth could the man's name be that was so elusive? "Please describe him," Alec requested.

"Is difficult. You look, you see English gentleman, not . . . I forget correct word."

"Individual?"

"*Da*. See gentleman, see good clothes—very proper but old, fair hair, good manners. Thin, not fat. Not tall, only medium, but holds self very straight. Face is . . . ordinary."

"Colour of eyes?"

"Grey, I think. Maybe blue."

"Moustache? Beard?"

"Not either. No hairs on face."

"Age?"

"Young. I make guess: twenty-one, twenty-two. Younger than Teddy."

"He went on calling after Devenish stopped?"

"*Da*. He, I think, believes he is in love, but is only because Teddy . . . Is hard to explain."

"You mean he fell in love with you because he thought Devenish was in love with you? Perhaps he saw that you disliked Devenish and he hoped to win your hand in marriage to prove himself the better man? Something on those lines?"

"Is possible, I think."

It was possible, and it would have set up a complex emotional situation if and when Clark found out that Devenish had cried off. "Tell me what he told you about himself."

"He tell to my father that his brother is lord."

"Did he mention his rank? Baron, viscount—"

"Means nothing to me. I do not remember."

"Or his hereditary name. That is, he's Lord Something-or-other."

"Not Lord Clark?"

"Possibly, but not necessarily."

She threw up her hands in despair. "You English say Russian names too complicated. Is nothing compared to English names. I not know name of brother. I know he was injured in

236

war and never recover. He is invalid, like my father, and does not leave estate. He is . . . stingy?"

"Mean. The opposite of generous."

"So. He will not pay debts of Mr. Clark when he spends more than his allowance."

"Sensible man."

Miss Zvereva smiled. "This I think also. To gambler, money is water."

"Clark gambles, does he?"

"He talks much of racehorses. Also talks that will be rich lord some day, but I think gamblers are never rich."

"Not often, certainly."

The second housemaid pattered down the stairs. "Please, Miss."

"What is it?"

"The master's asking for you, Miss. He's coughing something awful."

Jumping up, Miss Zvereva said, "I must go."

"Of course. Just one last quick question. Do you know where he lives?"

"Mr. Clark? No. Brother in country. Far from London, I think."

"Thank you."

"You will see yourself out, please."

"Certainly. Thank you, Miss Zvereva."

The maid stood aside to let her go up. Alec beckoned to her. "You want to talk to me, sir?"

"Yes. Doris, isn't it?"

"Tha's right, sir."

"Last time I saw you, you told me Mr. Devenish brought a Mr. Clark to call on the Zverevs. You couldn't remember his christian name, nor the first part of his surname. I wondered whether either has come to you since then."

She shook her head. "We talked about it, me and Nancy, but we couldn't neither of us remember. Funny thing, Miss called Mr. D. Teddy, but she never called Mr. Clark anything but

Mr. Clark, even though we reckon, me and Nance, 'e was really nuts over her. Like Nance said, she's of them fem fatals like in the pictures."

"He went on visiting after Mr. Devenish stopped coming?"

"Yeah, for a coupla weeks. Then— Lumme, that was funny, too, come to think. Nance popped out to the post office for Miss. She saw Mr. D. looking in the window of the antikew shop next door. He didn't see her, or 'e pretended not to. Not that she'd give 'im the time o' day after what 'e done to Miss! Then when she come back, Mr. Clark turned into the alley just ahead of 'er. He stopped by Mr. D. and they started talking. Nance had to pass them but she couldn't hear what they was saying 'cause they stopped talking when she was by. But she was dead sure they was quarrelling."

"Even the best of friends squabble sometimes."

"Don't I know it. You oughta hear me and Nance sometimes! The thing is, after that Mr. Clark stopped coming round. Me and Nance, we reckon Mr. D warned 'im off."

"Why—"

"Doris!" Miss Zvereva called from the stairs. "Come. I need you."

The maid fled, pausing on the bottom step to glance back, wink, and wave.

He didn't really need her answer. Nor was he surprised or disappointed that Ernie was no closer to an answer after interviewing the other maid downstairs. Why did Devenish do anything? Mostly, as far as Alec could see, just to be nasty, an accomplishment he had raised to a fine art.

238

TWENTY-SEVEN

As promised, Alec came home for dinner. Daisy could see he was not in a good mood, but he nobly suppressed his irritation until after Belinda had gone to bed. Then it burst forth.

"What the deuce does Petrie think he's playing at? The Ritz says he came in and picked up his messages, went to his room for just long enough to wash and brush up, and then left again. His car isn't in their garage."

"He had to go to Bristol, darling. Time is money."

"Damn Yankee slogan! He bloody well knew we want to talk to him. Wait, you heard from him?"

"He came to lunch and told me what he found out so that I can pass it on to you."

"Did you put him up to it, Daisy?" Alec asked suspiciously.

"Certainly not! Phil knew if you got him to the Yard he'd be answering questions for hours, and . . . well, time is money. In Mr. Arbuckle's eyes, at least."

"All right. Tell me. No, wait, he came to lunch? That's hours ago. Why the deuce—"

"Because we had a domestic emergency, with which I didn't want to trouble you, but if you go on behaving like a bear with a sore head I shall not only give you all the details of the exploding boiler, I shall likely forget everything Phillip told me."

Alec laughed. "A dire revenge. Sorry, love. It's been a frustrating day. Another frustrating day, I should say. I hope you took notes."

"As soon as he left. And then the boiler—"

"I promise to listen to the sad fate of the boiler, but it'll have to wait."

"I'll fetch my notebook. I want to make sure I get the details right, such as they are."

When she returned, he was pouring a brandy. "Liqueur?" he offered.

"Yes, please. Orange Curaçao, if there's any left. With soda."

He brought it to her and sat down with his brandy cradled in his hand. "Go ahead."

"As I told you before, Phillip was at his club—"

"The RAC, you said? Very appropriate."

"Isn't it? He's kept up his membership in spite of living in America. Teddy was a member, too. Phil was playing billiards with friends—or perhaps just acquaintances, I'm not sure. Fellow members, anyway. They were gossiping about Teddy." She repeated what Phillip had said, as nearly as possible in his own words.

"Ricky! No one used any name other than Ricky?"

"If they did, Phillip didn't hear it. But I asked him if they'd mentioned whether Ricky was the athletic type. Someone had commented that he was bad at billiards but pretty good at squash, so I'm quite certain the secret job Teddy found him was working with Fay Fanshawe, and he's Mr. Hyphen-Clark."

Alec frowned. "A reasonable deduction, but far from certainty."

"Remember," Daisy argued, "Miss Fanshawe said 'Ray Richmond' was very sensitive about keeping his real identity secret. I bet Teddy held it over him, told him he'd blow the gaff if Ricky didn't do what he said."

"Yes, that would explain . . ."

Daisy waited a moment, then: "Explain what? Don't be exasperating, darling."

"Explain why Ricky hyphen-Clark, or anyone else, would agree to join Devenish in the nanny caper, for one thing."

"And?"

He gave her a would-be innocent look. "Oh, nothing."

"It's something to do with Miss Zvereva, isn't it? Did Teddy make Ricky pretend to court her?"

"How the deuce do you know about that? Don't tell me Ernie—"

"Of course not! She herself told me her father was encouraging a second Englishman after Teddy backed out. The prince wanted her to marry a rich aristocrat, and that's what Ricky will be when his brother dies."

"Pure speculation."

"Deduction. Am I right?"

"Perhaps. No pretence about it, though, as far as we can gather. Just a minute, Petrie said Ricky is in line for a peerage? You didn't mention that. It agrees with what Miss Zvereva says."

"Phil didn't exactly tell me. It was an aside, on the lines of 'Ricky can't have murdered Teddy because he's going to be a peer,' implying that peers don't do such things."

"Don't they just! I take it Petrie didn't get the brother's title?"

"No, 'fraid not. He decided you wouldn't like it if he was nosy."

Alec sighed. "We'll have to get in touch with these gossips. I hope you took all their names."

"Oh, darling, I'm so sorry. I didn't think to ask him."

Alec groaned. "Tell me you're joking!"

"It just didn't cross my mind. He referred to them as 'the fellows,' or 'one of the chaps,' didn't even mention any names."

"And now he's in Bristol. I bet you have no idea where he's staying or whom he's visiting."

"Oh, but I do, and I should have thought of it for Sunderland.

Mr. Arbuckle likes him to stay at the most expensive places. It makes a business man look serious."

"Good thinking. I'll ring up the Yard and get someone on to it." He glanced at the clock on the mantelpiece. "A bit late to disturb him, but once they've run him to earth, they can leave a message that he'll get first thing in the morning." He went out.

When he returned, Daisy said, "You're pretty sure Ricky is the murderer?"

"I'm not at all sure. The nets are still spread wide, though at present he's our focus, mostly because he's so difficult to pin down, to mix a few metaphors. At least we know the names of the others on our list!"

"Ricky—Richard? Most likely. Richard hyphen-Clark."

"Probably not Richard. The maids wouldn't have had any trouble remembering that. Until we've got his name—or his brother's—we can't find him. To tell the truth, I get the wind up whenever I think about a murderer who will be a rich lord 'when his brother dies.'"

The following day, a note in the post informed Daisy that the designs for her jewelry were finished and she could go to the shop to look at them any time. After breakfast, she rang up Sakari and invited her to accompany her. Sakari, breakfasting in bed, said she was free all day and Daisy should ring again when she knew what time she wanted to go.

Next she rang Lucy to invite herself to morning coffee. Lucy wasn't up yet either. She left a message with the butler, who said Lady Gerald had no prior engagement as far as he knew.

Then she helped Belinda with last-minute packing—including the inevitable last-minute dash to the shops—of bits and pieces that hadn't made it into her trunk before the railway carter came to fetch it. She drove Bel in the Gwynne Eight to Liverpool Street to catch the school train.

On the platform, Bel gave her a hug and a kiss before she was absorbed into the chattering swarm of her schoolfellows. Daisy waited to wave good-bye as the train chuffed out amid clouds of steam, with children's heads and waving arms poking from every window.

She returned to the car to find a policeman eyeing it with disfavour. When he saw her approach, however, he saluted and gallantly opened the door for her. Whenever such things happened, Daisy always wondered whether it was a tribute to a reasonably attractive, moderately young woman, or the bobby in question had recognised her as a chief inspector's wife.

She might even have met him sometime, so she said warmly, "Thank you, Constable."

He beamed, stood back, saluted again, and held up a taxi so that she could pull out.

Alec's day had started badly with a summons to Superintendent Crane's office. "I assume you have an excuse for not having pulled anyone in for the Devenish case?" the Super greeted him.

As the latest report was on his desk in front of him, Alec took this as rhetorical sarcasm. "My men have done an excellent job of whittling down the numbers, sir. I'd like to commend DI Mackinnon in particular."

"Been cooperative, has he?" Crane grunted. "His divisional super wanted us to leave it to him."

"Much too big a job for a division force, especially with most of the investigation outside their bailiwick after the initial securing of the scene and search of the Palace park. We've had as many as forty possibilities to consider. We're down to half a dozen or so. Today I'm going to see those I haven't already spoken to."

"No, you're not, you're going down to Leicestershire to explain to Sir James Devenish why no one has been arrested for his son's murder."

"Sir, that will only slow things down." Alec's memories of the baronet were not fond.

"I'm aware of that, Fletcher. The Assistant Commissioner is

aware of that. Ordinarily that would settle the matter, baronets not having the pull of peers. However, the Home Sec. hunts in Leicestershire and Sir James is Master of his favourite hunt. Enough said?"

"Enough said, sir. I'd like to point out that we do appear to have a peer involved."

"But you don't know who he is, and a nameless peer has even less influence than your average baronet. No, you don't like it, I don't like it, but we'll have to like it or lump it. Any forrarder on discovering who he is?"

"I'm pretty sure I know how to find out, but I'd have to be in London to do it, and it's not something I can delegate. Of course, I could set a man to going through every entry in the peerage looking for a hyphen-Clark."

"Lord knows how long that would take!"

"Exactly, sir. I have better uses for their time, especially considering that if I just stay in town I can—"

"Leicestershire," the Super said firmly. "Today."

"Yes, sir. As a matter of fact, I'll be quite glad to have a word with Sir James. It's odd that he spent only one day in town. I haven't had a chance to talk to him."

"Gently, Fletcher, gently."

"He did ask to see me, sir, not vice versa."

"Which does not give you licence to ride roughshod over the Home Sec.'s favourite Master of Foxhounds!"

"Sir! I never ride roughshod over suspects."

"And don't treat him as a suspect."

"From what I recall of him, he's far more likely to ride roughshod over me. After all, he's Master of—"

"Yes, yes. All the same, I wouldn't bet against you, Chief Inspector. You'd better get going. You may be missing a train at this very moment."

Alec got going, only to be told by Piper that he had in fact just missed the best train of the day.

"I'll drive," he said grumpily. "You come with me, Ernie. You're in charge, Mac."

TWENTY-EIGHT

Daisy drove straight from Liverpool Street to Lucy's. Her ladyship was expecting her and she was ushered directly to her ladyship's boudoir.

"I'm out to anyone else, Galloway," she told the butler. "Sit down, darling, have a cup of coffee, and tell me."

"Tell you what?"

"Whatever it is you're being mysterious about," Lucy said impatiently.

"I wasn't being mysterious! I haven't even spoken to you today."

"You've been mysterious for a week, darling, and Galloway said you sounded positively urgent when you rang up earlier."

"I did not sound urgent! So unladylike."

"As if you ever cared about that, Daisy. It has to be something about Teddy. Come on, you came here to tell me so tell me."

Daisy laughed. "It is, but a question not a report."

"I told you I've steered clear of Teddy for years."

"It's not so much about him as one of Alec's suspects—"

"Did Alec send you?"

"Heavens no. He wouldn't do that."

"Does he know you're here?"

"No. I would have had to explain and he'd have insisted on asking you himself, and you'd have been difficult and set his back up. It seemed easier just to come and ask you myself."

"You're not still expecting me to go to an artsy party with you, I trust."

"No," Daisy said regretfully. "It's too late for that."

"Ask away, then, though I can't imagine what you think I might know."

"Darling, you have the peerage at your fingertips."

"So does *Debrett's*. Why doesn't Alec look it up?"

"I knew you were going to be difficult. He hasn't got the whole name, nor the rank, so looking it up in an alphabet-based book would take forever and a day. What's known is the second part of the hyphenated family name, which is Clark, with or without an E, and the nickname of a younger son, Ricky, who's not much above twenty."

"Honestly, darling, you can't expect me to know all the nicknames of all the younger offshoots!"

"I don't. Stick to hyphen-Clark."

"Pour me another cup, will you. Hyphen-Clark? That would be Wrexham-Clarke with an E, Lord Ledborough. He's about our age, I think, crocked up in the war and never seen in town. I can't remember his christian name and I don't know the younger brother's, though Richard would be the obvious answer. Gerald has a *Peerage* in his study. Shall I send Galloway for it?"

"Don't bother. The names you've given me will be enough for Alec. I'm sure they have *Debrett's* at the Yard." Daisy glanced round the room. "You haven't got a copy here? Your favourite reading material?"

"Don't be sarky, darling, it doesn't suit you. My knowledge comes from people, not books. Mostly. Do you want to ring Alec and tell him? There's a phone on my desk."

"Yes, I'd better. When he's not telling me off for acquiring information, he's castigating me for not passing it on immediately."

The desk was an eighteenth-century drop-front, inlaid with beautiful marquetry in a lighter wood. A very modern telephone perched incongruously on top. Daisy asked for Scotland Yard and was put through at once.

Alec was out. Mackinnon took her call.

"Good morning, Mrs. Fletcher. What can I do for you?"

"Good morning, Inspector. You're back from Yorkshire."

"Aye. I came back yesterday but I had division business to catch up with, so now I'm catching up with the reports here."

In view of his unexpected chattiness, doubtless prompted by boredom with endless reports, Daisy ventured to say, "May I enquire . . . ?"

"Miss Angela Devenish?"

"Yes."

"She's off the hook. Her presence at the kennels all that day is vouched for by her assistant, her volunteer helpers, and the dogs."

Daisy laughed. "Thank goodness."

"If that's all—"

"It's not actually what I rang about. I don't know if you've got to the report about Ricky hyphen-Clark yet?"

"I have."

"Good. I've discovered his complete last name. It's—"

"Just a moment, let me find my notebook among all these papers. All right, go ahead, Mrs. Fletcher."

"It's Wrexham-Clarke." She spelled the first part. "And Clarke with an E. My informant doesn't know his christian name, but that will be easy to find now. His brother is Lord Ledborough."

"Thank you. Your informant was Lady Gerald Bincombe?"

"Yes, how did you guess?"

"The Chief Inspector was going to consult her ladyship if we hadn't found the information by other means before tomorrow."

So she had spared Lucy and Alec an interview that would

247

certainly have brought out the caustic side of each. She had also been spared a lecture from Alec for meddling.

She said good-bye to Mackinnon and hung up. "Alec was bracing himself to tackle you about Wrexham-Clarke, darling. Now he doesn't need to."

"He'll probably find some other reason to harass me."

"DI Mackinnon says your cousin Angela is in the clear."

"They thought Angela might have bumped off her brother?" Lucy said incredulously.

"They had to consider it. She gets all Teddy's money. Which I'm sure I shouldn't have told you so keep quiet about it. May I give Sakari a quick ring?"

"Of course."

Sakari suggested half past three to go to the jeweller's and Daisy agreed. Ringing off, she told Lucy about having her aquamarines reset by the Zverevs. She didn't mention their connection with Teddy, but Lucy was interested in the quality of their work.

"I had a Victorian ruby ring reset and I wasn't at all happy with the result. You must show me your necklace when it's done and perhaps I'll see what they make of the ring."

"Miss Zvereva wears a lot of rings. You can probably look at them and know whether you want to try the firm. The goldsmith himself worked for Fabergé."

"That's promising, if it's true."

"Oh! I hadn't considered that it might not be, though I did wonder if her father is really a prince."

"Darling, how naïve, and you an amateur detective!"

"Don't let Alec hear you say that," Daisy retorted absently.

Was she naïve, as she had accused Phillip of being? If the Zverevs were lying about the princely title and about the goldsmith's credentials, what else might they be lying about?

With Ernie Piper as his navigator and good roads all the way, Alec reached Saxonfield, the Devenish estate near Market Harborough, just before noon. He turned in between the two wrought-iron gates, standing open. The gravelled drive ran slightly uphill between an avenue of lime trees with pale new leaves. The park on either side was beautifully kept, grazed by recently sheared sheep, fat despite their near nakedness, and woolly lambs.

At the top of the rise stood a large, foursquare Georgian house, its red brick almost hidden by the fresh foliage of Virginia creeper. Sir James's ancestors had not indulged in the expensive frivolity of a pillared portico. To all appearances, generations of squires had husbanded the land on which they no doubt hunted, shot, and fished, as did their present descendant.

In fact, Saxonfield shouted a worthy prosperity. Whatever their problems in the way of rebellious offspring, in spite of death duties and income taxes, the Devenishes were very well-off.

Alec parked the Austin Twelve on the sweep in front of the house. As soon as he turned off the motor, a chorus of bays could be heard from somewhere behind a screen of evergreens off to the right.

"Foxhounds," said Piper with a shudder. He was a townsman through and through. "I'm glad I'm not a fox."

"You'd rather be a lamb? A clean but certain death at a young age or the chance of a grisly death when you can't run and dodge as fast as you used to."

"I'm glad I don't have to choose. There's Sir James, Chief, coming round the corner."

They both recognised the baronet from a previous case. A large man, red-faced and bristly moustached, at sixty or there-abouts he was running a little to fat about the midriff but still vigorous, as his stride attested. He wore boots, breeches, and an old tweed jacket, with an ancient cap of a different tweed.

The sheepdog at his side barked once, alerting him to strangers.

"Down, Shep." Shep lay down and fixed his commanding gaze on Alec and Piper, clearly ready to herd them if they strayed. "Mr. Fletcher?" The squire's gaze was equally commanding. "Detective Chief Inspector Fletcher? They told me you were coming. We've met before, I believe."

"On another distressing occasion, I'm afraid, sir."

"A pretty idea of my family you must have!" he said bitterly. "I won't ask— But come indoors. We can't talk here. Come, Shep."

He led them into the house, straight across a high-ceilinged hall, along a passage, down a few steps, to a room obviously in use as an estate office. The window looked out to a cobbled yard with stables on two sides, one side in use as garages in this age of internal combustion, the other still occupied by horses. On one wall hung a map of the estate and detailed plans of three farms to a larger scale.

Sir James motioned them to chairs, backs to the window, and sat behind his desk. Having demanded Alec's presence, he sat in silence, staring down at his brown, sinewy hands, laid flat on the scratched and battered desktop.

"Sir, you said outside you wouldn't ask . . . something. Do you care to complete the sentence?"

The hands clenched. "I wasn't going to ask what my son did to provoke someone to kill him. But I need to know. Was it— one of his stupid practical jokes taken too far?"

"We don't know for sure. When we find out who, we'll find out why. Sometimes it's the other way round, but in this case we have a large number of people whom Mr. Devenish had offended in one way or another. Often trivial-seeming, but what looks trivial to an outsider can be of desperate significance to the person concerned."

"I see," the baronet said heavily.

"He had a great many—acquaintances, and I'm afraid he seems to have"—what was the tactful word?—"to have affronted most of them. The sheer number is sufficient reason for our slow progress, added to the public nature of the scene of the crime. If we understood his behaviour, it might help us understand the mind of the murderer. Will you tell me about him?"

250

Sir James looked up for the first time. His faraway gaze seemed to pass through the detectives, beyond the stable yard, across his broad acres, and into the past.

"His mother claimed he was fragile and cosseted him. She and his older sisters indulged him, spoiled him. I assumed he'd grow out of it. He did grow stronger. I tried to take him in hand, but he had no interest in manly sports, no interest in the land his ancestors farmed for centuries, that would have been his one day." He sounded incredulous and the face he turned to Alec was bewildered.

"Difficult to know what to do," Alec murmured.

"If he'd had an intellectual bent, if he'd wanted to go to a university, I'd have let him, though I believe a young man in his position learns more that's useful right at home on the estate. But he wasn't interested in his studies. The only thing he had a spark of interest in was flummery like poetry and painting. All very well for girls, though most of them have more sense these days. Edward wouldn't even settle to one of those! He wrote little, painted a little, played the piano a little . . . Tchah!"

"A would-be Renaissance man, sir?"

"A dabbler! And didn't those fellows include swordplay among their skills? Edward wouldn't know—wouldn't have known the hilt from the blade. I should have put my foot down and made him stick to something. But what?"

"Difficult to know," Alec agreed.

"I let him go to London. Sow a few wild oats, I thought, then you can get serious. Next thing I know, he's hanging on the skirts of a divorcée ten years his elder! Maybe you remember that, Chief Inspector. It was at the time of my mother's death."

"I do." Alec clearly remembered trying to get hold of the divorcée and her rowdy entourage to confirm Teddy Devenish's alibi.

"He went straight back to her before his grandmother was in her grave. That was too much even for my wife. When he refused to give the woman up, I washed my hands of him. Not that it called him to heel, of course, as Mother left everything to him. Nothing I've heard of him since suggests any amendment in his character." He dashed a hand across his eyes. "So much for the glorious career of my son and heir," he said harshly. "Enough?"

"Thank you, sir."

"I can't see how it'll help you lay hands on . . . his killer."

"Nor can I at present. All I can say is that, put together with a great deal of other information, it may at least speed things up. Don't worry, sir, we'll catch him." Alec stood up, Ernie following suit.

Sir James heaved himself to his feet, leaning with both hands on the desk. "You don't suppose Edward was killed by that woman's ex-husband, or a jealous lover of hers?"

"That was four years ago, sir," Alec protested. "We've come across no sign Mr. Devenish was still in touch with her."

"You're sure?"

"Pretty sure. I can't recall her name, though. Can you?"

"No. My wife— No, we mustn't remind her of that dreadful time. She has enough to bear. You don't want to see her, do you?"

"I spoke to Lady Devenish in town, thank you. We'll be off, then."

"Thank you for coming. I'm afraid I was growing rather impatient. I realise you're doing everything possible and having seen you work at Haverhill, I'm glad you're in charge, Chief Inspector. Do you mind showing yourselves out? You can go through this door to the yard and round to your motor."

As they crossed the stable yard, Alec looked back and, through the window, saw him slumped at the desk, one hand covering his face.

"Whew!" said Ernie. "That was all right. I thought we were sent to have our knuckles rapped."

"We were lucky."

"What a waste of time, though, half a day on the road for half an hour's chat."

"Not entirely a waste of time." He ought to have talked to Sir James sooner. Mackinnon's report had been excellent, but

252

the baronet had not been nearly as frank to the Scot. Somehow, knowing what made Teddy tick ought to make it easier to understand the murderer.

A couple of horses whickered at them as they passed; a stable hand glanced out from a stall and waved a sort of salute, without a pause in his whistling. Everything was was spotless, the cobbles wet from a recent washing. Alec wondered what would happen to the place without a direct heir to keep it going.

An archway led on to a back drive, which they followed round the house to the front.

"You drive, Ernie."

"Right, Chief. D'you think there's anything in the divorcée business?"

"A jealous lover from the past? It doesn't seem at all likely. I suppose we'd better find out her name and do a bit of digging. As if we need any more suspects!"

"I know her name: Rendell. Called herself Mrs. Genevieve Rendell so I don't know her husband's first name."

Alec frowned. "Does any Rendell, male or female, turn up in any of our lists?"

"No. But a lover—"

"Don't waste time over it for the present. If we come to a dead end, we'll take another look. We're not desperate yet."

"You reckon this Clark bloke, Chief?"

"I reckon he's our first priority, if only because of the possibility of danger to his brother. But I'm not losing sight of the Russians."

TWENTY-NINE

Daisy drove down Hampstead Hill to St. John's Wood. Sakari was ready for her, bright eyed after her postprandial nap. She was wearing a particularly fetching sari, turquoise figured with black and gold. Daisy admired it as her friend struggled, with the aid of her turbaned footman, into a very English coat.

"Yes, is it not a pretty colour? It is new." Sakari sighed. "My husband says it is the last new sari I may buy unless I lose some pounds. Fat is a sign of prosperity in India, but enough is enough, he says. The doctor also orders me to slim unless I wish to drop dead one of these days."

"Darling, how grim! You must know all about slimming diets, though. Aren't people forever giving lectures on the subject? And you go to a great many lectures."

"However, I have always avoided those about dieting, Daisy." She sighed as Kesin helped her into the car. "It is not a subject that appeals to me. Let us change it. How is Alec doing with the Crystal Palace case?"

"He tells me hardly anything. As a matter of fact, I've given him more information than he's given me. You remember Mr. hyphen-Clark?"

"You have spoken of him."

"I found out his name!" Daisy said triumphantly.

"Good gracious, how?"

"It was easy, actually. His brother is a lord, so I simply went and asked Lucy. She knows everyone who's anyone, by repute if not in person."

"But could not Alec have asked her?"

"Of course, but the police hate to bother the aristocracy if they don't absolutely have to. They're so apt to complain, and they know the right people to complain to."

"Was Alec pleased?" Sakari asked with a twinkle in her eye.

"He couldn't possibly object to my talking to Lucy! As it happens, he wasn't at the Yard. I spoke to DI Mackinnon, and he was delighted."

"Did you suggest that he did not need to reveal his source to Alec?"

"No. I can do that with Ernie Piper, but I don't know Mackinnon half well enough."

"He seems to be a pleasant and competent officer."

"Oh yes, I like him. But I wouldn't want to put him in the position of withholding information from his superior. Ernie Piper and Tom Tring know what Alec will put up with—if he finds out! And they know me, of course. I'm so very glad we had Tom with us when I discovered Teddy's body."

"Indeed. Mr. Tring's presence was a great comfort."

"How long ago that seems! I know Alec and his crew have been working non stop but if they're any nearer an arrest I haven't heard about it. I wonder if the Zverevs are still suspects."

"Perhaps we ought not to go there, Daisy."

"Alec knows they're doing some work for me and he hasn't told me to stay away. Besides, they have no reason to want to harm us. By now the police must know much more about them and their connection with Teddy than we do."

Sakari sighed. "I suppose so. Well, here we are," she added as Kesin turned into the narrow passage and stopped before the jeweller's.

"You're very pessimistic this afternoon."

"I will tell you why. I am thinking that after your business we will go to that nice little coffee room round the corner and we shall have a nice cup of tea, but I, for one, will not have a nice pastry to go with it."

"Too frightful, darling! I'd forgotten."

"You may have one. It is not your waistline. Or rather, lack thereof."

"I do still have a waistline," Daisy agreed, "though I daresay by the time fashions allow one to display it, it will have vanished."

Sakari sent Kesin to run an errand. "I have told him to return in twenty minutes, Daisy. It should be enough time, and if not he will wait."

They went into the shop, jangling the bell on the door. Sakari sat down immediately.

"They are right, my husband and my doctor. It is possible to look too prosperous."

Daisy went to the counter and stood there watching the curtain in the corner. It didn't stir. Perhaps the door behind the curtain had been shut accidentally so that the bell on the front door couldn't be heard. If so, rapping on the counter with her knuckles would only serve to damage her knuckles.

"Jiggle the street door," Sakari suggested. "'Jiggle' is a good word. I learned it only recently and I have been dying to use it."

Laughing, Daisy jiggled the door. The bell obligingly clanged again, and she kept it going for longer than its usual course. There was no response from the curtain.

Impatient, she went over and lifted the curtain a little. The door behind stood open. She stepped just across the threshold and glanced round the room.

"No one here," she reported to Sakari. Raising her voice, she called, "Hello?"

Hurried footsteps on the stairs presaged the arrival of a maid-servant. She stopped on the landing, peered down at Daisy, and said, "Oh, I'm awf'ly sorry to keep you waiting, ma'am. The master's ill and everything's at sixes and sevens. I'll just run up and tell miss you're 'ere and I'm sure she'll be down in 'alf a tick. What name?"

"Mrs. Fletcher. I'll wait in the shop," she called after the girl as she scampered upward.

She went back and told Sakari what the maid had said.

"Miss Zvereva will not want to discuss your jewelry if her father is ill."

"No, I won't press her."

"She may not come down, whatever the maid told you."

"But as she may, we can't just leave. I hope she's not too long." Daisy perched on a stool and leaned back against the counter.

They had been waiting a couple of minutes when the street door was flung open with a jangle and a man rushed in.

"Zinochka—*Ach!* I beg your pardon. Where is Zinaïda Stepanovna?"

"Miss Zvereva?" Daisy queried, recognising the goldsmith, though he was wearing a dark suit and white shirt, not the Russian blouse she had seen him in before. "The maid went to tell her we're here."

"Now is not good time for— Zina!" He burst into Russian as Miss Zvereva came through from the rear. Daisy picked out the word "taxi," though it might mean something quite different in Russian.

The woman answered briefly, then turned to Daisy. Dressed for outdoors, she looked excited and anxious. "Excuse, please, Mrs. Fletcher. Here are your designs." She handed over a large envelope. "One minute, please." Another flood of Russian ensued.

The goldsmith replied, shaking his head vigorously.

Daisy was dying to examine the designs, but she hesitated to remove them from the envelope when Miss Zvereva appeared to be about to go out.

"Let us look at them, Daisy," said Sakari, heaving herself to her feet.

"I think Miss Zvereva—"

257

"Mrs. Fletcher, Mrs. Prasad, I ask of you now great favour. Will you come with us?"

"Go with you? Where? Why?"

"Is urgent." She cast a harried glance back at the curtained door, and a pleading one at the goldsmith, who stood silent, his face grim. "Hired car waits. Is not far, will not take long. An hour, maybe little more. I will explain, but please! Come now!"

Curiosity overcame common sense. Daisy allowed herself to be herded outside, with Sakari following close behind, protesting, "Daisy, do you think it wise to go?"

But the car had backed in and stood right at the door. Daisy found herself inside it before she could reconsider. The goldsmith handed Sakari in beside her and Miss Zvereva joined them, while the goldsmith—Daisy didn't think she'd ever heard his name—got in beside the driver. He spoke in Russian to the driver, who answered in the same language, and they were off.

After a stop for a bite to eat, Alec and Piper reached the Yard in mid afternoon. Leaving it to Piper to brief Mackinnon on their visit to Saxonfield, Alec started reading through the reports that had come in during their absence.

"Clarke! Alaric Wrexham-Clarke—what a mouthful! And his brother is Lord Ledborough? Mac, how the devil did you get hold of this?"

The inspector avoided his eyes and said to thin air, "Mrs. Fletcher telephoned, sir. She said she asked Lady Gerald Bincombe."

"I was certain Lady Gerald would know."

"Pity Mrs. Fletcher got there first." Ernie sounded sympathetic but looked as if he were suppressing a grin. "What next, Chief?"

"I suppose we still don't know where to find him, Mac?"

"No, sir. I was waiting for your authorisation to set enquiries in train, seeing he's ain brother to a laird. But if he's gone to earth in London using a false name, it's going to be verra difficult to find him, and knowing his full name won't help, either."

"Where's the family seat?" Alec glanced back at the page in front of him. "Marsh Abbey, near Shrewsbury. He may be there, or they may know where he is. Ernie, put through a call to Lord Ledborough. Mac, get busy with those enquiries. Hotels, clubs, you know the routine."

"Ye're thinking he's oor man, sir?"

"I'm thinking, first catch your hare. He's the only person we've wanted to talk to that we haven't been able to find. We'll worry about whether he's the one we want when we've got him."

At the back of his mind, insistent, was the possibility that, if Alaric Wrexham-Clarke had killed Teddy, his brother might well be in deadly peril. He knew all too well that once the taboo against murder is broken, it is never wholly restored.

It was much too soon though to write off the rest of the names on his list. He went back to ploughing through the new reports, making occasional notes but not finding anything of much interest.

As he turned the last but one face-down on the pile, the telephone rang.

Ernie answered it. "DS Piper." He listened for a moment. "Let me ask." Handing over the mouthpiece, he announced, "Lord Ledborough is not at home, Chief. D'you want to speak to his butler?"

"Yes!"

"Yes, we'll take the call. Hello? . . . Right, Mr. Maxwell, hold on just a minute while I transfer you to the Chief Inspector."

"Mr. Maxwell, Detective Chief Inspector Fletcher here. This is a matter of considerable urgency. Is his lordship unwilling to take the call, too ill, or actually away from home?"

Through the crackling on the line came a measured voice. "His lordship is in London, Mr. Fletcher."

"Since when?"

"He drove up yesterday."

"Where is he staying?"

"At a private nursing home. You appear to be aware that his lordship is an invalid. He finds travel extremely debilitating."

"Then I wonder why he has undertaken it at this moment?"

"I am unable to enlighten you."

"Again I ask, unable or unwilling?"

"His lordship did not take me into his confidence."

"But you can make a very good guess. Could it be something to do with his brother?"

After a momentary silence, the butler admitted cautiously, "It could be."

"Which nursing home is he at?"

"I can't possibly tell you that, Chief Inspector."

"You have the address?"

"Ye-es."

"I realise you would be taking a great deal upon yourself by disclosing it. While I don't want to sound melodramatic, it could be a case of life or death."

"What! You can't be serious, Mr. Fletcher."

Alec mentally added butlers to his list—solicitors, doctors, club secretaries—of those out of whom it was extremely difficult to extract information. "I am deadly serious, Mr. Maxwell. The police do not joke about such subjects."

As if reading his mind, the butler said, "I had better refer you to his lordship's solicitor."

"My dear chap, I haven't time to be hunting down solicitors!" It was going to be bad enough trying to get into the place once they had its address. Nursing sisters, if not quite as obstructive as doctors when it came to information, could be quite obstructive enough when it came to letting one see their patients. "Time is of the essence."

"Caller, do you want another three minutes?"

"Yes, please." No good ever came of swearing at telephone operators. This reminded Alec that Marsh Abbey was probably on a village exchange. Bored local operators had been known to eavesdrop . . . and to gossip. Whatever the butler said might be all over the district by tomorrow, another reason for his caution. "Look, Mr. Maxwell, I understand your reluctance. Suppose you give me the postal district and the name of the street."

Grudgingly: "I could do that. Just a minute. Right, here we are. The district is South East Twenty-three and the street is Canonbie Road."

"SE23," Alec repeated. "Canonbie Road. Thank you, Mr. Maxwell."

"My division," Mackinnon noted.

"Sydenham!" said Piper. "Right back at the Crystal Palace." He reached for a directory.

"Canonbie Road, that's Forest Hill, a very respectable area so I don't know it well. I recall the street because of the Scottish name. It's a steep hill, as far as I remember."

Maxwell was saying mournfully, "I don't know if I've done right, Mr. Fletcher."

"Don't worry, we won't reveal where the information came from unless it becomes absolutely necessary, which I don't foresee."

"That's poor consolation, if you don't mind me saying so. Well, no use crying over spilt milk. Good-bye, Chief Inspector."

"Got it!" Ernie said triumphantly. "The Fairlawn Nursing Home. D'you want me to get them on the phone, Chief?" he added, seeing Alec hang up.

"No, I think we'll arrive unannounced. If he doesn't want to see us, I don't want to give them time to find a doctor who'll say we can't see him. Get hold of an official car and a driver. Mac, I'd like a couple of your men unobtrusively on hand, possibly for the next few days. Could you set that up? I'll brief them when we get there."

While they were busy, Alec skimmed through the last report and crossed another name off his list.

Half an hour later, they crossed the river and headed southeast.

The Fairlawn Nursing Home was a large, late Victorian detached house in a street of large detached houses. The steep hill provided views north across London and south to the Crystal

Palace, though it would make exercise difficult for convalescent patients.

Mackinnon's men were lurking in an unmarked car a few doors away from the nursing home. Alec described the man they were after, what little he had found out about his appearance.

"That's not much to go on," one muttered. "Must be hundreds—"

"But the chances of more than one visiting this place . . ."

"Oh, right, sir."

"His name is Wrexham-Clarke, Alaric Wrexham-Clarke, but he's quite likely to give an alias. He's to be held for questioning. Division HQ? No, straight to the Yard, I think. If by some improbable coincidence he should arrive while we're here, you can let him enter, but be alert for an attempt to cut and run. Let me warn you, he's a gymnast and an acrobat, fast and agile. Not known to carry weapons but beware of an unconventional attack. One front, one back, and stay out of sight."

They waited five minutes to let the man behind the house get into place. Then Alec led the way up the garden path and rang the bell. The door was opened by a young nurse in a stiffly starched apron and cap. She backed away as Alec stepped over the threshold.

"Detective Chief Inspector Fletcher and Detective Inspector Mackinnon," he said, leaving Piper, unannounced, to sidle in inconspicuously after them.

"Ooh," she breathed, round-eyed.

"No need to be alarmed, Nurse. I just want a word with a patient, Lord Ledborough."

"Ooh, are you going to arrest him?"

"Good heavens no, just talk to him."

"I'll have to ask Sister." She scurried away. By this time Ernie had made it to the stairs at the back of the hall and was to all appearance studying with great interest a portrait of Florence Nightingale.

Sister was a formidably large woman, even more stiffly

starched than her subordinate. Rustling, she stalked towards the policemen. "I am Sister Bessemer, Chief Inspector. You want to see Lord Ledborough? Out of the question, I'm afraid. Quite apart from the fact that he is a sick man, he is at present in consultation with his brother, Dr. Wrexham-Clarke."

THIRTY

The hired car bore Daisy, Sakari, and the two Russians westward. Both Miss Zvereva and the goldsmith started talking urgently to the driver, a grey-bearded man who could have been the one Daisy saw at the Café Royal, or his twin. They spoke in Russian, of course.

"Where are we going?" Daisy asked.

"One moment, please." Miss Zvereva plunged back into the urgent talk, which began to sound more like a vigorous dispute.

The car slowed to a crawl. Daisy had half a mind to hop out while the hopping was good, but Sakari wasn't capable of hopping so Daisy stayed put.

"Where are we going?" she said again.

"Is not far." Miss Zvereva peered out of the rear window with an anxious look. "I explain when we are there."

The incomprehensible argument resumed, but the car speeded up as much as traffic allowed. The driver turned on to the Embankment. Where on earth were they bound? Charing Cross Station? No, they passed the station and continued towards Whitehall. Scotland Yard? Surely not Scotland Yard!

"Are they going to confess to your husband?" Sakari whispered.

"Who knows? Perhaps they have new evidence to report?"

"Who knows! Why do they bring us?"

"Who knows?"

But the car drove on. At Parliament Square, a policeman on point duty held them up. Daisy considered appealing to him for help, but how on earth would she explain that while she could easily have got out, Sakari was insufficiently mobile?

Victoria Street. Victoria Station?

They passed the station approach and turned into Buckingham Palace Road. A moment later, the car pulled up in front of a church. Daisy and Sakari exchanged glances of mutual bafflement.

"We are here." Miss Zvereva's announcement could not have been less enlightening. "Please, we get out now."

Daisy was more than willing. While Miss Zvereva helped Sakari and the goldsmith paid the now sullen and silent driver, she glanced at the notice board announcing the name of the church and the hours of services and was startled to find it written in both English and Russian.

"It's Russian Orthodox!" she exclaimed as the car drove off, watched by both the Russians.

"Please, you will come inside now. We have tell driver you want to see Russian church, but he is suspicious. Perhaps he go to my father. We must be quick."

"I shall be happy to see the church," said Sakari. "However, you have another purpose, do you not?"

A joyful smile transformed Miss Zvereva's face. "We marry! If you wish, will be witnesses? Will make Vasya and me happy."

Daisy was too surprised to speak.

"We shall be delighted," Sakari acquiesced. "Shall we not, Daisy?"

"Oh, yes, of course."

They went in, Vasya giving Sakari his arm up the steps with great solicitude.

In the vestibule, Vasya said gravely, "You will wait here, please. Only baptised in orthodox faith are allowed inside. I will make doors to stay open so you can see. Wedding ceremony is short."

He opened the doors. Even by candlelight, the interior was dazzlingly colourful. The reredos was painted with images of saints and angels, and icons bright with gold hung on the walls and pillars.

"It reminds me of a Hindu temple," Sakari remarked sotto voce. "We too like colour."

"Where is the altar? No pews?"

"We stand for service."

"Come, Zina."

The Russian couple went on into the nave. Daisy and Sakari watched them light candles and place them in holders before one of the icons. The central doors at the rear opened and a priest in elaborate vestments came through, allowing a glimpse of the altar before the doors closed. He advanced down what would have been the aisle had there been any pews. Miss Zvereva—Zina—and Vasya went to meet him.

Behind Daisy, the door opened and a couple came in. The man spoke to Daisy in Russian, then noticed Sakari and blinked. "Excuse, please."

The woman, looking into the nave, said something in the midst of which Daisy thought she made out "Zina" and "Vasya." The two hurried into the church.

"Best man and bridesmaid," Sakari suggested.

Though Daisy didn't understand a word the priest said, she watched in fascination as the wedding proceeded. The couple exchanged rings, apparently several times, and shared a goblet of wine (at least Daisy assumed it was wine). The best man and bridesmaid placed wreaths on their heads. The priest gave each a candle to hold and led them in a procession three times round the small table on which all the paraphernalia had awaited them.

The wreaths were removed. The priest blessed the newly-weds and their friends wished them joy, or a long life, or, for all

Daisy knew, many children. She and Sakari uttered their own good wishes in hushed voices.

"*Doctor* Wrexham-Clarke?" Alec frowned. "I've heard a good deal about him but not a whisper to suggest he ever qualified as a doctor. He was once a medical student, I believe. What the deu— What on earth is he up to?"

His astonishment and alarm impressed Sister Bessemer. "He's not a doctor? Oh dear! Nurse, go up to Lord Ledborough's rooms and ask if he'll see these . . . gentlemen. And hurry." As the young nurse scampered off, she continued, "But he is his lordship's brother?"

"If he's who he announced himself to be."

"Sir," Mackinnon chimed in opportunely, "Sergeant Piper has followed the nurse up the stairs."

"He has?" Alec, having watched Ernie follow his instructions, mimicked annoyance. "We'll have to go after him."

They split up to circumnavigate Sister Bessemer. Ignoring her expostulation, Alec took the stairs two at a time. Mackinnon was close behind, their rubber-soled shoes almost soundless despite the linoleum treads.

At the top, Alec glanced right, then left, spotted Ernie, and turned left into a wide passage with several doors on each side. As he closed in on Ernie and the nurse, she stopped at one of the doors. Raising her hand to knock, she glanced round, took alarm at the sight of three large men rushing towards her, and backed away, eyes wide, hand covering her mouth.

"You two, one each side of the door," Alec ordered in a low voice. "I'm going in."

Slowly, silently, he turned the knob, opened the door a couple of inches, and kept his grip so that the latch didn't click as it retracted. Through the gap, he saw the foot of a bed, draped with a white coverlet. He guessed the patient was not in it, nurses being apt to remove and neatly fold the bedspread of occupied beds.

267

Someone spoke, his tone full of suspicion. "What is it?"

"A very simple preparation. That's why doctors don't like to prescribe it: they can't charge much for it. It's completely harmless, and it could cure both the tremors and the irregular heartbeat."

"What is it? What's it made of?"

"Just potassium chloride and water. You could sprinkle potassium chloride on your scrambled eggs like salt, which is sodium chloride, and you wouldn't notice a thing except a slight bitterness."

"Why are you so eager to improve my health? Even a complete cure wouldn't persuade me to throw away yet more money I can't afford on your gambling. You'll just have to save up your allowance to pay your debts."

"Call me an optimist. I hope—"

"Optimist! What gambler is not an optimist?"

"Listen, damn y— Dammit!" The second voice sounded sulky, with a touch of a whine. "I hope when you're feeling well, you'll be in a better mood, not so damn crotchety. You never used to be like this."

"I used not to be a cripple. And you used not to be a gambler. Oh, all right, go ahead with your damn injection! It can hardly make me feel worse. But don't count on changing my mind."

"You'll be glad. No more pain. Open your pyjama jacket and I'll swab with iodine to disinfect the skin. I brought some with me. There we are. You'll feel a bit of a prick, I'm afraid."

Alec shoved the door open, crossed the room in two strides, and knocked up the syringe just as it touched Lord Ledborough's abdomen. It flew from his brother's grasp and across the room, where the ampoule smashed to pieces.

"Piper, see what you can save of the contents. Don't touch the stuff."

"Here," cried Wrexham-Clarke, "what do you think you're doing?"

"Arresting you on suspicion of practising medicine without

a licence. Further charges may be preferred. Mackinnon, read him the warning. Lord Ledborough, I apologise for—"

"Look out!"

Mackinnon's shout came too late. Wrexham-Clarke darted out of the door, bowling over the little nurse who had crept back to see what was going on. The inspector set off in hot pursuit. Alec sped after them, emerging into the corridor in time to see Sister reach the top of the stairs, blocking the way with her bulk.

Wrexham-Clarke elbowed her in the ribs. She gasped and shuddered but she was too heavy to be displaced by such mistreatment. Gamely, she reached out to grab him. He flung himself at the landing rail, grasped it with both hands, did a twisting back flip, and disappeared from Alec's view. A thud announced his landing.

Running footsteps told the pursuers his escapade had not interfered with his escape.

"Look out!" bellowed Mackinnon. The Scotsman's lungs were in good shape. Alec resolved to ask him later whether he played the bagpipes.

Somehow Alec and Mackinnon managed to move Sister aside without further damage to anything but her dignity. They raced down the stairs. The front door stood wide open.

From outside came a triumphant shout of "Gotcha!"

Alec and Mackinnon stopped on the threshold. At the foot of the steps, Wrexham-Clarke sprawled face-down with a hefty plainclothesman sitting on him.

"Heard your shout, sir. Stuck out me foot and over he went, arse over tip."

THIRTY-ONE

"*Darling, sorry* to interrupt but I've had a letter from Mrs. Gilpin."

"For pity's sake, Daisy, that's not sufficient reason to ring me at the Yard!"

"Just wait till you hear what she says. I should have thought it's exactly what you want to hear. But I can save it till you get home if you—"

"Great Scott, Daisy! Just tell me, will you?"

"She's recovered her memory."

"That much I guessed."

"And she says she's certain she would recognise the other nanny—the third one, unless she was the second—if she saw her again."

"She can?" Daisy could practically hear Alec sitting up and taking notice. "I humbly apologise. That's just what we need."

"You mean you've got someone in custody for her to recognise?"

"You know I can't discuss that. Is she coming up to London?"

"Her sister's doctor says she needs another week's rest."

"I'll send Ernie down with a selection of photos for her to

look through. He won't cause alarm and despondency and he can get her statement at the same time. Thanks, Daisy. Anything else useful?"

"I don't think so."

"Then thanks and good-bye."

"Will you be home for dinner?" She spoke into a dead receiver. Sighing, she hung up.

Alec came home at last just before ten. Mrs. Dobson had kept dinner hot for him so Daisy fetched a trayful to the dining room. He dug ravenously into the food, while Daisy relayed the main points of the rest of Nurse Gilpin's letter.

"She came out of the lavatory cubicle and saw the other nanny come out of one farther along. One averts one's eyes, as she delicately put it, but she noticed that she— It was a woman?"

"Don't fish."

"Well, all the *she*'s are confusing so I'm going to assume it was another man like Teddy and call her him. He didn't appear to be going to wash his hands until he saw her approach the basins. And then it was more of a quick lick and a promise, so she was close behind when she followed him out."

"You're not telling me she followed him all the way to the far end of the park to upbraid him for not washing his hands properly?"

"No, though I admit to thinking the same for a fraction of a second, before I read on. It seems on her way to the ladies' she had noticed a pram with a baby sleeping, parked in the end passage."

"As a matter of fact, Mackinnon's men found the pram. It was an extremely lifelike doll."

"No, was it? Part of their disguise, of course. She assumed the nanny would turn that way when she—I mean *he*—left the ladies', but he went the other way. Naturally she assumed it was a mistake, that he'd realise and go back. She stopped to watch for a moment to make sure. When he showed no sign of reversing course, she hurried after him to point out his error."

"And he went on so she went on, and the children saw them and went after them—luckily for her."

"Yes! I'm still not happy about her going off like that but she swears she was thinking of the twins as well as the abandoned baby and decided they would be perfectly all right with Bertha. The rest of us were due to meet there, after all. I have to tell you, also, that her sister considers that she was infected by the detecting spirit after living so long in the household of a detective."

Alec gave a snort of laughter. "She does, does she? I never thought of my job as contagious."

"I suppose it's not unreasonable. After all, I caught it."

"Oh no you didn't. You were already detecting the first time we met!"

Daisy decided to ignore the dig. "Anyway, I can reasonably recommend Mrs. Gilpin to Lucy, don't you think?"

"That's entirely up to you, love."

"I knew you'd say that."

Alec finished eating and sat back. "Just what I needed."

"Thank Mrs. Dobson, as always." Daisy put the empty dishes on the tray. "Cocoa or whisky?"

"Whisky. I'm celebrating."

Daisy took the tray to the kitchen and rejoined him in the back sitting room. He had poured her a half and half vermouth with soda.

"To celebrate. All right?"

"Fine." Daisy pursued her own train of thought. "It was naughty of the children to go chasing Nanny Gilpin, too, but one couldn't scold them properly after they saved her life. Life is more peaceful without them but I miss them, especially Belinda."

"You have plenty of time for your writing. Didn't you say you had fallen behind?"

"Yes, but that's partly because I promised Mr. Thorwald an article about the Crystal Palace, and I just don't feel like writing it after finding Teddy."

"Understandable."

"It's unsettled me. I keep finding other things to do. This

afternoon, Sakari and I went back to the Russian jeweller's to see the sketches."

"Not that they have anything to do with Teddy," Alec said dryly.

"You don't still suspect them, do you? Because what happened today absolutely proves Miss Zvereva had no reason to want to marry Teddy."

"Oh? What happened?"

Daisy managed to tell the story of the exotic church and the fascinating ceremony without revealing that she had been half-convinced she and Sakari were being kidnapped. "They explained the hurry and the secrecy after we signed the register. They've wanted to get married forever but the prince was dead against it and would have absolutely forbidden it if he'd guessed they were in love, just because Vasya—Mr. Petrov—isn't a nobleman. Or rather wasn't one in Russia."

"Sounds familiar."

"My mother." Daisy sighed. "Zina didn't want to have to go against an express order and she was afraid if he discovered their plans he'd find a way to stop them. Then he fell ill. The doctor prescribed sleeping medicine that made him sleep like the dead."

"An unfortunate choice of words, love."

"You have murder on the brain! All right, he slept very heavily the first night he took it. The next day Vasya got a marriage licence and arranged things with their priest and their friends and a hired car. And the day after, today in fact, Zina gave her father a draught after lunch. When he was sound asleep, they were just about to rush off to church when we turned up. Oh blast, I must have left the designs in the car!"

"As long as it was a hired car, not a taxi, I expect the driver will return them to the Zverevs."

"I hope so. But he was a friend of the prince. He tried to argue them out of going. They were afraid he'd find a way to stop them. Well, they're well and truly married now, so it's too late. You didn't say whether they're still suspects."

"No-o . . . No, not really. We're virtually certain we've got the man."

"It is a man? Not hyphen-Clarke— What's his name? Wrexham-Clarke?"

"Alaric Wrexham-Clarke."

"Alaric? Outlandish! That would explain 'Ricky,' wouldn't it. So you found him?"

"Once we knew his name it was just a matter of time. But we caught up with him just in time. Another five minutes and his brother would have been dead or dying."

Daisy listened in amazement to the story of Lord Ledborough's narrow escape. "Two extraordinary coincidences, your arriving at exactly the right moment to save him and Sakari and I being on the spot to attend the wedding."

"We couldn't have planned it better if we'd had a week's notice of everyone's movements. I saw him actually in the act of attempting murder. I would have looked pretty silly, though, if he'd turned out to be properly qualified after all."

"What was really in the syringe? Did you find out yet?"

"Yes, they analysed it in no time when I told them it was said to be potassium chloride. A dilute solution is, as Wrexham-Clarke claimed, completely harmless to anyone in normal health. It might even help under certain conditions. But the contents of the ampoule were highly concentrated and would have caused a heart attack to a man in Ledborough's condition, probably fatal and certainly debilitating, even if his charming brother hadn't intended to stick the needle directly into the heart, as he used the hatpin on Devenish. It was a large hypodermic, intended for veterinary use."

"Ugh! What about Teddy's murder? Do you have evidence other than Mrs. Gilpin's recognition? Assuming she does pick him out."

"On second thoughts, that would help, but it might be hard to persuade a jury to take it seriously if the defence hammered on her loss of memory, as they surely would. Of course, the prosecutor can make use of motive, which tends to sway juries. Also, though the hat pin has no—"

"You found the hat pin? No one told me."

"Good lord, we managed to keep something from you?" Alec teased. "I'm amazed. An alert gardener found it stuck in a potted palm. Bloodstains but no useable fingerprints. However, the discarded handbag is covered with Wrexham-Clarke's dabs. It was part of the costume Devenish hired from the theatrical costumer. Hired in his own name, so no difficulty proving that part."

"Isn't that plenty of evidence? You don't sound satisfied."

"All in all, it's not the most robust case I've ever presented to the prosecutor, but I wouldn't despair of it. It won't surprise me, either, if we get a confession. He's a weak, whiny sort of fellow. Little as prosecutors and judges like confessions, juries love 'em."

"Sakari's theory makes sense. I'm sure she's right."

Alec sighed. "I suppose you've told her everything."

"Of course. She was there when it happened, and—"

"Yes, never mind, what is her theory?"

"We know Ricky was very sensitive about what people thought of him. That's how Teddy blackmailed him. And Teddy didn't give two hoots what people thought. In fact, he courted scandal. Invading the ladies' room wouldn't amuse him if it didn't cause havoc."

"Very likely not, except insofar as it embarrassed Ricky."

"But how much more embarrassed Ricky would be if they were publicly unmasked! Which would also cause a terrific uproar. Suppose once they were in there Teddy announced that he was going to start undressing as soon as a suitable audience arrived. It would be much more humiliating to Ricky than his job as an acrobat."

"He could have left," Alec objected. "Teddy might be annoyed enough to reveal the acrobat business, but Ricky would have escaped the disrobing."

"Still, he'd lose face either way. The threat must have been the last straw that snapped his inhibitions."

"It's conceivable. A prosecutor could make much of it. But please don't go telling Sakari I said her theory is correct!"

"I won't." Daisy reserved the right to tell her friend that Alec admitted the reconstruction was plausible.

"Will Bel and the boys have to give evidence?"

Alec frowned. "I hope not. It'll be up to the counsel for the prosecution, of course. They don't like to call children. Given the connection between those children and the investigating officer—"

"You."

"—Not to mention the chief witness in the attempted murder of Lord Ledborough, I'd guess they'll avoid it like the plague, if at all possible. Would it upset them?"

"Belinda, yes. Not the boys. They'd revel in it, especially Charlie."

"True." Alec laughed. "What's more, I can imagine Bel not finding it such an ordeal if Ben and Charlie were there too."

"What I absolutely cannot imagine is what Mother will say when she hears her step-granddaughter and her fourth or fifth cousins several time removed may testify in a murder trial. Did I tell you she's coming up to town next week?"

"No-o-o! Let's pop over to France. I'm giving the case back to Mackinnon, and I'm getting a week's leave before I start work as superintendent."

"Darling, you got it!" Daisy jumped up and plumped down on the arm of his chair to give him a congratulatory kiss. "Not that it's any surprise, of course. It must be perfectly obvious even to Mr. Crane and the Assistant Commissioner that you're far and away the best man for the job."

HISTORICAL NOTE

The Crystal Palace was erected in Hyde Park for the Great Exhibition of 1851. At that time it contained the first public ladies' "convenience" in London, a concept previously considered unworkable because no lady would want to be seen entering or leaving a place with such intimate connotations.

A couple of years later, after the Exhibition, the huge glass and iron Palace was carefully dismantled to be re-erected in Sydenham Park in southeast London, with the addition of two new wings.

In 1936, the Palace burned down in a spectacular fire visible for many miles. Despite many proposals to resurrect it, all that is visible today are the foundations. Their impressive extent can only suggest the impact of the huge glittering building.

Charlie's monsters are still to be found in the park, lurking among bushes and trees, in the ponds, and on the island. They are large concrete depictions of prehistoric mammals, created by Charles Waterhouse in accordance with the latest theories derived from fossilized skeletons then available.